Barbarian Voyage

Leda Palmer

Copyright © 2025 by Leda Palmer

Published by Werner Ink

Norristown, PA

All rights reserved.

No portion of this book may be reproduced in any form without written permission from the publisher or author, except as permitted by U.S. copyright law.

Cover Art by Miblart

Edited by Courtney Umphress

Paperback ISBN: 978-1-960073-09-9

Library of Congress Control Number: 2025906272

Contents

Dedication — VI

1. Dirty Heathen — 1
2. Short-Lived Relief — 7
3. Open — 18
4. Double Blessed — 24
5. Endless Summer — 31
6. Deficient — 41
7. Afternoon Delight — 44
8. Not For You — 52
9. Swirly — 59
10. Frolicking — 66
11. Forbidden Fruit — 74
12. Good To Know — 81
13. Watch Your Step — 86
14. Her Favorite Songs — 91
15. Peckish — 99

16.	Sunlight	104
17.	Snake Oil	115
18.	Full Dark	124
19.	Relax	130
20.	Mounted	137
21.	Riding Bitch	144
22.	Come and Get It	152
23.	Worth Waiting For	159
24.	Dumb Joke	170
25.	Campfire Confessions	176
26.	Onatel	182
27.	Serious Wooing	194
28.	Delayed	199
29.	Breathtaking	214
30.	Lies of Omission	225
31.	Pouty	232
32.	Complete Panic	237
33.	Breaking Her In	252
34.	Taken	257
35.	Sitting on a Gold Mine	260
36.	As You Wish	268
37.	Unearthing Secrets	277
38.	Spit it Out	284
39.	Heavy	288

40. Focus   295

41. Boinking Like Crazy   301

42. Fun Reunion   310

43. The Proposition   317

44. Surprises   329

Also by   334

About the author   335

This one's for all the girls who need a little sunshine in their life.

PS: For the music lovers who adore a soundtrack while reading, I highly recommend *Endless Summer* by the Elovaters. Our hero Jalen wouldn't have turned out quite the same if I'd never discovered that album.

-Leda

1

Dirty Heathen

Ren

"You've gotta be fucking kidding me." I snagged Karsen's elbow and ducked down a side hall on Oraxis Station, praying that tool bag Travis hadn't spotted me.

"Hey. What's the matter?" Karsen pulled her arm free but blessedly followed.

No chance in hell was I answering *that* loaded question. "I just want to get out of here so we can head to Dionus."

The half-truth seemed to satisfy my new crewmate. She went back to gawking at the station, eyes wide and a permanent grin painted on her face. Since joining our crew as a replacement for her sister, Karsen hadn't missed a chance to explore whenever we stopped somewhere new.

Me? I was just trying to get in and out without running into anyone I knew. Well... more like one particular person. *So far, so good.*

The truth was, if this mission had been for anyone other than my boss and best friend, I would've never agreed to it. But after Arda gave me my ticket out of my own personal hell, I owed her. It was the least I could do to repay her for hiring me when no one else wanted to take a chance on a nobody from a tiny tin can floating in the middle of nowhere.

Karsen side-eyed me as we trailed down the metal corridors of the space station I'd once called home. "What are we looking for, again?"

"There's a planetary landing code for Dionus. I need to grab it real quick, and then we'll be all set."

Karsen shrugged. "Sounds good to me." A man wearing a mechanic uniform rounded the corner ahead, and her gaze zeroed in on his muscled arms. Then she sent the guy a megawatt smile.

I ducked my head, thankful for Kar's flirting. His gaze slid right past me in my baggy skinsuit and glided over Karsen, devouring her curvy frame like a starving dog would a feast.

Speeding up, I snagged her arm again. "Come on. We're almost there."

"Sheesh. Can't let a girl window shop?" Karsen snickered.

I rolled my eyes. Kar and I were about as opposite as it got. It wasn't just that she loved to flirt, while I would rather gouge my eyes out with a laserspanner. She was bubbly and sweet to my surly and scowling. And Kar took great care with her appearance, her long black hair and makeup perfectly highlighting her gorgeous features. Her light-brown skin practically glowed, and her dark-brown eyes popped, framed with glittery eyeshadow.

Not me. The only paint on my face was engine grease—and I liked it that way. I mean, who needs to look cute when you spend most of your time fixing broken machines?

I stopped in front of a hatch. "Here it is." I punched in the code, not bothering to knock.

"Is this your place?" Kar asked.

I shook my head. "Nope. My brother's."

Kar stiffened. "You have a brother, too?"

I didn't miss the hint of accusation in her tone. My crewmates had been surprised to learn I had a sister the first time traveling to Dionus came up, and I told them Cassidy lived there.

Yeah, I didn't talk about my family a lot. I'd learned long ago that sharing too much was a recipe for disaster. Anyway, no one wanted to hear the pathetic mess that was my past. "We're not blood related. He's more like a... foster brother."

Her eyes widened. "Oh."

I pushed open the door and strolled in. Demetri's apartment was a wreck, but that was nothing unusual. My fingers itched to set everything to rights, but I ignored the urge, heading straight for his bed.

"This is... cozy." Karsen's nose wrinkled as she took in the haphazardly stacked piles of books, clothes, and other junk littering every surface of the closet-sized room.

"Cut the shit, Kar. It's a pigsty. Demi has always been a dirty heathen." Kneeling on one knee, I dug underneath the cot for the lockbox he kept his important paperwork in.

Karsen giggled. "I wasn't going to say it..." She stopped in front of his desk and lifted a framed photo, tilting it so I could see. "This him?"

Demetri stared out of the frame, looking handsome with his sparkling hazel eyes and the light catching the dimple in his chin just right. His arm was wrapped around a stunner with long blonde curls and a shy smile on her face. "Yep. That's him."

Karsen turned the frame over and pursed her lips. "You look so different in this photo." She brightened. "Oh, it's the hair. I'm totally digging you with long hair! You should grow it out again."

I dragged a hand through my signature short locks. A pang of regret struck me that I shoved aside violently. Now was not the time to think about why I'd worn it short for years. Or to remember the reason I cut it in the first place. Especially not *here*. "It's not the hair. That's not a picture of me. That's my sister."

Karsen gasped. "Shut up, Ren! Why didn't you tell us you were a twin?"

"It's a long story." The lockbox clicked open, and I dug through the contents. I lifted the code triumphantly. "Look at that. We got what we came for."

"Cool." Karsen pouted as she set the photo down.

I knew Kar was eager to learn more about me. That was just who she was—absolutely brilliant and obsessed with learning. At just over eighteen, she was smarter than any teen had a right to be—with multiple degrees to prove it—and it was because she soaked up knowledge like a sponge.

But I couldn't let her suck up what I had on offer. Not unless she was ready to wipe up a whole lot of decay.

I shoved the lockbox under Demetri's bed and stood. "Let's get out of here."

"I get the feeling you don't like it here much," Karsen said as we exited into the hall.

I chuckled dryly. "You could say that."

"Do you want to talk about it?" Kar leaned in, looking so damn earnest I almost wanted to spill.

I shook off the urge. "Nah. It's all in the past." Still, I'd be much happier when we were back on the *Verne* and we put a few thousand light-years between us and Oraxis Station.

We were headed to a world far away from this little asteroid-belt-orbiting space station. A jungle world filled with wild creatures and a humanoid species rumored to be the most uncivilized that'd achieved faster than light travel. I couldn't say I was too thrilled with that part of the plan. Still... I'd take just about anywhere over staying here.

"Excuse me, ladies!" The familiar voice behind me instantly made my skin crawl.

Karsen started to turn, but I wrapped an arm around her shoulders and dragged her forward into the station's docking bay. "Shouldn't we—"

"Oh, look, there's the *Verne*. Right where we left it." I hustled across the busy bay, pulling Kar in my wake. The ugly exterior of the mid-class vessel we called home was visible outside the bay window, and I breathed out a sigh when I spotted the docking port still attached.

My heart pounded in time with the footsteps slapping the floor behind us. I couldn't let that sorry excuse for a man catch up to us. *Not today, Satan.*

"Wasn't that the chief engineer? You sure we shouldn't see what he..." Karsen trailed off as my hand darted out, snagging a bottle of clear transmission fluid off a cart we passed.

I flicked the lid open and casually splashed the contents on the floor behind us. "Who?"

Kar glanced pointedly over her shoulder, but before she said anything, Travis yelled again. "Ren? That's you, isn't it?"

Karsen's brows shot into her hairline. I didn't slow. Didn't acknowledge the man who *clearly* recognized me. Thankfully, my genius crewmate got the hint and let me drag her away. And when Travis's footsteps sped behind us, she winced but didn't speak a word to warn him.

Crash.

I stopped beside the docking port leading to the *Verne* and slowly turned. Travis writhed on the cement, clutching his back and howling in a puddle of tranny-fluid. I watched him flailing as I waited for the docking port to pressurize, and my racing pulse finally slowed.

Kar hissed in my ear, "What was that about, Ren? Do you know that guy?"

I looked Travis dead in the eyes and raised my voice, hoping the asshole could make out my words over his cries of pain. Pain that was *much* less than he deserved. "I didn't hear him."

2

Short-Lived Relief

Ren

The docking bay hatch slammed behind me. Within seconds, I engaged the unlock sequence and tapped my neck, activating my personal comm device.

Yeah, I'd made fun of Arda when she first opted for a transplant, but after it saved her ass on that Garcuk ship, I'd changed my tune. You never know where a little extra tech might come in handy. Like now.

"Mission accomplished, Capt. Let's blow this joint."

"I knew you'd come through! You wanna celebrate before we leave in the Oraxis Station mess? My treat."

Normally, I was never one to turn down a free meal. Just not when I still could feel phantom eyes on my back like a hellish caress.

"Is there any way we can get the fuck outta here instead?" I flinched and a million anxious thoughts flooded my mind. Arda would demand I explain. She could even insist on staying. Then I might have to actually talk to that scumbag instead of just injuring him.

But Arda barely paused a second before she replied, "Got it. Fucking off as we speak."

I sighed. Arda was the best. She had my back, no questions asked. That was exactly why I was doing this. Well, one of the reasons. Fact was, I understood her plight all too well. She deserved the full truth about her family lineage.

If only we could all be so lucky...

But the relief was short-lived. A clatter near the hopper drew my attention, and I instantly tensed. Wait... I cocked my head, listening carefully. The bang repeated and my pulse soared. That wasn't next to the hopper. It was coming from inside.

"What the actual fuck?" I abandoned Karsen beside the docking bay hatch and stalked across the shuttle bay. The *Verne* shifted, and since Arda was fucking off in the cockpit, I knew exactly who I was about to kill for messing with my baby.

My hands clenched into fists as I spotted a pair of massive legs peeking out from underneath.

"Lux, if you've messed up a single bolt on my baby with your four-fingered hands—" Arda's alien mate slid out, and the panicked expression on his normally stoic face made the words die unsaid. "What's wrong?"

"It's Smudge. She's stuck in the engine." He dragged a hand through his long golden hair, silver eyes flashing with distress.

Holy crap. Did his lips just quiver?

You can tell a lot about a man by how he treats his pets. Lux loved his like a baby.

"Move. I'll get her."

Karsen caught up to us. "Did I hear that right? Is Smudge—"

Lux cut her off. "Stuck. Yes." He hopped off the rolling platform, and I didn't waste any time taking his place.

"Don't worry. I've got this."

Karsen wrung her hands. "Arda asked for an update, but I better stick around and make sure she's not injured."

"Her cries are not those of pain, merely annoyance. I do not think she's injured."

I heard Lux's reply, but my vision filled with the hull as I slid under the hopper. I bit my lip, wishing I could see the conflicted look on his face as he debated ignoring Arda's wishes. The only thing Lux loved more than Smudge was Arda.

He sighed. "Give my mate her update. The *Verne* is small. We'll hail you if we need you."

"Okay. If you're sure." Bootsteps faded away.

I thrust a hand out. "Laserspanner."

"Do you see her yet?" Lux whined.

Yep, you read that right. The seven-foot-tall alien lord who'd been hired to represent his entire species in diplomatic relations with Earth just whined like a toddler. If I weren't so eager to save Smudge, I might have laughed at how much of a puddle Lux became over his ugly alien pet.

Smudge was definitely not winning any pet food endorsements anytime soon. Honestly, though, she was actually kind of cute. Like a cross between a bunny and a cat—only one that was hairless and as gray as a faded oil stain.

"Not yet." I unlocked a panel with the laserspanner. "Don't worry. I'll find her."

Fact was, I wasn't just worried about Smudge. I had to save the poor hopper's wiring from being clawed, nibbled on—I shuddered and choked down a gag—or worse, turned into a litter box.

I'd always been more comfortable around machines than people, but the obsession I had with the hopper—hell, with the whole *Verne*—ran deeper than most. I wouldn't be able to fall asleep tonight without assessing the damage and plotting a dozen different scenarios to fix them with the limited supplies we had on board.

The panel slid off, and I set it on the floor beside me. Then I stuck my head inside, breathing a huge sigh when I spotted Smudge immediately. "I see her." The little critter was acting strangely, purring like a freight train and rubbing against a warming block in the engine's center.

Luckily, she was close enough for me to grab her. I tensed, waiting for her to dart away the moment I touched her. That was her normal skittish response to being startled.

Not today. I grabbed her torso, and she whipped around with a bloodcurdling hiss.

I snagged my hand away instinctively. "The hell?"

Smudge speared me with a look that made me shiver. Then she went right back to rubbing against the warming block.

Lux choked out, "Was that Smudge? What did you do to her?"

"I barely touched her."

"What are you waiting for? Pull her out of there." Lux's voice shook with worry.

"Give me a sec." I buried my shock and reached inside. The silly fucisera might want to rub on the engine all day, but I couldn't let her. She could get hurt in there.

I grabbed her as fast as I could and pulled her out of the engine. She hissed and flailed in my arms. Pain shot through my hands as her claws sank into my flesh. "Shit. Take her!" I rolled out from under the hopper's hood and shoved Smudge at Lux.

Lux snatched her out of my arms, and she instantly quieted. But while she'd stopped hissing and scratching, she wasn't at all still. She squirmed, trying to leap out of her daddy's arms.

Lux frowned. "I think she's trying to go back inside."

Ignoring the stinging cuts on my hands, I slid back under the hull. "I'll reattach the panel real quick." We didn't need her jumping in there and getting stuck again.

"I will put her in her carrier."

Minutes later, I slipped out from under the hopper and found Lux staring at Smudge inside her carrier. She yowled, alternating between throwing herself at the locked door and rubbing herself against the sides of the box.

"What's up with her? I've never seen Smudge act like this."

Lux shrugged. "I have no clue. I would call her vet, but with the time difference, everyone on my home world is likely sleeping at this hour."

I glanced at the clock. "I know someone who can help who's a lot closer than Pheria." I grinned, strolled to the comm unit in the corner of the docking bay, and placed a call to Earth.

"Hello, Zenda speaking." My former crewmate happened to be one of the best animal scientists on Earth. If anyone in this system knew what was up with Smudge, it would be Zen.

"Something's wrong with Smudge," Lux blurted before I could sneak out a greeting.

"Oh no. Is she hurt?"

I cut in when I heard the panic in her voice. "Hey, Zen. She's fine physically. Just acting really strange, and the vets on Lux's home world won't be open for hours."

"Hey, Ren." Zen sighed. "Okay. I bet I can help. I did a lot of research on fuscieras when I was trying to convince Smudge to warm up to me. Describe her symptoms."

"I found her snuggling with a warming block inside the hopper's engine just now. And when I pulled her out, she scratched the hell out of me." I waved at Lux, urging him to bring the carrier closer. "And listen to the racket she's making."

Lux complied, and after a moment's silence, a sound I hadn't been expecting echoed through the comms. Stifled giggling.

"Why are you laughing?" Lux scowled.

"Sorry," Zen replied. "It's just, I think I know what's happening."

"Care to enlighten us?" How Zenda could know sight unseen, with only a few symptoms, what was bothering Smudge was kind of freaky. But that was why I'd called her. She was smart as hell and obsessed with animals. Even alien ones.

"When fuscieras reach sexual maturity they seek partners during times of peak fertility. I'm willing to bet the warming block was the closest thing Smudge could find to hump that was the right temperature for a fusciera." Zen cleared her throat. "Put simply, Smudge is in heat."

"What?" Lux barked, his eyes widening.

I chuckled as the critter's actions began making sense. "You can relax, Lux. Your baby is just horny."

Lux's scowl deepened, and the stare he sent me was so hot it could melt lead.

Zenda giggled. "She's right. It's perfectly natural and nothing to worry about. Let me send you some of my research, Lux. Then you'll know how to help Smudge through her heat since you won't be around any males of her species. I can answer any questions you have, as well."

I backed away. That sounded like more information than I needed to learn. "I'm gonna leave you to it." I lifted my scratched hand. "I better have Karsen look at these." The hopper's repairs could wait until the alien biology lesson ended.

"Tell my sis I said hi!" Zenda insisted. "Arda, too."

"Will do. Later, Zen. Lux." With that, I made my escape. I strolled down the *Verne*'s central hall, passing the white walls accented with silver and dotted with a handful of doors—including the empty med-bay—on my way to the bridge.

Karsen was probably still filling Arda in on what went down on Oraxis Station. I'd grab her and ask her to fix me.

As soon as I drew close enough to the bridge hatch, their voices murmuring proved my guess true. I picked up my pace, ready to deal with the stinging cuts. Then I stopped short, and my stomach sank.

"I'm telling you, Ren was acting really weird," Karsen said. "She deliberately spilled that fluid. Then she said she didn't hear him afterward. There was no way she didn't hear the guy yelling for her. He called her by name, even."

Arda replied softly, "I know Ren keeps things close to her chest, but trust me, Kar. If she didn't want to talk to that guy, there must've been a reason."

My speeding pulse slowed a tiny fraction. At least Arda was sticking up for me.

"What could be enough of a reason to make the guy eat it like that? You should've heard how hard he fell. And the way he screamed afterward. I bet he broke something."

If only she knew... But with how judgmental Karsen was being, I wasn't feeling inclined to share the full story.

Arda's voice rang with confidence. "I trust Ren. Sure, she doesn't like men, but she's never been the type to go around dropping dudes for the hell of it. I'm willing to bet this guy deserved it. She'll fill us in when she's ready. Let it go for now, okay?"

"If you say so, Capt," Karsen replied grudgingly.

And... that was my sign to leave. Suddenly, the cuts were the least of my worries. I couldn't step onto the bridge and face my crewmates' questioning stares. I'd dredged up about as many memories from the past as I could face for one day.

I spun on my heel and hightailed back the way I'd come. I paused outside the docking bay, but with Lux still in there chatting with Zen, I couldn't escape to my happy place just yet. So I opted for the next best thing.

The hatch to my quarters opened without a sound. Sighing, I settled on my bed and stared at the blank walls. The room wasn't anything special. Honestly, I didn't spend much time in it. My waking hours were normally spent in the docking bay. Or the engine room. Anywhere I could keep my hands busy and my mind occupied.

Here, my mind tended to wander. And today that was the last thing I needed. Not when all I could think about was Cassidy and how much I didn't want to see her.

We were twins, but only in the genetic sense. I hadn't been close to Cassidy since the day we were torn apart as children. When she'd returned looking for me as an adult, I'd been less than receptive to her attempts to reunite. Especially after her engagement—and the awkward visit when I met her fiancé.

I shuddered, forcing the memory aside. What the hell was the matter with me today? I couldn't go two seconds without being bombarded with another memory I'd do anything to forget.

A knock on the door made me flinch. "Who is it?"

"It's me."

My skin prickled and my shoulders tensed. "What do you want, Karsen?" I wasn't in the mood for her sunshiny bullshit after she ratted me out to Arda.

"Lux told me Smudge scratched you. I need to take a look at you."

"I'm fine. Go away."

She was silent for a moment, and I started to wonder if she'd actually listened. But then her voice rang out again. "Don't make me bring Arda in on this. Or I can order the *Verne* to unlock your hatch with my medical clearance."

Karsen might be younger than me, but she was as stubborn as Zen. Didn't know why I even bothered trying. "Fine." I crossed the room and opened the hatch. "Come in. Let's get this over with."

Karsen peered around curiously as she walked inside, carting a portable med kit. My fingers twitched as I realized this was the first time she'd seen my room. Kar had only replaced Zen a few months ago, and we weren't exactly besties yet.

Couldn't say that I blamed her for not being super close. I wasn't exactly the best at making friends. Been the same story my whole life.

"Nice room. A bit plain, but—" Karsen stilled as her gaze trailed over my bed. "What is that? Or should I say *who*?"

I followed her gaze. "Oh, that." She was staring at the ridiculous pillowcase I'd been gifted on my last birthday. It featured a headshot of an old Earth film star from the nineteenth century. He was on a beach, flashing a sultry look, his black shirt half undone and showing off an impressively hairy chest, despite not being what most women—me included—would consider classically handsome.

"It's Nicolas Cage," I answered nonchalantly, sinking back on the bed.

Karsen's brow furrowed. "Ooo-kay. He a friend of yours or something?"

I chuckled. "No. It was a gag gift. From Zenda."

"That sounds like my sister. But why him?" She eyed the pillow once more before kneeling and digging into her med kit.

"When we first started working on the *Verne*, she talked me into watching this ridiculous old Earth flick from about a century ago called *Face Off*. I mean, the movie wasn't terrible, if you could get past the crazy premise."

She grabbed my arm and attached a portable med-bot. "Which was?"

I smirked. "The two main characters *literally* change faces."

Karsen giggled. "People back then really believed that was plausible? That's still not possible, even with all our medical advances."

"Yeah, I don't know. The plot's not important, though. Me and Zen got into a debate about who was hotter out of the two main men. She said it was the other guy, John... something. I can't remember. But I liked my man Nick better."

Karsen snorted. "I kinda want to see the other guy now."

I leaned in. "Spoiler alert—he's got nothing on Nick." Truth be told, neither of the guys really got my motor going. But it had been fun arguing about it with Zen. Looking back, that was the moment our friendship first blossomed.

"If you say so." Karsen side-eyed Cage's chest hair and shook her head.

"Anyway, for my birthday, Zenda tracked down this gem from an antique shop." I grabbed the goofy thing with my free hand and squeezed it. "We all had a good laugh about it." I grinned as the memory washed over me.

I might not have the closest family, but the friends I'd made on the *Verne* were the best. And I would do anything to keep them, even make nice with Zen's little sister when she thought the worst of me.

"Listen, Kar." I frowned at my boots. "I'm sorry about how I acted back there when we were leaving the Oraxis. But that engineer... let's just say I would've rather cut off all my fingers than talk to that asshole."

"You have history. I get it." The med-bot chimed three times, and Karsen pulled it off my hand, revealing smooth, scratch-free skin. "If you ever want to talk about it, I'm all ears." She smiled softly, and all the suspicion from before left her eyes.

Maybe she doesn't think the worst of me after all...

I sighed. "Thanks. I'll remember that." But I wouldn't be taking her up on that offer. *Not unless hell freezes over.*

3

Open

Jalen

"That's it." Liquid heat pulsed through my veins as my gaze locked on the glorious vision before me. "Open for me, beautiful."

I'd waited for this moment for so long. Caring for her. Lovingly tending to her every desire. All for this. My mouth watered as more of the lush pink prize I'd been desperately waiting for was slowly revealed. It was even more beautiful than I'd imagined.

"Yesss," I crooned. "I can't wait to taste you." I licked my lips and leaned closer.

A shadow fell over the delicate flower, and the bud snapped closed.

"Hey!" I scowled at the massive ontania bush beside my rare canides plant. "What in ellios's name is this, Tani? I thought we talked about this? If you keep sucking up Candy's light, she'll never bear fruit! Don't make me grab the clippers."

I paused, glaring at the stupid plant like it might actually respo—

"Don't hurt me."

Eyes widening, I jolted. "Wh-what?" That plant did *not* just talk back to me.

In the three years I'd been stuck on this tiny spit of land, I might have adopted the habit of talking to my plants. I might have even given them nicknames. Could you blame me for making friends with a few bushes when I spend ninety-nine percent of my time with no one to chat with? But no matter how much I'd grown to think of my plants as friends, they'd never talked back.

Not until now.

No. It didn't talk.

That was crazy...

I must be overheated from sitting in the sun all morning. *Yes... that's all this is. I just need a drink.*

"Please, don't clip me," a disembodied voice whispered. "Please!"

"Harlx's ghost!" I backed away slowly, my heart pounding. This wasn't happening. I was going insane. I—

A flash of blue caught my eye between the bush's branches. I shook my head and circled Tani. Before I'd taken two steps, laughter rang out, confirming my suspicion.

"By Harlx's beard, you should've seen your face!" Cruz brayed, his long blue hair swinging in his face as he chuckled heartily. "I had you going there, didn't I?"

I rolled my eyes, but a smile creeped across my lips. "Laugh it up." I leaned against the chest-high fence bordering my yard and scanned Cruz up and down. His abs flexed beneath his pocketed vest as laughter spilled out of his mouth. His violet eyes glittered, and it was hard for me not to join in with his merriment, despite being the butt of the joke.

But my smile faded when I registered his nearly empty pack. "I wasn't expecting you for another week."

Cruz was my lone contact with the outside world. As tribe runner, he had the unenviable task of braving the harsh jungles of Dionus to bring supplies to outcasts like me. Normally, his visits were as predictable as a sundial. He'd show up, his pack bursting with the supplies I'd need for another month of seclusion.

But not this time.

"Please tell me you just came here to poke fun at your favorite recluse." My heart thumped heavily in my chest and my thoughts raced as Cruz fought to control his laughter.

What if my home village burned down? Or off-worlders caused trouble? So many things could have happened while I was stuck here, and I'd have absolutely no idea it was occurring.

My stomach sank. What if something had happened to Rhelt or his mate?

We might not be the closest family—they were the whole reason I was in this mess to begin with—but that didn't mean I wished them ill. If anything happened that I could've stopped, that would be a far worse punishment than my years of seclusion.

"Nothing's wrong." Cruz wiped his eyes and cleared his throat. He nodded into my yard. "Karln begged me to fetch her more of those herbs you just sent."

"Truly?" My speeding pulse finally settled, and a huge grin spread across my face. "I told you they'd work like a charm." I waved at him. "Come in and grab some?"

Cruz rolled his eyes, but the sly half-smile he flashed told me he'd play along. "Can't." He coughed, a pathetic, weak sound that was clearly forced. "Got a tickle in my throat. Wouldn't want you catching it."

"Oh. Too bad." I headed for the herb garden I planted along the far side of the fence. I liked to play around, inviting Cruz inside, but the truth was, he couldn't come in. No one could. And I couldn't leave the confines of my yard. Not until the ruling was lifted.

Cruz trailed me along the perimeter. "So what was that all about?" He stared at my prized canides plant. "With the way you were talking, I thought I'd find you covered in drool."

"You'd like that, wouldn't you?" I wiggled my brows, making him chuckle. "Just waiting for the day I finally get to taste the fruits of my labor."

He shook his head, his gaze trailing across my garden with a perplexed frown. "I don't know how you do it."

"Do what?"

"Make the best out of... everything."

A wry grin curved my lips. "What am I supposed to do instead? Sit around crying all day?"

"Pretty much." Cruz scratched his chest. "It's what everyone else I run for does."

My stomach clenched. *Been there...* I brushed off the memory before it fully formed.

I bent beside the herbs and plucked a few orange stems with my fingers. "Not my style. You know what they say. Life throws you shit, either you sit there stinking or make manure."

"No one says that." Cruz chuckled.

"You must not know many planters."

"Nope. Just you and Karln."

I stood, the fragile reddish leaves crinkling in my hands and contrasting against my bronze skin. I could pass them over... but what was the fun in that? "So... what did you bring me?"

It was another game we played. We both knew I wasn't planning to hold out on him. Knowing the plants I grew were helping people back home kept me going. But I wasn't exactly playing by the rules. Never had, and I likely never would. Bartering with my runner was a gray area I'd learned to exploit—a necessity for my sanity as a castaway.

"What?" Cruz nodded back to Tani. "Playing puppet master with your brood wasn't payment enough?"

A hearty laugh rumbled out of my chest. "That *was* the best entertainment I've had in months..." And yes, I was being completely honest. Pathetic, I know.

"Well, I haven't passed any pretties to snag you some new seeds."

"You didn't take that hike I was telling you about?"

He hefted his pack on his shoulders. "You think I have a burning desire to tromp through the jungle *more*?"

Not everyone could enjoy exploring as much as I did. Or... as much as I used to. "Fair point."

Cruz leaned in, lifting a brow. "Would a rumor whet your appetite?"

"Depends how juicy it is."

"It's practically oozing." He backed away suddenly, a look of mock horror crossing his face. "Wait... I forgot. You're not interested in the comings and goings of city folk, am I right?"

Like ellios I'm not. That was where Rhelt was. My only cousin, who'd turned up his nose at me after a single mistake. I'd burn my garden to the ground for a chance to understand what went wrong... *Nope. Not going there.*

I adopted a casual grin that hopefully disguised my inner turmoil. "Eh, it might be good for a giggle."

Cruz stretched out his hand expectantly.

I slapped the leaves into his waiting palm.

"So, word from the city is that someone in space used the planetary landing code." His grin turned smarmy. "And... they're from the Terran system. I know how much you *love* those humans."

My heart clenched as the lovely face of the only human I'd ever encountered flashed in my mind's eye. Honestly, I'd be happy to never see another off-worlder again after what happened with her.

But Cruz didn't need to know that. And I refused to let him see that his playful dig had hit its mark. "What can I say? I have a type." Not like there was a chance I'd have any interactions with them, but curiosity got the better of me. "Any news about why they've come?"

"Not that I've heard. Want me to keep an ear to the loam for you?"

That request was gonna cost me... But I wasn't kidding about entertainment being sparse. "Why not?"

His eyes lit up. "You got any more of that stuff from last time?"

"Why do you think I became a planter in the first place?" I chuckled and pulled a burner from my vest pocket.

Cruz grinned as I passed the paper-wrapped tube to him. "Thanks, Jalen. Don't work too hard now."

I waved. "Me? Never." I pulled another burner out and dug through my pocket for a light. "See you around."

A Terran linguist had arrived a few months ago, and he hadn't stirred up any trouble. If the rumors were true, he'd even managed to upgrade our translators a bit since he'd started studying the intricacies of our many tribal tongues. More humans landing on Dionus might not mean anything. Even if it did, there wasn't much I could do to stop them. But it couldn't hurt to learn what they were here for, either.

As the first warm blast of smoke filled my lungs, all my worries washed away. I turned, my gaze landing on Candy. I licked my lips and sauntered over. "Now... where were we, beautiful?"

4

Double Blessed

Ren

*C*hime.

My muscles burned as I worked the wrench, fastening the last of more than a dozen nuts. The hopper's sluggish motor was about to become a thing of the past.

Chime.

I frowned at the insistent ping coming from my neck and slipped out from under the hull. Slapping a hand against my skin, I silenced the sound. "Why the fuck is my neck ringing? Verne, you listening?"

The *Verne*'s androgynous computerized voice answered me. "How may I be of assistance?"

"Did someone set an alarm on my implant?" It sure as shit wasn't me...

"Captain Arda requested you be alerted when the next meal cycle began."

My brow furrowed at the same time my stomach rumbled loud enough to wake the dead. "Huh. Guess I am a bit hungry…"

I set my tools aside and brushed my hands down my stained blue skinsuit as I stood. Honestly, I couldn't blame Arda for hacking my implant. I got a little hangry when I skipped meals. And since I was always laser-focused on whatever task I was working on, I missed my fair share of them.

Luckily for me, I had my captain—and best friend—looking out for me. Today it was more important than ever that I was in a good mood. After spending the better part of a week cruising at sub-light, we were finally close enough to land. Within hours, we'd set foot on a new world.

A tiny thread of excitement tugged at my chest. Sure, I was happiest when I had my hands in an engine, but I couldn't deny that exploring the universe got my motor pumping, too. If only I didn't have to meet with Cassidy, then I could really enjoy it.

I slipped out of the docking bay and headed to the mess hall. There wasn't much I could do to stem the discomfort boiling in my veins when I pictured seeing my sister again. But I could cure the hunger gnawing at my belly.

"Hey, Ren."

"Capt." I smiled at Arda as I ducked into the mess. "Thanks for the reminder. I would've probably forgot again." I sidled up to the food processor and quickly keyed in one of my go-to orders.

Arda chuckled, making her long brown curls swish against the shoulders of her pink skinsuit. "Don't mention it." She sipped from her teacup, frowning as she pulled it away from her face.

"Something wrong with your drink?"

"Fucking oolong." Her mouth puckered like she'd sucked something sour. "That damn upselling sales agent was full of shit."

A chuckle rolled off my tongue even though I had no clue what had her steaming. "About what?"

"The so-called greenhouse they sold me on during the *Verne*'s renovations is defective." She scowled into her cup as she swirled the brown liquid. "He claimed it was so easy a baby could grow their own veggie purees with the press of a button."

"Or you have a black thumb."

She sighed. "Maybe..."

"Hey." With a hunch that deep furrow in her brow wasn't only from a subpar cup of tea, I sank into the seat across from her and planted my elbows on the circular table. "What's really bothering you?"

Her bright-blue eyes flashed to mine. It wasn't a surprise she'd snagged an alien lord for her very own. Arda was a smoke show, petite and curvy in all the right places. And as captain, she was normally confident enough to bark orders until her throat was hoarse... but right now, a sliver of vulnerability shone in her gaze.

She chewed on her lip, then leaned closer, lowering her voice. "How the hell am I gonna keep a kid alive if I can't even grow a plant properly?"

My eyes widened before flashing to her stomach. "Are you..."

"No. I'm still packing." She tapped her arm where the birth control implant practically everyone used these days—myself included—rested under her skin. "But Lux wants kids one day. It was the whole reason he voyaged to Earth to begin with. And I want them too—eventually."

I couldn't blame her for waiting. Arda was younger than me by a few years. At twenty-eight, I *still* didn't feel ready for kids. Especially not when I'd have to raise them by myself. There wasn't a man in the universe I trusted enough to be my kid's daddy. At least Arda would have Lux to help her.

Her arm shot at the wall, toward the defective greenhouse. "Shit like this makes me worry I'll never be ready."

I scoffed. "You can't hang the fate of your future children on how well you kept a stupid plant alive. I'm sure there are plenty of women who can't grow a damn thing, but their kids turn out okay." I frowned, wishing I could offer a personal anecdote to really prove my point.

Yeah... that ain't happening. My history with maternal figures wasn't the type of thing you brought up to convince someone kids were easy...

I settled for reaching across the table and snagging her hand. "What are you worrying about this for? You said yourself you aren't planning to have kids anytime soon. You'll have plenty of time to figure it out."

Arda twisted her lips. "You're right. I guess I'm just feeling bad about not being helpful with Smudge."

"Oh... that." Apparently fuscieras' heat lasted a good long while. It might be a month before she was done yowling and hiding in the ship's nooks and crannies. Lux had been practically tearing his hair out, trying to get his beloved pet to settle—with little success. "I wouldn't worry about it. She'll be back to normal before you know it."

Arda sighed again.

I couldn't stand seeing her so dejected. *Fuck... Better change the subject.* My gaze darted around the mess before landing on the tablet in front of Arda. From my spot across from her, the lettering was upside down, but it looked like she was reading a research article. I nodded to the tablet. "So, what're you investigating today?"

"Oh, that's some info on Dionus." She brightened. "I've managed to track down the exact location of the facility we need to search."

"That's great news."

Arda had been on the hunt for information about her genetic heritage for ages now. Around the time she got together with Lux, she discovered some pretty interesting facts hidden in her family lineage that pointed to illegal genetic tampering on what might be a massive scale. The latest clue we uncovered pointed us to a spot on the jungle world we were about to touch down on.

She leaned back in her chair. "It wasn't too hard once we were in orbit. But it looks like the building is surrounded by some pretty rough terrain. Think your sister can connect us with a local guide?"

"We'll find out soon enough." The food processor chimed, and I took advantage of the distraction, hopping to my feet. The truth was, I wasn't entirely sure what to expect when we met with Cassidy. We hadn't exactly left things on the best terms...

"Oh yeah, and get this." Arda kept talking, seeming not to notice the way my shoulders had stiffened as I pulled a tray loaded with a chicken-and-cheese burrito from the food processor. "I dug up an article from one of the leading cultural researchers on Dionus. Sounds like a lot of those rumors floating around about the planet being overrun with barbarians are exaggerated."

I sat, plunking my tray on the table. "Really?" We'd all heard the stories. It wasn't only their strict visitation laws that kept travelers from vacationing there. The local people were said to be superstitious and vicious to outsiders.

She swiped her fingers over her screen. "Yep. The planet has a fascinating history. A few centuries ago, they were invaded by space-faring scavengers who wanted to use the planet's resources for their own ends. They spread tales about the populace to keep others away—but that was after the locals ran them off and stole their tech."

"And that's how they learned to travel the stars?" I shuddered as I pictured how traumatic that must've been. The Dionions were just merrily living their lives before aliens appeared out of nowhere. It was like something out of a retro invasion vid.

"Wild, isn't it?"

"Yeah…" I didn't know if that made them any less barbaric, though. Frankly, that they could overpower a technologically superior foe had to say something about their brute strength. "So, they don't still live in huts in the jungle?"

"That part is true. They have some cities too. That's where we're landing to meet your sister. But the old research facility is pretty far from civilization."

I smiled as I lifted my burrito. "We'll find a guide. Don't worry." Hot sauce stung my tongue and made my eyes water.

Footsteps clattered in the hall. "Hey, you two ready for landing?" Karsen poked her head in the mess, an expectant look on her face. "Lux wanted me to tell you we're beginning our descent in five."

Arda stood. "I better head to the bridge before he fucks up my controls."

I chuckled around a bite of burrito. Arda and Lux were always giving each other a hard time about who was the better pilot. "See you later, Capt."

Karsen slid into the chair Arda had vacated and activated the retractable seat belt. "Shouldn't you stow that for landing?" She nodded to my tray.

"One sec." Opening wide, I shoved the last third of my burrito inside my mouth.

"Impressive." She cocked a brow. "Do you swallow that whole, or is chewing required?"

I rolled my eyes, my mouth too full to come up with a snarky reply. Karsen and I had turned a corner after the whole fiasco on Oraxis

Station. Now, she was back to teasing me—which was better than assuming I was on a one-woman mission to take out every man I met.

My empty tray clattered as I slipped it inside the dish sanitizer. Then I sank into my seat and slapped the button to trigger the straps. After swallowing, I said, "You ready to step foot on an alien world?"

Karsen's face lit up. "Of course. I'm looking forward to meeting a new culture. I might even let one of those Dionion men get to know me real close, if you know what I mean."

I nearly rolled my eyes again. "So the blue hair does it for you?"

"Please. Like I care what color their hair is. I'm more interested in what they're packing elsewhere. Don't know if I'll ever have another opportunity to land a guy who's been double blessed."

My insides twinged at the reminder. Since I'd learned about Dionion men's unique anatomy, I'd been a bit curious, too. But I wasn't planning to ask any of the locals for a test ride. In fact... "You might want to reconsider that. They mate for life. Aren't you a little young to settle down?"

"Who's to say there won't be some guys looking for a bit of fun before they meet the love of their life?"

"From what my sister told me, it doesn't work that way. They don't do casual. And once they find their mate, that's it." At least... that was how it was *supposed* to work.

Karsen pouted. "Damn. Well, a girl can dream, can't she?" She fluffed her black curls just as the *Verne* started shaking.

My fingers tightened on the armrests while the ship slowly sank into the atmosphere. The shaking finally receded, and once the telltale clack of the landing gear descending rang out, I sighed. And yet, the relief didn't stick around. Because I knew landing safely on an alien world wasn't the most nerve-racking thing I needed to face. "Let's go meet my sister."

5

Endless Summer

Ren

I tugged the neck of my skinsuit as we wove through the crowded streets. "Fuck, this planet is like a sauna."

Despite the humidity, I couldn't deny the place was charming, with the same small-town vibes you'd expect from any off-the-beaten-path vacation spot on Earth. We'd landed close to the city center of Dionus' capital, Harlxston, and so far there hadn't been much to see besides neatly swept roads and throngs of scantily clad blue-haired Dionions roving the streets.

Their species resembled humans enough that you might mistake them for one from afar. But only if you ignored how their skin shone like metal in the sun, in a shade of bronze no human had ever been born with. Their oddly shaped teeth flashed when they talked, the canines so long and sharp they made chills run down my spine.

The people gave us a wide berth, wandering past us with bundles on their backs, likely on their way to some market. Others eyed us warily as they disappeared into airy wooden structures lining the roads.

Arda chuckled, shading her eyes from the blazing sun. "At least we're not stuck waiting for nightfall." We'd been forced to leave Lux on the ship. His species was vulnerable to strong sunlight, making it impossible for him to walk outside during daylight hours.

Karsen tipped her face to the sky. "Apparently, it's like this all year round. Endless summer." She grinned. "I could get used to it."

I gave the buildings lined with windows by the dozen a closer inspection—every window was wide open. I buried the groan that tried to fight its way out of my throat. "Doesn't look like air conditioning is a thing here."

Arda clapped my shoulder. "Relax, we have the *Verne*, remember? You can hop on board if you need to cool down."

I nodded, fighting to brush off the discomfort swarming me. A bead of sweat trailed down my forehead, but my skinsuit took care of the rest. The planet's temperature wasn't what was truly bothering me. I just didn't want to talk about what was.

"Ren?" A high-pitched squeal pierced my ears.

Crap. Speak of the devil...

"Cassidy." I spun around just before my sister thudded into my chest, wrapping her arms around me like a vise. I wiggled, unable to escape, so I settled for freezing in place until she saw fit to set me free.

"I was so excited when I heard you were coming!" She pulled away, and pale-blue eyes brimming with tears met mine.

My heart twinged. I wasn't sure what I'd been expecting, but a tearful welcome wouldn't have been my first guess.

"Holy shit. It's like looking in a mirror." Arda's gaze darted between our faces.

We were identical, with the same high cheekbones, slim stature, and tanned skin, but that was where the similarities ended. Cassidy wore a dainty sundress like the natives favored, her long blonde hair styled in a waterfall of curls hanging down her back.

Me? I looked like I'd spent all day wrestling with an engine—as always.

Cassidy stuck out her hand. "Hi! I'm Cassidy."

Arda shook it with a smile. "I'm Arda, captain of the *Verne*. And this is Karsen, our medical officer."

Karsen grabbed Cassidy's hand next. "You can call me Kar."

"It's so nice to meet you! Come on, let's get out of the heat." Cassidy flashed a blinding grin as she led us down a curving side street. "When I heard Ren was working as a ship's mechanic, I knew she'd found her calling. She's always had a knack for fixing things—even as a kid."

I cleared my throat. "Where did you hear about my job?" Last time we'd talked, I was still stuck on Oraxis Station, and we hadn't exactly kept in touch since then.

"From Demetri," Cassidy explained. "He accepted my invitation to visit Dionus way before you did. You might even see him if you stick around long enough."

"For real?" Guess that explained why Demi hadn't been at Oraxis when we'd swung through.

"Well, if he ever drags himself out of the jungle." She glanced at Arda and Kar. "Our brother is studying to be a linguist. He's been working with tribes all over the planet to better understand the nuances of the Dionion language. It's his work that's helped the translators become a thousand times more accurate."

Arda nodded. "We uploaded the language upgrade to our devices you sent to the *Verne* earlier this week."

Cassidy's eyes lit with pride. "That was all Demi's doing." She leaned in conspiratorially. "When I first met Rhelt, half the things he said came out like grunts. If it weren't for the pair bond, I would've likely never given him a chance."

"Pair bond?" Karsen asked.

"It's what happens to Dionions when they find their mate." Cassidy stopped in front of a wooden house with bright red and yellow potted plants hanging in the windows. "To be honest, I'm not entirely sure how it works. Something to do with pheromones... All I know is the minute I met Rhelt, I knew he was the one, even though he scared the pants off of me."

Scary sounds about right. Shivers coursed down my arms.

Karsen's brows lifted. "So the pair bond affected you even though you're different species?"

Cassidy giggled. "That's putting it mildly, but yeah. I've chatted about it with a few of the women here, and they described everything I experienced perfectly."

"Fascinating. I'd love to hear more—"

I cut Kar off before she convinced Cassidy to spill her life story. "How about we focus on the reason we're here before we get wrapped up in research projects?"

Cassidy glanced at me. "Sure." The wooden porch stair creaked as she climbed and then opened the door. "Come inside. I'm happy to help however I can."

Arda and Karsen ducked in the doorway without hesitation, while I hung back with a lump in my throat.

You can do this, Ren. Maybe he won't even be here...

Cass led us into an airy living room decorated in shades of green and blue. The open floor plan revealed a small kitchen on the opposite side of the house, complete with a food processor and wooden table and chairs. A pleasant breeze wafted around us, at least ten degrees cooler than the air outside. I scanned the ceiling, hunting for the machine responsible for it, but only spotted some ordinary fans.

"Have a seat." Cassidy waved at two blue oversized couches that faced each other with no entertainment in sight.

What do they do for fun, stare longingly at each other all night? With how head over heels Cass acted the first time she introduced me to her mate, I wouldn't put it past her. As for her mate... after what happened back then, I wasn't so sure.

"Can I grab you something to eat or drink?" Cassidy asked.

"Ate before we landed." I perched on the corner of a couch, fighting to shove the unwanted memory to the back of my mind.

Arda glanced at me shrewdly before turning to Cass. "Thanks for the offer, but we're fine. What we really need help with is finding a jungle guide."

Cass sat across from me. "You don't want to go into the jungle, trust me."

"Can't be avoided." Paper crinkled as Arda pulled a map out of her pocket and unfolded it. Then she sat next to Cass, spreading the page across both their laps. "We're looking for an old facility located somewhere in this area." She pointed to a region covered in thick foliage. "According to the *Verne*'s scans, there's nowhere close by where we can land our ship."

"They don't like clearing trees to make landing strips," Cassidy explained. "The tribes are very protective of their land."

"That's why we need a local to guide us." Arda pointed to a different spot. "If we land here, then it'll be about a week's journey on foot to the facility."

Karsen pursed her lips. "Can't we fly the *Verne* low over the trees? Then a few of us could rappel down."

"No," a masculine voice boomed. "I'd strongly advise against that."

I stiffened, but luckily everyone missed it since they'd turned toward the tall, muscular Dionion emerging from a darkened doorway.

Cassidy beamed, stars in her eyes. "This is my mate, Rhelt."

Rhelt strode into the room, dressed casually in long brown shorts that hit below the knee, and a pocketed vest that left most of his chest and abs on display. Arda smiled politely, and Kar gave him a cool once-over that would've likely ended with a flirtatious smirk if Cassidy hadn't just introduced him as hers.

Honestly, I couldn't blame her. Like most Dionion men, Rhelt was fit and stacked like a bodybuilder. But that didn't stop a shiver from running down my spine when he finally locked eyes with me.

My brain screamed, *Look away*, but I viciously rejected that notion. I had no reason to hide and absolutely nothing to be ashamed of. Even so, holding his gaze burned like clasping a red-hot ember. Yet as much as I wanted to throw the fire in his face, I wouldn't. Not when the sparks would singe Cassidy too.

Rhelt's violet eyes flashed with some emotion I couldn't pinpoint before he tore his gaze off mine and scanned the map. "In the time of our ancestors, when the invaders came, they dropped from the sky. After they'd been routed out, we set up a network of defensive drones to patrol the jungle."

"Yikes. I hadn't heard about that," Karsen admitted.

"I did. The safe flying zones were included with the landing instructions." Arda pointed to a cleared spot on the map. "I figure we can land here and hire a guide to take us the rest of the way."

Rhelt frowned. "Where do you need to go?"

Arda's finger trailed across the paper. "Here."

"Impossible." Rhelt's dark brows disappeared beneath the blue bangs dangling over his forehead. "There aren't any guides who will take you *there*."

I crossed my arms. "Why not?"

Rhelt flicked a glance in my direction before returning his attention to the map. "It's in the middle of dradhowler territory."

"What's a dradhowler?" Karsen asked.

"You don't want to know." Cassidy shuddered.

A trickle of fear wormed up my spine.

Arda cut in. "I've read about those, too. Sounds like they're only a problem during certain moon cycles. Won't the right guide know how to avoid any run-ins?"

Rhelt snorted. "There's no one senseless enough to chance it."

Cass tilted her head. "Are you sure about that? Because if I'm remembering correctly, there is—"

"No." Rhelt spun on his heel and bolted into the kitchen as abruptly as he'd entered.

"Just... give me a sec." Cassidy hopped out from under the map, the paper crinkling as we leveled dumbfounded stares at Rhelt. He poured himself something out of a pitcher, but instead of drinking it, he clenched the wooden cup so hard the sides buckled in like they might snap.

After Cass crossed the room and rubbed her hands across the big guy's shoulders while speaking softly, Arda leaned in, lowering her voice. "You know what that was all about?"

"No clue." My eyes narrowed. "When were you planning to tell us about those howler things? What the hell are they?"

Arda shrugged, seeming unperturbed even when the mere mention of visiting the creatures' territory had sent a local man running—literally. "Some big beasties that prowl around the jungle when it's fully dark."

"Beast?" Karsen blanched. "Oh, *hell* no. I am not in the mood to be mauled."

"Could've fooled me. Weren't you just saying you wanted to get up close and personal with a new species?" From the way Kar's lips pressed into a thin slash, I gathered she wasn't amused by my quip.

Arda muffled a chuckle behind her fingers. "Relax. There won't be any mauling going down. Did you two forget this planet has three moons?"

"What's that got to do with anything?" I asked.

"The dradhowlers only come out when it's fully dark, which doesn't even happen every night. They're easily avoided by seeking shelter during the rare times when none of the moons are visible."

Karsen drummed her nails on the armrest. "If that's true, then why did Rhelt freak out when you brought it up?"

We turned our gazes to the kitchen as Cassidy clapped and let out a delighted squeal. "Thank you, babe. This'll work out great." She rocked up on her toes and planted a peck on Rhelt's chin.

A small smile painted Rhelt's lips while he gazed at his mate, but the moment Cassidy sauntered in our direction, his face hardened. Then he slipped out of a side door without bothering to say goodbye.

Cassidy sat beside Arda again. "We have the perfect guide for you."

My pulse raced. I was not expecting it to be so easy. Judging by Rhelt's reaction, I'd thought Cass would tell us to pack up and go home.

"That's fantastic!" Arda grinned. "So, when can we meet? And where?"

"May I?" At Arda's nod, Cassidy grabbed the map and carried it to a nearby desk. Picking up a pen, she scrawled some directions on the back. "I'm writing you directions to his cabin. It's a short walk from the landing site you chose."

"That's convenient," Karsen said.

"And he knows the way?" Arda asked.

"Mm-hmm." Cassidy's pen stopped scratching. "He's definitely your best shot at making it in and out in one piece." She held the map out but stopped before she reached Arda's side and scanned her with a serious stare. "It'll still be dangerous. Are you sure—"

Arda snagged the map. "I am. Thank you, Cassidy."

"Anything for a friend of Ren's. You should wait a few hours before you head over there. Rhelt's out hiring a runner to send your guide a message with the trip details."

"Not a problem." Arda folded the map neatly. "It'll give me time to pack for the hike." She stuffed the paper into her pocket and thrust out a hand. "I really appreciate your help. Let me know how I can return the favor."

Cassidy ignored Arda's hand and pulled her into a hug. "It's nothing. But I wouldn't mind a few moments alone to catch up with my sis."

My heart stuttered as Cassidy's words bounced around my skull. *What do we have to catch up on? Does she know? Did Rhelt tell her?*

Arda met my eyes. "You cool with that, Ren? We can wait for you on the porch."

Might as well get it over with... "Yeah. Meet you outside in a few."

Cassidy sank onto the couch beside me as the front door swung closed. "I'm not even going to ask why you came. It doesn't matter. I'm just so glad to see you, Ren."

Oh, fuck. Were those tears in her eyes? "It's nice to see you too."

Not like I didn't see her face every time I looked in the mirror. Who cared if I spent half my life wondering where she'd disappeared to? It was like she expected all that hurt to slide away when she grabbed my hand.

But things weren't always so simple. And twins weren't always inseparable, ready to finish each other's sentences. Especially not when they spent their childhoods in vastly different places.

"Did you have something else you needed to say to me?" I asked cooly.

Cassidy retracted her hand. "You're not going with Arda, are you?"

I eyed her warily. "Why? You don't think I can handle a hike through the jungle?" Honestly, I hadn't planned on it. There was plenty for me to do on the *Verne* while Arda was off searching for that facility. But seeing Cassidy so leery about it almost made me want to dig out my hiking boots.

"It'll be a rough trek. And the guide is a little... eccentric. I don't want you getting hurt."

Wow. How clueless can she be?

I scoffed. "Trust me. I can handle whatever I need to just fine on my own—like always." I stood, ready to race out the door, but Cassidy snagged my sleeve.

"Wait. I didn't mean—" She shook her head. "I'm sorry, Ren. Just be careful, okay? And maybe when your friend finds what she's looking for, you'll come back for a longer visit? There's still a lot of stuff I'd love to talk about with you."

I tugged my arm free. "Sure... maybe." With one last nod, I fled through the door, hoping Cass was smart enough to realize that *maybe* was really a *no*.

6

Deficient

Jalen

"Can you believe this, Trivet?" I spun toward my companion, shaking the note I'd read about a dozen times in his face. "What did I tell you? I knew everything would turn out all right."

The midday sun shone on the garden as Trivet's gaze shot to mine, though he didn't bother lifting his head out of his food bowl. Still, I could tell from the way his tail wiggled he was happy for me.

Yes, I was talking to an animal. I was starved for company, remember? But that was about to change. I just had to do one thing, and then I could bust out of my cage for good.

I dragged a hand through my chest-length blue hair. "My bag's packed already. Got the route all planned out."

A smile crossed my lips as I pictured stepping out of the fence for the first time in three long years. I'd get to travel the jungle again! Before I'd landed myself in captivity, I'd always loved hiking to far-off spots, seeking new seeds and plants to bring to Karln.

This wouldn't be exactly the same. For one thing, I was about to venture into one of the most dangerous spots in the jungle. And I'd have a Terran in tow... One I'd been explicitly warned to keep safe—and not to touch.

"Why do you think Rhelt was so worried I keep my hands to myself? Do you think he's still hung up on what happened?"

Trivet finally lifted his head, his long purple tongue darting out to clean his lips, showing off a row of off-white teeth. I'd befriended the furry critter my first year here, when his mother holed up in a makeshift nest that I'd discovered while planting. Trivet had been the runt of his litter, with a lame back leg that hadn't formed properly in the womb. When his siblings took off, he'd stuck around, making a home in my garden.

I probably should've shooed him away. His species, lormates, were nimble, black-furred mammals that grew to about the size of an infant. And they were omnivores, which made him a menace in the garden. But I couldn't help feeling a bond with the puny guy. While all the other lormates were out in the wild, living their lives and finding love, he'd been left behind. No female in his species would ever settle for a mate with such an obvious deficiency.

Guess we were kindred in that. After what happened with Rhelt and Cassidy, it was clear I was pretty deficient, too.

But I'd made peace with that long ago. Not all Dionions were destined to find love. Suppose I was one of the few who fit in that category. That didn't mean my life had no purpose. Like Trivet, I'd keep my head up and make the best with what I'd been handed.

"You know what? I'm not going to worry about it." I folded the paper in two and shoved it inside one of my vest pockets. "If Rhelt wants me to take Cassidy's friend to find something in the jungle, that's all right with me. And hopefully after I'm done, I can fly out of here."

There was once a time when I'd dreamed about exploring off-world. If I were being perfectly honest, those dreams never faded completely. Even while confined with no sign of release, I occasionally pondered what it'd be like to travel the stars.

It looked like I might get my chance after all. I just had to obey that note to the letter. Keeping my charge alive wouldn't be an issue. I knew the jungle like the back of my hand and had an uncanny knack for tracking moon cycles. I'd spent many days in my youth holed up in some nook, waiting for safe passage.

The other part might be a tad trickier. I'd gone three long years without any female companionship. But no matter how nice the female Rhelt sent was—no matter how tempting—I wouldn't touch her.

It won't be that hard, will it?

I just had to endure a week alone with a stranger, and then I'd be free to pursue anyone I'd like. Ellios willing, I might even find a mate one day. If not on Dionus, then perhaps somewhere out in the stars.

Trivet crossed the room, twining his lithe body around my ankles with a halfhearted *mew*.

"Hey, don't worry. If I find a ride off this rock, I'll take you with me. How does that sound?"

With a flick of his tail, Trivet hopped onto the fence and leaped out of the garden. I watched him go with a sigh. "See you out there, buddy."

7

Afternoon Delight

Ren

"Are you sure you don't mind?" Arda's voice reached my ears before the slam of the shuttle bay doors rang out.

"Of course not," Karsen answered. "You shouldn't have to be stuck with a stranger for a week all alone."

I popped my head out from the hopper's hood as they passed me. "What's going on?"

Kar yelped, a hand pressed to her heart. "Holy crap, Ren! I didn't see you there."

"Pro-tip: Assume Ren is always hiding somewhere in the shuttle bay, even if you don't see her." Arda chuckled as she adjusted the pack on her back. "Especially if you're trying to sneak in a little afternoon delight."

"Really wish you'd take your own advice." I carefully settled my favorite laserspanner back in my tool case. "Might be a *delight* for you and Lux, but the rest of us... not so much." I'd lost count of all the times they'd started getting frisky without realizing they had an audience.

Arda had the gall to look insulted. "Hey, don't knock it till you've tried it." She nudged my shoulder playfully. "Why don't you take some time off this week? I bet Lux won't mind dropping you at your sister's place. You two can catch up some more while we're gone."

Yeah… No thanks.

We'd flown to the spot on the map where Arda would meet with the guide. Only I hadn't realized one thing. "*We're* gone?"

Karsen spun sideways, and I finally clocked that she had a bag strapped to her back too. "I volunteered to tag along after we got the go-ahead from your brother-in-law and saw his warning."

I frowned at Arda. "Warning? What warning?"

Arda bit her lip and lowered her voice. "Look… Don't tell Lux, but it sounds like the guide we're heading to meet is a weirdo. Honestly, I'm not too worried about it, but it would freak Lux out if he knew."

My heart raced. "You're kidding, right?" Why the hell would my sister send us a nutcase as a guide? "What is it about him that's so weird?"

Arda shrugged. "Rhelt didn't explain it fully. He just mentioned that the guy has been living in seclusion, and this would be his first time leaving his home in a few years."

I leaned against the hopper. "Sorry I saddled you with a week-long trek with some grumpy recluse."

"Hey, not a problem." Arda squeezed my shoulder gently. "I've dealt with my fair share of grumps."

Is she talking about me? Suppose that was fair. Then again, Lux could be a bit grumpy from time to time.

Still, I couldn't ignore the twinge of pain in my chest. Arda would rather bring Kar than me. Suppose that made sense, too. Karsen was personable, and skilled with medicine to boot. If anything went wrong on their hike, she'd be helpful to have around. And me? I'd probably only be a buzzkill, like usual.

I didn't know why I didn't accept it and move on like I always did. This wasn't the first time I'd been left out of something. It wasn't the first time I'd been picked last. Even forgotten. I'd learned at a young age to make do with the scraps of affection I received.

So, when the next words popped out of my mouth, the person most shocked by them was me. "I'll tag along too."

Arda's eyes widened. "Really?"

No, not really. Take it back. You can spend the entire time with your hands in an engine instead of sweating in the jungle and listening to some alien grumble about being dragged out of his house.

But even though Arda's incredulous response was the perfect excuse to backtrack, I doubled down. "Yeah. Sounds like fun."

Okay... the *fun* bit clearly went too far. Karsen's gaze narrowed and her lips twisted like she'd eaten something rotten.

"Fuck yes!" Luckily, Arda had no qualms accepting my bald-faced lie. "This is gonna be epic! I've been meaning to get us together for a girls' trip."

Karsen's severe expression lifted, and she let out a breathy laugh. "Strangest girls' trip I've ever been on."

It would actually be my first, but I wasn't about to showcase how lame my previous life was by bringing up that sad fact.

Arda clapped her hands. "If you're coming, you better pack quick. Daylight's wasting."

Despite the reservations swirling in my head—mostly that this was a terrible, idiotic mistake—my lips curved into a smile. Arda's obvious excitement had chased away that twinge like it never existed. And that was enough to make me hustle out of the shuttle bay to my room.

As I stuffed some extra clothes and provisions into a pack, I drew in a few deep breaths. Had I just signed myself up for a miserable week hiking through a sweltering jungle ripe with danger? Yep. But on the bright side, at least I wouldn't need to worry about visiting Cassidy. That in itself was enough reason to follow through.

Ren

"Fuck my life," I whispered under my breath a couple hours later.

"Problem?" Karsen gamboled beside me, a perky grin on her face as she navigated the dense jungle with ease.

I jerked my leg free from the third thorn bush that'd assaulted my skinsuit since I'd stepped outside. "Just trying to keep my clothes from shredding before we get there." I winced as the fabric tore, leaving the outer half of my ankle exposed to the scorching heat.

"If you didn't wear your skinsuits so baggy, they wouldn't catch on everything," Karsen unhelpfully stated.

"Can't help it if I don't want all my nooks and crannies on display like the rest of the universe." Virtually everyone wore skinsuits these days. The ingenious fabric wicked away sweat and kept body temperatures regulated. And yeah, they worked best if they fit snug against the skin. But I'd rather endure a shoddy fit than deal with the alternative.

Arda wrapped a hand around my shoulders while scanning the map. "It's fine. I have a sewing kit in my pack. Anyway, we're almost there."

I slapped my neck. "Good. I'm getting eaten alive out here."

The constant buzzing was certainly annoying, but I couldn't deny the planet was beautiful. Blue-tinged leaves topped most of the trees, and countless fragrant blossoms littered the forest floor. Dewy fruits and berries dotted branches, and bright bird-like creatures with leathery wings flitted around, sampling them.

Soon the dense jungle path opened up, revealing a fenced-in yard bursting with so many strange plants it was hard to see the small cabin on the back of the lot. "This is it." Arda folded the map and stuffed it into her pocket.

"Guess we should knock on the door," Karsen said.

I frowned at the chest-high fence. "Where's the gate?"

Arda grinned. "Oh, I almost forgot." She tugged her pack off and unzipped it, pulling out another folded piece of paper. "Rhelt gave me the code to get in." She paced along the fence. "He said the gate was... ah ha. Here." Arda stopped after she turned the corner, and I hurried to follow. By the time I caught up, she'd already tugged the gate open.

We piled inside the yard, wandering through the neatly planted rows of flowers. Karsen whistled. "Fancy garden."

"Wonder what all these plants are for?" Arda bent beside an enormous yellow blossom the size of her head and sniffed deeply. Her face scrunched as she rubbed pollen off the tip of her nose. "It's definitely not perfume."

Another bug whizzed past my ear, and I snagged her arm. "Doesn't matter. Let's see if this guide has some damn insect repellent."

"All right, hold your horses." Arda giggled as I led her toward the cabin. "Have you ever ridden a horse before?"

How random. "Um... no."

Karsen said, "Me either."

"I have. Well, kinda." Arda swatted a low-hanging purple blossom away from her face.

I lifted a brow. "How do you *kinda* ride a horse?" With the majority of land back on Earth developed, it was pretty rare to see big animals like horses.

"There's this bar I've been to that has an antique bucking bronco machine." She leaned in and stage-whispered, "I think the pervy owner only kept it around to watch girls bouncing."

I chuckled as we approached the door. "Remind me not to go there."

Arda slapped my shoulder weakly, flashing a lopsided grin. "Nah! It was fun." She squinted at me. "You should let loose more often, Ren. Can't let the pervs keep ya down."

Oookay...

Karsen lifted her fist and knocked firmly on the cabin door. My pulse kicked up as we stood there waiting. Nothing.

Karsen knocked again. Still nothing.

"I'm gonna head around back," Karsen announced. "You guys wanna stay here in case he comes to the front?"

I shrugged. "Sure." As she disappeared around the side of the house, Arda lifted her fist and pounded again.

Where the hell is this guy? An unsettling feeling took up residence in my gut.

As Arda lifted her fist to pound again, the door swung open.

"Hello?" A steamy, fresh-scented man busy wringing long blue hair peered out of the house, aiming a disarming smile at Arda.

I blinked repeatedly, and it took everything in me not to gasp at the towel-wrapped hunk in the doorway. Water droplets clung to his flesh, and the pitter-patter of running water made it clear we'd interrupted his shower. My gaze trailed down miles of bronze muscled skin to the considerable bulge tenting the fabric tied at his waist. Or should I say, *bulges.*

Holy double dipstick.

Heat flashed, searing me so unexpectedly I wobbled on my feet. An insane urge to run hit me, but my body refused to listen. I just stood there, dumbstruck and more than a little lost.

Wake up, Ren. He's not the first hottie you've seen, and he won't be the last.

Arda cleared her throat. "Hey, nice to meet you. Rhelt said you'd be expecting us."

That was the instant the guide noticed me. Our gazes met, and I swear something indescribable poured through me. It was like every synapse in my brain fired at once. Tingles shot through my limbs, flashing through my flesh and burrowing into my core, setting off a wave of yearning that nearly had me panting.

What in the fuck is that? *Is something wrong with me?*

I shook off the feeling, but then warm hands landed on my shoulders.

Huge hands.

Emerald-green eyes bored into mine. "Cassidy?" The man shook me, making the gasp trapped in my throat finally escape. "Where is Rhelt?" he asked, panicked. "What happened?"

Thank god Arda was there. She shoved the hulking half-naked stranger back. "Hey! Get off of her. That's not Cassidy."

The guy's brow scrunched up. "Not Cassidy?" His gaze snagged on my short locks before he searched my face. "But..."

"We're twins." My voice escaped in a thready timbre I didn't recognize.

"This is Ren, Cassidy's sister." Arda giggled, her laughter seeming at odds with the tense situation. "Jeez, it's like I'm in a brothel. You wanna put something on?"

"Uh... Certainly. My apologies." The guy turned as if to walk inside, but flipped back before he'd taken a step. "I'm Jalen." His gaze slid off Arda and back to me, his smile slipping. "Be right back."

The door slid closed, and it finally felt like I could breathe normally again.

"You all right?" Arda asked. "I'm sorry he grabbed you. I know you don't like strangers touching you."

Gulping, I forced a smile. "It's fine. Honest mistake."

But as the words rang out, I couldn't help worrying. Because if I was being completely honest, at that moment, having Jalen's hands on me hadn't felt like a mistake at all.

What the hell is happening to me?

8

Not For You

Jalen

I eased the door closed, fighting the impulse to tear it back open for another glimpse of the blue-eyed beauty in my garden. The moment I'd spotted Ren, the universe shifted. My breath came hard and fast, my flesh alive as if awash with the invisible caress of dainty fingers. It was all I could do to stop myself from tearing the door off its hinges.

Not again! This isn't happening.

Tearing through the cabin, I shut off the shower and threw on my clothes while attempting to bury the wave of attraction pulsing through my body. There was only one reason I'd merely look at a female and have such an intense reaction.

But I'd been fooled before. I wouldn't go down that path again. Especially not with *her*.

Harlx's bane! I couldn't even go a few heartbeats without breaking the conditions my cousin had set for me. My hands shook as I recalled the heat of Ren's arms beneath my palms. I'd barely touched her, all while assuming the worst had happened. Who could blame me when she showed up shorn, looking just like Cassidy?

Twins. It was just my rotten luck...

It didn't matter. If I wanted my freedom back, I couldn't touch her. She was off-limits.

I might've already ruined things. What if they were out there, reporting back to Rhelt? They could be telling him I grabbed one of them before we'd even been properly introduced.

No... I couldn't think like that. Everything would be all right.

Get yourself together, Jalen. I had to show them my reaction was a solitary slip-up. That I could be trusted to lead them into the jungle, and I had no intention of repeating that stupid mistake—no matter how much I wanted to.

After donning my shorts and vest and stuffing my feet into boots, I headed for the door. *She's not for you. Remember that, you imbecile.* I sucked in a deep breath, willing the thought to take root and flower. Then I stepped outside.

Ellios deliver me... Where were they? I stared at my garden with a frown. Had I dreamed the whole thing? Had the years of isolation finally driven me insane?

Muffled voices drew my attention to the side of the cabin. I followed the sound, keeping my steps light. Before long, two distinct voices became clear, both feminine, but only one made my loins tighten uncomfortably.

"What do you mean Arda's not with you? She went to find you." As my pulse kicked up, I knew that was her—Ren—even before I'd turned the corner.

A different female answered, "I bet she's in the backyard. If she walked around the other side of the house, then she probably missed me coming back."

I rounded the corner and grunted as a warm weight smashed into me. My hands fell instinctively to her hips as her cheek pressed flat to my bare chest, and a nervous breath ghosted across my skin. Shivers erupted and my fingers tightened.

Yes. My—

"Get off of me!" Ren squeaked.

A fragrant puff of some alien flower smacked me in the nose before she scrambled back. "My apologies." I pulled my hands back, holding them up in surrender. "I heard voices."

Our gazes clashed, her pale blues full of something I couldn't name. My skin thrummed, that unwanted sensation tearing through me with renewed vengeance.

No... No, you can't trust it. You're wrong, just like last time.

I furiously buried the urge to tug her back against my chest as a voice cleared beside me.

I'd practically forgotten someone else was present. "You sure weren't kidding, Ren." A voluptuous dark-haired female sheathed in a purple one-piece outfit thrust out her hand and aimed a sultry smile at me. "I'm Karsen, but you can call me Kar."

Did she want me to take her hand? *Don't do it. You've already groped one of them—twice.*

Ren saved me from making a decision when she pushed between us with a scowl. "Finish the introductions after we find Capt."

Karsen shrugged and retracted her hand, following Ren around the cabin's perimeter. Both were practically jogging, paying no mind to the flowers they trampled. "Hey!" When Ren whipped around and aimed a glare at me, I wanted to wither, but stood firm. "Watch where you walk. Some of these took years to grow."

"What's with the plants?" Karsen slowed, taking more care with her steps. "We were all wondering."

"Most are very rare. The blooms can be made into medicines, dyes, and other useful things. I harvested the seeds while traveling through the jungle to seldom-visited locations."

Karsen grinned. "Huh. Guess that's why they picked you to be our guide."

"Not to brag—" I began.

Ren snorted.

"But I have more experience in the jungle than most."

"That's reassuring." Karsen scanned me with an appreciative glint in her eyes. "You look like someone who's always up for an adventure."

I grinned. "I am. But there's something I should warn you about before we leave. There's this minor issue with—"

"Yeehaw!" a voice called from ahead.

That, along with Ren's gasp as she approached the backyard, made the rest of my words die unsaid. My mouth snapped closed, and I hurried to her side. Then, blinking furiously, I tried to make sense of the scene we'd stumbled upon.

"What the fuck are you doing, Capt?" Ren planted her hands on her hips, staring incredulously at Arda, who had climbed my pi-lock tree and perched above our heads atop one of the gnarled black branches. She rocked on the thick branch, a silly grin painting her lips, while rolling her pelvis so much the golden leaves rustled around her madly.

What in the universe...

Laughter sliced through the garden. "What did I tell ya? I know how to ride 'em right." She wobbled sideways and another manic chuckle slipped out of Arda's mouth as she lifted one hand, swinging it in a circular motion. "I'm a rodeo queen!"

"Watch out," I warned. "Those branches are slipper—"

Thump. Snap.

I winced, expecting the Terran to scream after she tumbled out of the tree and landed hard in the dirt. Especially once I spotted the puddle of blood pooling beneath Arda's unnaturally bent ankle and realized the branch wasn't what had snapped. Yet, somehow, she only stared with a stunned expression at the bone peeking out of her pink coveralls before laughing again.

"Arda! Stay still." Karsen rushed forward, tugging her bag off her back.

"Why so bossy? Thought *I* was the boss?" More giggles spilled out of her lips.

Ren took a step forward, then turned aside, averting her eyes. "Fuck! Is she okay?" Her skin paled, and she sucked in a few deep breaths.

"Her leg is broken." Karsen pulled out gauze, tubes covered in odd writing, and various other supplies from her pack. "And her pupils are enormous."

"Goddamn horse threw me." Arda glowered at the tree. "You said you'd make me look good!" Hardly a moment passed before more laughter erupted, spewing out of her so forcefully tears pooled at the corners of her eyes.

What is she talking about? I just stood there wearing an inane smile while the females took action. It was all so incredibly... strange, and honestly, kind of funny. But I suspected if I joined in with Arda's laughter, it would not go well, so I choked down the urge.

Karsen spoke slowly and firmly. "Arda, I need you to call Lux. We have to get you back to the *Verne* so I can set the bone and put you in the med-bot."

Arda covered her mouth, muffling her laughter. "I can't call Lux. I'll have to admit I was riding *him*." She squinted at the tree. Then her face brightened, and she tugged Kar's sleeve, waving frantically. "Wait... that's what went wrong. It's not a horse, it's a camel! You can't hump a hump!"

A sound somewhere between a chuckle and a scoff burst out of Ren's throat. "Great. She's high as a kite."

Kar tugged her arm free. "Arda, please stay still. I need to stop the bleeding. This is gonna hurt."

"Hurt? I feel amazing!" Arda eyed the tree with a goofy pout, even as Karsen poked and prodded at her wound. "Sorry I humped you, Steven. I just wanted to show them my bronco busting."

"Who the fuck is Steven?"

With her back still turned, Ren missed the accusatory glare Arda threw her way when she answered. "The camel. Duh."

Ren wrung her hands. "Did she hit her head, Kar?"

Arda gasped loudly. "You cheeky fucker!" Her eyes, the pupils so large and black you could barely see the blue ring of her irises, met mine as she jabbed a thumb toward the tree. "Did you hear what that perv said to me?"

"No visible head wounds," Karsen replied while Arda continued arguing with the tree like it was talking back. Honestly, she sounded completely insane. And no, I didn't miss the irony...

I strolled closer, my brow furrowing. It was clear from the distress on her friends' faces, Arda's behavior wasn't normal. But what would make someone act delusional while also unaffected by pain? I racked my brain, but it wasn't until I kneeled in front of her and spotted a shimmery spot on her nose that everything clicked. "She didn't sniff a big yellow blossom near the gate, did she?"

Ren stiffened, her eyes widening. "Why?" It was pretty clear from her reaction that my guess was accurate.

My stomach sank. Two things. Rhelt had asked for two simple things, and I'd already dug myself a hole I wasn't sure I'd be able to climb out of.

I forced a smile. "Looks like your friend just inhaled the strongest hallucinogen on Dionus."

9

Swirly

Ren

"She... what?" I couldn't have heard him right. Then again, we did just catch Arda rocking a tree's world. One she seemed to think was a camel. A *talking* camel.

"Stop mumbling, Steven. Sounds like you're gnawing on a mouthful of dicks," Arda yelled at the tree, then burst into a fit of laughter.

Jalen shook his head, his mane of damp blue hair shifting across his broad shoulders. "She'll be out of it for a while."

My heart raced as Arda's bizarre behavior began to make sense. Even now, she was ranting and raving at the tree she'd tumbled out of like she wanted to throw fists. And with Karsen busy stemming the—deep breaths—sickening blood flow, it was up to me to make sense of what happened.

"Is she gonna be okay? Shouldn't you have posted a warning or something?" I crossed my arms, squaring off in front of the big bronzed alien—who, despite my taller-than-average height, topped me by more than a head. "And why the fuck are you growing hallucinogens in your garden?"

The bastard had the audacity to chuckle. "I don't get many visitors. If I'd known Rhelt had given you the gate code..." He winced. "I'm sorry. It doesn't matter what I thought. But your friend will be all right. Most of the effects of the drosse should wear off within a day, though she might experience brief flashbacks for a week or two."

Karsen said, "Drosse. I've heard of that. It's similar to LSD, but naturally occurring instead of chemically derived."

"Fuck." I chanced a glance back and released a sigh. Kar had wrapped Arda's ankle with gauze, hiding the nauseating sight of bone poking out of her skin. "Let's concentrate on getting her to the ship. The med-bot can flush that crap out of her, right?"

Standing, Karsen brushed the dirt off her knees. "Unfortunately, no. At least, not completely. There's only been a few preliminary studies about those flowers back home. The *Verne*'s med-bots won't be equipped to deal with it."

"Like I said, she'll be fine in a few days. Dionions have been using drosse for centuries. She just needs to ride out the effects," Jalen stated calmly.

Karsen nodded her confirmation, and only then did the anxiety pinging through my chest begin to settle.

I dragged a hand through my hair and turned back to Jalen. "Fine. We need to postpone our hike until she's back to normal."

Jalen rocked on his heels. "If that's what you want."

Crossing the garden, I ignored the bloodstained dirt and the roiling in my stomach and kneeled beside Arda. "Hey, Capt. I'm gonna call Lux. Once the sun sets, he can bring the hovercart to take you back to the ship."

"Your face. It's so... *swirly*." Arda patted my cheek, grinning absurdly.

I glanced at the sky. "Is she stable enough to wait until nightfall?"

"Yeah. Better she doesn't put any weight on her ankle." Karsen studied Arda shrewdly. "And the pain doesn't appear to be bothering her."

"That's one reason we use drosse," Jalen explained. "She won't feel a thing."

"Great." I straightened, lifting my hand to my neck, ready to activate my comms implant. "We'll be back in a couple weeks when her flashbacks are over." The last thing we needed was a repeat of this madness when we were in the middle of the jungle.

"About that..." Jalen twisted his lips. "You might want to reconsider waiting that long."

My hand fell at my side. "Why?"

"It has to do with that issue I brought up earlier. If we don't leave today, it will be months before we can safely hike where you want to go."

Karsen lifted a brow. "What are you talking about?"

"There's a river we need to cross. It's only passable on a few days each year."

"Seriously?" I asked.

He nodded to the sky. "You can blame the moons and the tides. With all three moons in the sky, the waterline drops enough to wade through. That's happening again tomorrow night, and once again fifteen days from now. But after that, the rainy season will be at its worst. If we miss the current window, we won't get another chance for months."

"Months." I scrubbed a hand down my face. "Arda won't want to wait that long." And truthfully, she shouldn't have to. Not when she'd already been living in uncertainty for so long.

"Can't we swim across when the water's higher?" Karsen asked.

"Not safely." Jalen tilted his head. "Is whatever you need to find important enough to risk your lives?"

Karsen scratched her chin. "What about a bridge? We could chop down a couple trees."

Jalen chuckled humorlessly. "You don't know much about Dionus, do you?"

No shit, Sherlock.

"The jungle is sacred to my people. Any off-worlders who disrespect it are deported."

That was a little extreme. Cut down a tree and get kicked off-world? But we didn't come here intending to stomp on the natives' traditions.

"This has turned into one big mess, hasn't it?" Karsen sighed.

"While Arda's recuperating, I'll build something to help. There's more than one way to make a bridge." I'd think of something that would allow us to cross without disturbing the jungle. Couldn't be that hard, could it?

"What if you didn't have to?" Karsen's gaze flicked over Jalen in a way that made my skin crawl. "Arda was prepared to head out on her own. Really, only one of us has to make the hike. I'll do it."

Her cool announcement sent a bolt of unease straight through my insides. "But you're our medical officer. Who will take care of Arda?"

Karsen grinned. "Hm... you're right. But if I can't go, that leaves us with only one option."

A bead of sweat rolled down my temple. "Hell no."

Her smile fell. "I get it. If you don't want to go, we'll wait. Hey, at least you'll have lots of time to hang with your sister while Arda's recuperating. Bet the months will fly by."

Fucking hell...

I narrowed my eyes at Karsen, wondering if she'd sensed it somehow. Had I given my genius crewmate some inkling of my feelings when I'd first told her about the stupidly handsome man hovering behind us?

No. If I had, she wouldn't have volunteered to take a hike with him. Karsen just wanted to get the job done. And I was clearly the logical choice to go.

Double fuck.

Could I handle spending a week alone with a *man*? One who'd awakened feelings in me I'd been having a hell of a time fighting to tamp down since we met.

But was the alternative any better? There was no way Cassidy would stick to herself when she learned of our delay. She'd insist on visiting to help out, and then she'd corner me for that talk she was so desperate for...

I threw up my hands. "All right. I'll do it." I whipped around, spearing Jalen with my best icy glare while ignoring the way my flesh warmed under his gaze. "But I'm not interested in anything except finding what we need and getting back as fast as possible. Understood?"

Despite my frosty tone, his smile didn't dip in the slightest. "You're the boss, Ren."

A shiver chased up my spine as my name slipped off his tongue, and suddenly his gaze wasn't just warm anymore. Fire blazed, sparks crackling in the space between us so fiercely I nearly hyperventilated.

"Noooo. I'm the boss!" Arda's loopy voice broke through my trance.

"Course you are, Capt." Karsen kneeled beside her and eased the pack off Arda's back. "We're gonna wait here while Ren and Jalen go for a little walk. And we'll be just a comm call away if she needs anything." She tossed the bag to me, and I tore it open before sifting through the contents.

I'd call Lux once we left. Arda and Karsen would be safe waiting in the fenced-in yard until the sun sank and he could retrieve them.

"Oh... right. Later, Ren." Arda blinked, her gaze flicking to Jalen. "Wow! When did we get a hottie?"

Karsen's lips tightened like she was holding back laughter. "That's Jalen. The guide." She jerked her head at me, clearly wanting us to leave.

"Ooohhh." Arda's head lolled on her shoulders, and I thought that was the end of it. But just as I finished rummaging through her pack and stuffing the few things I might need into my own, Arda leaned closer. "Don't worry about Nicky-boy. I won't tell if you don't," she sing-songed.

God, how embarrassing. What the fuck did I do to deserve this?

"Come on." I tossed Arda's pack on the ground and spun toward the gate.

"Who's Nicky-boy?" Jalen asked, that seemingly permanent smile of his finally fading around the edges.

"The hairy man in Ren's bed," Arda blurted.

Are none of my secrets safe with hippie Capt unleashed?

Face burning, I snagged Jalen's elbow before Arda told him about the vibrators hidden in my bedside drawer. "Thought you said we had to leave right away?" I marched toward the gate, ignoring the sizzle where we touched as my friend's manic laughter reverberated in my ears.

10

Frolicking

Ren

Later that evening, exhaustion weighed down my limbs as I trekked through the jungle under the light of two enormous crescent moons. When night fell a few hours earlier, I'd marveled at how bright the world still was.

Jalen had warned me we'd need to travel well into the night to make it to the river tomorrow. And I had, without complaint. Still, the long hours of hiking were wearing on me.

Suddenly, a dim chime alerted me to an incoming message. I slapped my neck, activating my comms implant. "What's up?"

Jalen whipped around, eyeing me before hurrying forward a few steps like he wanted to give me some privacy.

"Hey, it's Kar. Just letting you know Lux arrived. He's loading Arda onto the hovercart as we speak."

"That's a relief." When we'd split, Jalen had stopped me from dragging him out of his yard and went back for his supplies while I informed Lux what was happening. It had taken a serious tongue-lashing to keep him from braving the burning sun until night fell. It was good to hear they'd finally reunited.

"So... how're things with the hot guide?"

"Fine."

"Just fine?"

I glanced ahead, spotting Jalen grinning ear to ear as he trailed his fingers across a pretty purple flower. "Yeah. Fine."

I couldn't blame her for being curious. Jalen had made a big impression on my crewmates. While I'd been talking Lux out of roasting himself to a crisp, Jalen had returned to the backyard with food and drinks and had even stripped the pillows off his own bed to ensure they'd have a comfortable stay in his garden.

A crackle over the comms made me wince. "If that's all, I better go. Lots of ground to cover tonight, I hear."

Karsen said, "Okay. Just remember, we're here if you need anything."

"Got it." With that, I silenced the call and sighed.

"Everything all right?" Jalen asked.

"Yep. Kar was letting me know Lux made it to your garden."

His smile brightened. "That's great!" He strolled forward, his steps so light they were almost a skip. If he wasn't so insanely hot, his muscles rippling with every step, his goofy walk would be enough to make me laugh.

It shouldn't have bothered me. I mean, if the man wanted to bounce through the jungle to his heart's content, who was I to stop him? But after another endless mile stretched out, I blurted, "Do you have to walk like that?"

His head tilted as he took another jaunty step forward. "Like what?"

"Like you're... frolicking."

He chuckled. "Frolicking. That's a new word for me, but it sounds fun." He shifted to face me but kept bouncing away while waving at himself. "Is this how you do it?"

I rolled my eyes. "Yep. That's a grade A frolick you've got there."

He laughed again. "I'm just soaking it all in. The sights. The smells. I don't see the problem with enjoying myself."

"The problem is that you're having entirely too much fun trekking through an insect-riddled jungle—"

"Is the repellent I gave you wearing off?" He started to dig into one of his vest pockets until I shook my head.

"No, I'm fine." He'd shared some cream with me earlier, and since slathering it on, I hadn't been bitten once. "The point is, you shouldn't be frolicking. No one else who got torn out of their house to drag some random girl through the jungle would be happy about it."

"I like hiking." He flashed a crooked grin that made my insides all gooey. "And you're not so bad. Even eased up on the whole not talking thing."

I bit my lip and fell silent.

That was right. I'd told him to shut it when he'd tried chatting me up when we first hit the trail. So sue me.

Fact was, Jalen turned out to be the complete opposite of what I'd been expecting. I started this trip thinking I'd be saddled with some isolated recluse.

Nope. Karsen might be sunshiny, but this man was what you got when two stars collided. Megawatt positivity blasted out of his pores, yet he maintained this aloof cool that stopped him from coming off as a complete boy scout. No, it drew everyone into his orbit—but I refused to be sucked in.

"Don't tell me I shocked the words out of you?" Jalen chuckled as his hand slipped into his pants pocket. "If it makes you feel better, I think we've made it far enough for one night. You won't have to watch me frolic while I sleep."

A flash of metal off the path diverted my attention. "What's that?" As we walked closer, more of it became visible, glistening in the moonlight where it wasn't shrouded beneath vines and greenery. It almost looked like a motorcycle, only with no wheels.

"That's one of the riders the invaders brought with them. There are a few of them scattered around the jungle. Guess they couldn't be bothered to take their trash with them when we scared them off Dionus."

Huh... Weird they just left them to rot. If I had a chance to—

A loud flick behind my ear made me jolt. "What the hell?" I spun around, my eyes widening. Jalen dipped his face into his cupped hands as a familiar scent drifted to my nose. "Are you *smoking*?"

"How'd you guess?" He grinned, blowing the aromatic smoke into the trees.

Fuck! Normally, I was the first one to perk up at the mention of drinks. And I enjoyed more than my fair share of weed. But didn't he realize now wasn't the time to relax?

"You want some?" After blowing out another fragrant cloud of smoke, he offered the joint to me with a smile.

"I'll pass." I barely knew this guy. And just because the smoke smelled like heaven didn't mean it wasn't laced with something. I wasn't about to get high with him alone out in the middle of nowhere.

He shrugged. "Okay. No pressure." He drew in a drag, smiling softly in the moonlight.

"Do you really think you should be smoking right now?"

He laughed, smoke spilling out his mouth and pooling around his sharp canines. "Of course." He took another long pull off his joint. Then, while holding the smoke in, he said, "Watch this."

Jalen strolled to a huge orb-shaped bush lining the far side of the path. It was one of the same stupid pricker bushes that attacked my ankle that afternoon. We'd passed dozens of them on our hike, and I'd steered clear each time, not wanting my entire skinsuit torn to shreds.

"What are you—"

The words died in my throat as Jalen bent, blowing smoke straight into the bush. Within a few seconds, the sharp needle-like growths receded, leaving behind a hole wide enough to fit an arm through. Jalen repeated the action several times, puffing on the bush long enough to widen the hole so much that one entire side was free from prickers. It reminded me of an old Earth vid I'd once watched, where beekeepers blew smoke into a hive so they could harvest their honey.

"Come on." He waved me forward. "It won't stay like that for long."

I gaped, first at him and then at the orange innards of the massive plant. "How did you know how to do that?"

Jalen grinned and took another toke. "It's not my first trek." He blew smoke out just as the first of the prickers sought to reform, making them retreat again. "Adventurers always sleep within the safety of the lionettle, if they're smart."

"So, is that what you are?" With cautious steps, I walked into the lionettle.

"Highly intelligent? Absolutely."

I scoffed as I settled cross-legged on the pillowy interior, which was surprisingly comfortable. "I meant an adventurer."

Jalen's ever-present smile fell. "I used to be." He sank beside me, taking a final puff before snuffing his joint out on the bottom of his boot and flicking the butt into the jungle.

I wanted to ask him why he stopped. Why someone with such an obvious love of the jungle, and travel, would become a recluse. But at that moment, the prickers started reforming.

"Holy shit. I can barely see!"

"It's all right," Jalen replied coolly. A heartbeat later, a light flickered to life beside me. "Hold this, would you?"

I grabbed the lighter, frowning as my fingers rubbed over the smooth white base that was definitely not plastic, or even metal. "What's this made out of?"

"Bone."

Revulsion pulsed through me so fast it was lucky I didn't drop the creepy thing. "Oh my god, are you serious?" I shuddered, praying I wasn't shacking up with a psycho who had crafty plans for my body parts.

Jalen chuckled as he dug into his pack. "Don't Terrans use all parts of the animals they eat?"

"These are animal bones?"

"Certainly." Jalen plucked the lighter deftly from my fingers and used it to light a small candle he'd pulled out of his pack. "Contrary to rumors floating around the universe, we aren't a bunch of savages defiling the bones of our enemies."

"You've heard about those?" With the candle spreading a soft glow across the small enclosure, my nerves settled slightly. If I squinted, I could almost believe we were in a normal tent.

His green eyes twinkled in the candlelight. "Heard about them? Who do you think spread them?"

"Wasn't it the aliens who invaded your planet?"

He shook his head. "We spread them ourselves. If the rest of the universe fears us, then they won't come looting again." He shrugged. "At least, that was the hope. Hasn't always worked out too well."

"Smart."

"Told you we were highly intelligent." He winked, then dug into his pack again.

"What are you looking for?"

"Food. I'm starving, aren't you?"

Yep. That was definitely marijuana. He totally has the munchies.

I chuckled wryly. "Not as hungry as you." As I watched the candlelight bounce on the flower's inner walls, a random thought snagged in my brain. "How hard is it to get out of here? What happens if I wake up in the middle of the night and need to pee?"

Jalen tossed a cloth-wrapped bundle into my lap. "Walk slowly and you won't get caught on anything. The spines won't stop you from getting out, just getting in."

Cautiously, I unwrapped the fabric. "It's that easy?"

Jalen hurriedly tore open his wrapper and crunched into his food before replying. "Yep. But if you do, wake me up so I can let you back in." He swallowed. "Better yet, hold off until daybreak if you can."

"Why?" I lifted a brown piece of... something to my nose and sniffed. *Is that cinnamon?*

"Dangerous when there's no moon," he said around bites.

"What's so dangerous?" I asked.

"The fiercest predators in the jungle are nocturnal. They come out during full dark, so it's best to seek shelter while they're active." He patted the flower beside him. "Don't worry. We're safe as long as we stay in the lionettle."

A shiver chased down my spine. *Great. I'm stuck in a flower tent with a stranger, and I can't even run away without the fear of being eaten.*

The thought should've made dread pool in my stomach and nausea bite the back of my throat. But for some reason, it didn't. Maybe it was the goofy smile Jalen sent me as he popped his last bite into his mouth. Something about the guy set my mind at ease—and that was more terrifying than any predator stalking the jungle.

It was bad enough trying to ignore the annoying attraction I just couldn't shake. I didn't need to start liking his personality and being comfortable around him too.

Shoving the thought aside, I took my first bite of the mystery snack. The tangy deliciousness exploded on my tongue, and I groaned.

"You gonna finish that?" Jalen asked.

I glared at him. "Get your own," I hissed, scarfing down half in one bite.

He laughed, the delighted sound echoing within the flower and making my skin prickle. "Here." Jalen plopped another treat on my lap. "I brought plenty."

11

Forbidden Fruit

Jalen

A delicious scent wafted around me as I came to. I breathed deeply, recognizing the familiar perfume of lionettle pollen mingling with something infinitely sweeter. My cocks stirred, waking faster than the rest of me. I rolled sideways, closer to the faint aroma lingering beside me.

As my eyes opened and my gaze landed on the empty spot that I'd watched Ren fall asleep in, it all came flooding back.

The trek through the jungle.

My beautiful companion, so guarded and prickly.

She'd warmed up, eventually. Even seemed to enjoy a few of my poor attempts at jokes, though you could hardly tell from the permanent scowl on her luscious lips. Lips I wanted so badly to—

She's forbidden, remember? I prayed the thought would snag in my brain and begged my loins to listen. I couldn't afford to trip up. Not if I wanted out of exile for good.

Where was she, anyway? Sitting up, I scratched my chest and gathered my things. Then I eased out of the lionettle, hoping Ren was just off in the jungle answering nature's call.

After ducking behind a tree to do the same, I returned to the road. "Ren? Where are you?"

My pulse kicked into high gear when she didn't immediately reply. *Harlx's bane. Did I lose her?*

I should've never fallen asleep. Not without making it clear what dangers lurked in the jungle. She could've easily gotten turned around if she wandered too far off the path. And who knew—

"Over here."

A huge sigh stuttered out of my lips. I rounded the path, back the way we'd come last night. "Ren?"

Her blonde head popped out of the trees, a vine tangled in her hair that she didn't seem to notice. Metal flashed in her hands as she briefly met my gaze before looking back down.

My brow furrowed. "What are you doing?"

She gestured to the abandoned rider. "Thought I might be able to fix this."

I paced closer, watching as she spun a silvery contraption around in a circle. The alien vehicle had been left in the jungle for so long I'd be surprised if it was salvageable. "So can you?"

She frowned. "Turns out... no."

"Too bad. Perhaps we should get going, then?"

With a deft flick of her wrist, she pulled a small component out and set it on a pile by her feet. "You said there were more of these, right?"

I leaned against the side of the rusted hunk of junk. "Yep."

"That's what I thought. I'm bringing some spare parts that look to be in good shape with me. Maybe I'll be able to fix the next one."

"As you wish."

She leaned over the open engine, the tip of her pink tongue poking out of the corner of her mouth. I couldn't deny she was fascinating to watch. So absorbed in her task and fully confident with every move she made. It had me wondering what it would feel like to be the subject of all that focus. To have her nimble fingers trailing across something much warmer than that cold metal, but just as hard.

Great... I'm jealous of a machine. "I don't mean to rush you, but we need to cross the river today."

Ren's brows dipped. "Can I finish yanking this one piece?"

"I suppose." I grinned and rounded the vehicle, bending beside her.

She edged away. "Um... What are you doing?"

I looked up, gulping when I noticed how close I'd gotten. With Ren bent inside the hood, and me kneeling beside her, my gaze lined up perfectly with her chest. She dragged in a shaky breath as my mind wandered, picturing what might be hidden under the loose fabric sheathing her torso.

Her hands stilled. "I said, *what* are you doing down there?"

Blinking, I aimed a sheepish grin higher—at her eyes this time. "Sorry." I pulled my bag off my back. "Thought I'd scoop these up while you finished."

"Oh." She visibly relaxed, her stiff shoulders loosening as her fingers flew into motion. "You don't have to carry them. I can—"

"It's not a problem." I dumped the last piece into my bag just as she tore a greasy box off the engine block. "Here." I stood, holding out my bag with the top uncinched. "Might as well keep everything together."

She shrugged and dropped it in. "Thanks." Then her gaze trailed over the ground. "Did you pack my tool kit too?"

I nodded. "Let me carry it. We'll make better time if you're not weighed down on the hike."

Her lips pursed, and I had the distinct impression she had to force herself not to argue. "Fine. Thanks again." She dropped the tool in my bag, wincing as metal clinked inside.

"Don't mention it." I jerked my head toward the trail. "Ready?"

"Sure."

We made good time that morning, most of it walking in silence. Until Ren shared some of her Terran rations with me. After I choked down half the bar with forced smiles between each bite, she laughed uproariously.

"You know, it's okay to admit they taste like garbage."

"Thank ellios! I was afraid you loved that stuff."

"Hardly." Her laughter tapered off as she nibbled her bar. "Hiking rations are made to meet our nutritional needs in as compact a space as possible. They're barely edible, but they'll keep your energy up."

I wrinkled my nose, shaking the chewy, tasteless hunk of food at her. "How about you let me handle the meals from now on? We can hold on to these, just in case."

"Be my guest. But don't come begging for more of the good stuff when you run out of the snacks you packed." She eyed my pack curiously. "What was that stuff you fed me last night?"

"Haldi bread. It's good, right?"

"Good?" She scoffed. "Almost better than burritos." She thrust a finger at me and cocked a brow. "That's high praise in my book, I'll have you know."

"I'll take your word for it." With a chuckle, I sped up on the path, hunting for a particular tree. It didn't take long to spot what I was searching for. "Ah, do you see that tree up ahead?"

She squinted. "The one with the diamond-shaped leaves?"

"Yes. See those striped balls hanging in the highest branches?"

She shaded her eyes and gazed up. "What about them?"

"Those are haldi fruit. We ferment them, then bake them into the bread we ate last night."

"That's interesting." She scanned the jungle. "Those trees are everywhere."

I nodded. "In this part of the world, haldi trees are quite common. You'll find every tribe has their own spin on haldi bread as well."

"What tribe did the bread we ate come from?"

"None of them. That was my own recipe."

Ren whistled. "And he cooks too. Is there anything you don't do?"

"You learn to be self-sufficient when you're on your own."

"Well, you can cook for me anytime. Can't say I have a knack for baking, but I love to eat."

"Yes, I noticed." I leaned closer, adopting a playful tone. "I thought you were gonna bite my fingers off when I asked if you were done with your portion last night."

Instead of laughing casually like I hoped she would, Ren inched further away from me. I straightened, backing out of her personal space, and she relaxed. "Yeah, I might've. Don't get in between me and good food if you value your life." She offered me a halfhearted grin.

"I'll remember that," I said softly, returning her smile with a much brighter one of my own.

Ren was an odd one. Beautiful, but not in the showy way that most attractive females had of primping their hair and painting their faces. Yet even though she downplayed her looks with a shaggy haircut and rumpled clothes, it couldn't disguise how naturally stunning she was.

Still, I couldn't quite get a read on her. At times, it almost seemed like she was afraid of me touching her. Was it just me she didn't want coming close? Or did she have an aversion to touch?

Whatever the answer, I should take her distaste as a sign. Rhelt had warned me to keep my hands to myself. This was one more reason to listen.

And don't forget the hairy male waiting for her in her bed…

Jalen

At midday, we stopped for lunch in a small hollow beside a creek. After doling out food—from my pack this time—we sat down to eat under the shade of a haldi tree.

"So tell me. What are we looking for, exactly?"

Ren shot me a confused look. "You didn't get the details from Rhelt?"

I shook my head.

"Arda's looking for clues to her genetic heritage at an old research facility. We got a tip that pointed us here." She flipped a piece of haldi bread in her hands. "You know the place?"

"Think I might. There are some old ruins right about where you have marked on your map. I've even been inside a time or two. I don't remember spotting any research in there, though."

She shrugged. "It could be hidden. We'll find out when we get there, I guess." After chewing thoughtfully, she turned to me with a raised brow. "How do you know Rhelt and Cass? You were pretty worried when we showed up on your doorstep and you assumed I was my sister."

I nearly told her the full truth. But she didn't need to know the grim place my mind had gone. "I never expected to see Cassidy there without Rhelt. I was worried something bad might've happened. Rhelt's family."

Ren cocked her head. "Are you brothers?"

"No. He's my aunt's son."

"Okay. Cousins, then."

"It's not quite so simple. We grew up as close as brothers since my aunt raised me. My parents died when I was very young."

"Oh." Ren blanched. "You were an orphan."

I grinned. "It's all right. I was so young when they passed I don't have strong memories of them. And Aunt Karln was amazing. With her raising me, I didn't feel their loss too deeply."

Ren sighed, her tone tinged with bitterness. "Lucky you."

"Something wrong?"

She shook her head and lifted the last bite of her bread. "I'm about done. You?" She popped it into her mouth and stood.

"Gotta get back to my frolicking." I hopped up and bounded off, forcing the same exuberance into my stride I'd used the first day when I'd been elated to break free from my walled-off existence.

Ren rolled her eyes. "Ugh. This again. I swear you're just doing it to annoy me."

I flipped around and shot her a cheeky grin. "Why would I want to do that?" But at least some color had flooded back into her face.

I wasn't certain why, but orphans seemed like a touchy subject for Ren. Perhaps there was more to that than she was letting on... Whatever the answer, it was clear I wouldn't be digging it up today.

12

Good To Know

Ren

The soles of my feet ached as we closed in on the river late in the afternoon. "Really wish I would've been able to fix that rider right about now," I muttered under my breath.

"You looked comfortable working with those tools." Jalen grinned, and I tried to ignore how warmth spread through my chest at the slightest hint of a compliment he gave me.

"Fixing machines is my life. I'm the head mechanic on the *Verne*."

"That's impressive."

I side-eyed him. "Why do you sound so surprised?"

He shrugged. "Guess it's easy to fall back into thinking about Cassidy when I look at you. She doesn't seem like the type who'd ever dirty her hands in an engine."

I snorted. "Never. She's always been more of a people person." A pang of resentment settled in my chest. Maybe if I'd been more like her, my life wouldn't have been so hard. I shook off the old regret.

Now wasn't the time to wallow about the past. "You sound like you know Cass pretty well."

"Not quite. I only met her when Rhelt brought her back to Dionus to be his mate."

I scoffed. "Fated mates. What a crock of bullshit that is."

"What do you mean?"

After spotting how much his smile fell, I grimaced. "Sorry. I didn't mean to dump on your way of life. The whole mate thing is just idiotic to me."

"How so?"

I fiddled with the sleeve of my skinsuit. "Doesn't it sound like something out of a kid's story? You meet someone, and wham—you just *know* that stranger is the love of your life, who will always be by your side and never leave you. That's how Cass described it to me."

"What's so wrong with that?" Jalen asked.

"You can't trust fate to find someone worthy of sharing your life with. It's not how the universe works."

Jalen blinked. "It's how it works for Dionions." He stated it so matter-of-factly, I knew he believed it.

"Sure it is." I couldn't explain how I knew not all Dionions were bound by the same ideals. Not without dredging up some memories I was desperate to keep buried.

"I don't understand why it's bothering you so much. Don't you have a hairy male waiting for you back on the ship?" he said jokingly, though his tone wasn't as laid back as usual.

The hell is he talking about? My brow furrowed. "What?"

"What did Arda call him... That's right. Nicky-boy."

A laugh startled out of me, and heat washed over my face. "Are you serious? You know Arda was talking out of her ass back there, don't you?"

His face screwed up. "Talking out of her *what?*"

I waved a hand. "It's a figure of speech. It means she was so hopped up on your stupid trippy flower that she wasn't making any sense." I chuckled humorlessly. "I promise you, there is no hairy man in my bed."

"Hm." Jalen met my eyes, and a slow smirk spread across his face that sent tingles down my spine. "That's good to know."

My mouth went dry, and my mind blanked. *Why is that good? He shouldn't care about who's waiting in my bed. Shit, maybe I should've let him keep thinking I had a man back on the ship. It would certainly make things easier if he thought I was off-limits. Wouldn't it?*

We rounded an enormous boulder, and a familiar sound suddenly became clear, wiping the disconcerting thoughts from my head. "Is that the river?"

"Sounds like it." Jalen jerked his head forward, a blinding smile on his lips. "Come on."

I followed him eagerly, ducking beneath a few low-hanging vines and around a pricker bush. All the while, the whoosh of running water grew louder. Finally, we wove through a stand of tall trees and emerged on the banks of an enormous river.

"*That's* what we need to cross?" Fear prickled the back of my neck. The river was so massive I had to squint to make out the far banks. I wagered we'd need to swim for at least an hour to make it across. What was worse, the current didn't look calm. Not in the slightest. I spotted a few places where rapids whipped between rocks and even a steep drop-off downstream.

Jalen gestured for me to continue walking. "We need to follow it upstream. There's a spot where it will be safe to wade once the moons rise."

"If you say so." Shivers racked my frame as I turned away from the rapids. We hiked in silence as the sun slowly sank below the tree line and shadows lengthened within the jungle.

I tugged at the neck of my skinsuit. "At least we'll get to cool down a little. Is it just me, or is it getting hotter out here?"

Jalen's eyes narrowed as he examined my face. "The day always cools when the sun starts going down. Are you feeling hot from exertion?"

"Maybe." I shrugged, but I must've been hotter than even I realized. My legs wobbled, and I almost took a tumble into a bush.

Jalen's hand shot out to steady me. I instinctively cringed back from his touch.

"Here." Jalen pulled his hand away and offered me his water bottle. "Have a drink."

"Thanks." I accepted it gratefully and gulped a few mouthfuls, though it didn't cool me as much as I would have liked. Heat radiated within me, like a furnace was trapped in my chest. As I handed the water bottle back, my gaze caught on my ankle. "I bet that's the problem."

Jalen asked, "What is?"

I lifted my leg, twisting it so I could show off the torn fabric at my ankle. "I forgot to mend this last night. My skinsuit must not be regulating my body temperature properly with this big rip." I tugged my bag off. "I took Arda's sewing kit before we left. I'll stitch this up quick—"

"I'm afraid we don't have the time." Jalen smiled apologetically. "Not if we want to make it across the river tonight. Think you can rough it for a tad longer? I promise I'll help you mend your clothing when we stop for the night."

"You know how to sew?"

"I'm the self-reliant recluse, remember?" He grinned.

"How could I forget?" I shouldered my bag. "I can wait. Lead the way."

13

Watch Your Step

Jalen

We reached the crossing just as the sun set. I bit back a frown as I studied Ren in the moonlight. Luckily, with all three moons in the sky, it wasn't hard to make out her features.

The flush on her cheeks worried me. Was she sick and becoming feverish? Or was it only a problem with her odd skinsuit, like she claimed?

Or it could be something else entirely...

Stop fooling yourself, Jalen. That's not *the reason.* I forced the thought aside. We had the crossing to worry about now. That required all my concentration.

"Huh, looks like you weren't kidding about the current calming with the moons out." Ren leaned over the riverbank, scanning the slowed current with a furrowed brow.

"Are you a strong swimmer?"

She bit her lip. "Not really. I can keep myself afloat in a pool, but there wasn't much opportunity to swim where I grew up."

"Shouldn't be a problem as long as we cross quickly. The water is only about thigh deep here, so we can walk. And you can hang on to me if you need help." I thrust out a hand, intending to lead her across, but she made no move to take it.

Instead, Ren scowled at my fingers like they were snakes. "I'll be fine on my own."

Only, she might not be... I swallowed the urge to insist she take my hand. It was clear she wanted no part of that. But I wouldn't feel comfortable knowing she could fall and be washed away at any moment.

"Hold on." I dug into my pack and pulled out a short length of rope. I handed one end to Ren and tied the other end around my waist. "Tie that around you. Just in case."

She secured the rope around her waist. "I'm ready."

"Good." I grinned. "Let's cool off, shall we?"

Ren blew out a deep breath. "Yep. Let's do it." She sighed deeply as she took her first step into the river. "Oh, that's refreshing."

"Watch your step. Some of the rocks are slippery."

I led the way, pausing every few steps to check Ren followed without issue. The rope made it impossible for me to get too far ahead, not that I wanted to. Within a few moments, the water rose, drenching my legs up to mid-thigh. "You doing okay?"

"Yeah. It's not too bad."

We walked in silence with the river's melody playing in our ears. If I hadn't been hyperaware of the danger waiting for us if we took a tumble and got washed downstream, it would've been quite pleasant.

I hadn't told Ren, but if we'd turned in the opposite direction when we reached the river, we'd have eventually encountered the biggest waterfall in all of Dionus. Occasionally, an unlucky animal tumbled off the edge, caught in the unyielding current. They never survived, either from the drop itself or from the hard landing on the sharp rocks littering the waters beneath the falls.

My stomach bottomed out as an unwanted image invaded my mind. Ren taking a spill and disappearing under the water. The rope snapping. I'd swim after her, but with the current so strong…

No. I couldn't think like that.

Looking back, I forced a smile. "You still good?"

"I'm fine."

Even so, my hands clenched warily around the rope. We'd made it about halfway, but there was still a long stretch to cross.

The reflection of three bright orbs bounced along the racing water. I dragged in a calming breath. *Harlx's boon, be with us.*

No sooner had the silent prayer filled my head than a sharp tug snagged the rope. I whipped around in time to spot Ren going under. Her wide eyes met mine before the dark water swallowed her.

I planted my feet in place, knowing what would come next. As the current caught her, the rope jerked my waist, seeking to knock me over. If I went down, then all was lost. I was a strong swimmer, but not so strong that I could save us both in the short time we'd have before reaching the falls.

Heart pounding, I leaned back and wrapped both hands over the rope. Then I began pulling, desperate to reel Ren closer.

How long can Terrans hold their breath?

The wayward thought made my stomach clench. She flailed underwater, her head still completely submerged. I had to yank her out. Fast.

Seconds that passed like years ticked by as I pulled the rope over and over. Finally, she surfaced with a gasp. I bent, lifting her under the arms. "Ren? Are you okay?"

Chest heaving, she clung to me, soaking my skin and clothes. I didn't complain. Not while fear still raced through my blood, searing me with its molten fire.

I could've lost her. Yes, I barely knew her. But for some reason, that felt like it would be the ultimate loss.

After a few shaky breaths, she replied hoarsely, "I'm okay. Thank you for saving me." She tipped her face up, and my heart stuttered as I met her gaze in the moonlight.

"You're certain you're all right?" Though the last thing I wanted was to pull away, I forced myself to. I scanned her carefully. "Nothing hurts?"

She shook her head, sending specks of water flying off her sodden hair. "No. I might have a bruise or two come morning, but I—" She gasped. "Oh my god! My bag. It's gone!"

"I'm sorry." I glanced up and down the river, carefully eyeing the banks, but spotted no sign of it. "Guess it's a good thing you already agreed to let me handle the meals."

She grimaced. "I didn't just lose those rations. My clothes were in there." She covered her mouth with a hand. "And the map."

I shot her a reassuring grin and tapped my temples. "Got the only map we need right here." Except, that statement didn't reassure her as much as I'd hoped it would.

"Great."

I wished I could think of something more to say, but I had nothing. And time wasn't exactly on our side. "You ready to finish crossing?" My gaze lifted nervously to the sky. Already, the largest moon was over halfway to its peak.

Ren nodded. "Yeah."

I lifted my foot to take a step, and jolted as a wet hand slipped against mine. Ren gripped my fingers with a sheepish grin. "What? I don't want to fall again."

"No worries." I squeezed her hand gently. "I don't mind."

14

Her Favorite Songs

Ren

I can't wait to rest. We'd finished crossing the river with no more embarrassing tumbles. After I made it safely on solid ground, I dropped Jalen's hand with another quiet thank you and kept my distance.

Don't get me wrong; I was grateful the guy saved me from certain death. I just didn't need to give him the wrong idea about how comfortable I'd be with him touching me—again.

My insides turned liquid at that thought, and I tried to bury the memory of his strong hand softly holding mine. What would it feel like to have his hands on other parts of me?

Shut it down, Ren. I couldn't start fantasizing about something that would never happen. Yeah, the guy was hot. Far too hot for a filthy mechanic like me. He probably had some delicate little lady back at his cabin who helped him plant his stupid flowers. She'd laugh at his dumb jokes and never cringe when he reached for her.

I gritted my teeth and focused on planting one aching foot in front of the other. It didn't matter who Jalen was fucking. After this trip, I'd never see him again.

My belly flip-flopped. "Are we almost there? My stomach feels like it's about to eat itself." Yep, I was just hungry. That was all.

"Your organs won't need to resort to cannibalism yet." He pointed ahead. "Our campsite is behind that split tree."

"Thank fuck." I raced forward, rounding the tree eagerly. "Um... there are no lionettle plants over here."

Jalen chuckled. "That's because we're not sleeping in one tonight." He nodded at a steep, rocky hillside covered in vines. "Come on. It's this way." He circled the base until we reached what might be an opening, blocked by an enormous boulder.

"Am I missing something?" I crossed my arms. "I don't see any way we're fitting past that."

"Don't be so quick to judge." Jalen crouched beside the rock and brushed some vines away. A flash of metal nearly made me gasp.

"Is that what I think it is?"

Jalen grinned. "If you think it's the locking mechanism, then yes." He flipped a switch inside a metal panel set into the boulder, then stood. "Can you back up, please?"

I stepped back, my eyes bulging as he shoved the gargantuan boulder, and it swung out of the way like it was a flimsy wooden door. "It's mechanical?"

"Something like that." Jalen scratched his chest nonchalantly. "Unlike you, I've never been technologically inclined. There are a bunch of caves with doors like this across Dionus, built centuries ago. Keeps the wild critters out. Everyone's taught how to use them when they're young."

I tried to pick my jaw up off the ground as I waited for Jalen to light a candle and lead the way inside. The universe might think his species was barbaric, but technology like this—built so long ago—proved they were far from it.

"There should be some lanterns inside," he said.

Trickling water filled my ears as I followed him into the cave. He located a lantern almost immediately, and I bit back a gasp as soft light washed over the huge open space. Several straw mats with rolled-up blankets rested against one wall, each large enough for a Dionion to sleep comfortably with room to spare. And in the back, a woven screen stood folded on the edge of the most inviting pool of clear water.

"Is that deep enough for bathing?"

Jalen blew out his candle after lighting a second lantern. "Yes. Most of the caves around here have them." He turned back to the cave mouth and grabbed a handle sticking out of the boulder. "Why don't you hop in?"

My heart pounded madly as the boulder door swung closed, locking us away from the outside world. "You want me to take a bath... with you right there?"

Jalen quirked a brow. "That's what the screen's for. Drag it over after you climb up and it should cover the pool completely."

I narrowed my eyes suspiciously. "And you'll be out here doing *what*?"

He chuckled. "Well, if you pass me your clothes after you get out of them, I can sew that ripped leg for you."

My gaze caught on the pool again. Why did the water have to look so inviting? It would be heaven to rest my aching muscles in there. To scrub off the river scum that had gotten caught in my hair.

And I was still so freaking hot. Unnaturally hot, even. I really hoped it was my skinsuit and not a fever setting in.

So even though the idea of getting naked with Jalen within earshot made my skin prickle, I could see there were more benefits to hopping in rather than chickening out. "Fine. But I don't want to talk while I'm in there. That would be too... weird."

"If you say so." Jalen mimed locking his lips with a key.

Rolling my eyes, I turned for the pool. The raised platform was clearly built and not natural. A deep semicircle-shaped tub was cut into the rock, fed by a trickling stream of water that rolled down the cave wall. I paused on the top step and dragged the woven screen sideways, blocking the rest of the cave. Within the quiet little bubble, I could almost imagine I was alone.

As I lifted my fingers to the zipper at my neck, Jalen rudely cleared his throat, breaking the spell. "What?" I barked.

"Sorry. I forgot to give you this." His voice grew louder as he spoke, making me sure he was walking closer.

"You don't need to give me anything."

The reassuring sound of his laughter made some of my tension subside. "Okay. Guess there'll be more soap for me. Are you certain you don't at least want a towel?"

I snapped the screen sideways and grabbed the items he held out with a smirk. "Thanks." When he didn't retreat, I speared him with a glare. "Are you going to stand there the whole time, or what?"

He chuckled. "No. But I am going to need your skinsuit if you want me to sew it."

"Ugh. Fine." I dragged the screen in place and quickly shucked off my skinsuit. Since I never wore a bra—when you've been blessed with less than a handful, there isn't much point—that left me standing there in just my panties.

Fuck. I can't believe I'm doing this.

Keeping my body behind the screen, I inched it open just enough to toss the damp skinsuit out. It landed on the stone floor with a plop at the same time I slammed the screen back into place.

"Got it. Thanks."

I breathed out a shaky sigh as the heavy clomp of Jalen's footfalls retreated across the cave floor. Then I slipped out of my panties and sank into the tub.

Oh, hell yeah. As the cool water enveloped me, I closed my eyes in relief. It was almost enough to negate the sheer awkwardness that I'd just experienced.

I lifted the soap to my nose, smiling as the light floral aroma eased my senses. Then I took my time lathering my hands before setting the bar on the tub's edge and attacking my short locks with suds.

Soft humming rose, and once again Jalen broke the illusion that I was alone. "Do you have to do that?" I asked grumpily.

"Hm?" The humming cut off, replaced with a soft chuckle. "Sorry. Old habit. Seems I've grown so used to hearing the sound of my own voice when I'm alone that I hardly notice it anymore. You're lucky I didn't break into song."

I don't know about that... Even that tiny glimpse of Jalen's humming made me certain he had a phenomenal singing voice. "I'll thank you to keep the singing to yourself."

"Do you like music, Ren?" he asked, his voice a low murmur that set my pulse racing.

"Of course. Who doesn't?" I brushed a stray bead of soap off my forehead before it dripped into my eyes. "I thought we weren't talking while I bathed?" I dipped below the water and rinsed, only to pop out and hear another question.

"Do you like to sing too?"

A tiny smile curved my lips. *He doesn't quit easily, does he?* "You don't want to hear me sing. I mess up the words all the time. Even to my favorites."

"I bet you look fine doing it, though."

Do I have water clogging my ears? I thought he just said... "What did you say?"

He cleared his throat. "I bet you have fun doing it, though."

"I'll have fun finishing my bath in silence."

He chuckled softly. "If you say so."

I picked up the soap and lathered my hands again. Yet just as I started brushing the suds against my skin, his voice rang out, humming once more. The soothing baritone rumbled through the air, making it impossible not to listen. To forget he was out there, a single thin screen separating us as my hands traced over my naked flesh.

I sighed but kept my mouth shut, fighting to ignore the throbbing beat of my pulse. Soon, I'd washed everywhere, making sure not to let my fingers linger on the spot where I could really use some relief right about now...

Nope. Not going there. No way in hell will I get myself off with him right there.

The delicious thought snagged in my brain and made the throbbing intensify. But I shoved the idea aside before I could sink my teeth into it. The last thing I needed was for him to hear me moaning and take it as an invitation. He could cross the room in a few swift strides and tear down that flimsy screen like it was nothing...

I shivered as I stood and wrapped the towel around me, forcing the naughty image to the back of my mind. At first, I wasn't sure I could banish it, but then a new realization dawned on me, and the shiver turned into a full-out shudder.

"Um... are you done with my skinsuit yet?"

Shit! How didn't I see this coming? With my bag gone, I had nothing to change into. My only article of clothing—except for a tiny pair of panties—was out there, in Jalen's hands.

"About that... This garment is still very damp. Are you certain you want to sleep in it?"

"What?" I squeaked. "I have to. That's all I have to wear."

"You could stay in the towel until you lie down. Then you'll have a blanket to cover with. In the morning, it will be dry enough to put back on."

"Oh, you'd like that, wouldn't you?" I couldn't disguise the disgust in my tone.

Jalen's laughter rang out. "What? For you to get a good night's sleep so you're not so grumpy in the morning? I certainly wouldn't mind if that happened."

I scoffed. "And what about you? You'll just ignore me all night?" I found it hard to believe any guy who spent years as a recluse would overlook a mostly naked woman in the same closed space with him.

"Yes. I'm too tired for anything else." Footsteps echoed in the cave again, making me tense. "If you want your wet clothes, you can have them. Or I can turn my back while you walk out of the screen and cover up. Then I'll hang this to dry, take a bath of my own while you eat your dinner, then go to sleep—on my own pallet."

As he finished speaking, the clomp of his footfalls grew so loud I knew he was just on the other side. I held my breath, my heart speeding so fast I grew dizzy.

"I promise I won't bother you while you sleep. What do you say, Ren?"

Fucking hell. I *really* didn't want to shove my limbs into that wet skinsuit now that I was clean and dry. And I couldn't keep standing there forever, half-naked and hungry.

But could I trust him to keep his word? *For fuck's sake, the guy did save my life...* "Turn around *and* close your eyes."

"Doing it as we speak." Shuffling sounded behind the screen. "Ready."

With the damp towel wrapped around my torso, I eased the screen open. Jalen stood just beyond it, my balled-up skinsuit in his hand and his back facing me.

Now or never...

I darted across the cave floor and kneeled on a mat. Then I shook out a blanket, keeping my gaze glued to Jalen the entire time. He didn't move a muscle, just stood there silently until I said, "Okay, you can look."

He turned slowly and aimed a soft smile at me as I lay on the mat with the blanket pulled to my chin. "That wasn't so hard, was it?"

I scowled. "Maybe for you." He took a step closer. My eyes narrowed and my heart sank. "Where are you going?"

He held up my skinsuit. "I'll hang this next to where you're sleeping. Then you'll be able to grab it first thing in the morning."

"Oh. Thanks."

Jalen hung the garment quickly. Then he met my eyes as he towered over me, so close I was intensely aware of my near nakedness under the thin blanket. "Not a problem. I left some dinner out for you." A moment of weighted silence fell over us, with neither of us moving. Then Jalen scrubbed a hand down his face with a chuckle. "Pleasant dreams, Ren."

I swallowed thickly as he headed for the pool. "Goodnight."

15

Peckish

Ren

G od, who knew a straw mat in a cave would feel so freaking good? A smile curved my lips as I woke the next morning. It was one of those times you're so warm and comfy and the absolute last thing you want is to get up. But before I could convince my subconscious to take over and lull me back to sleep, something odd invaded my senses.

First there was the comforting smell, laden with subtle notes of leather and smoke. If it had been only that, I might've been able to ignore it. But just as I started to drift again, my pillow twitched.

Eyes popping wide, I choked down a gasp. A bare male chest lay beneath me, clearly visible in the dim morning sunlight seeping around the cracks of our boulder door.

I'm in his bed. How the fuck did I get in Jalen's bed?

My first instinct was to blame him. Because no way in hell would I consciously decide to crawl into my hired guide's bed—while almost completely naked. Nope. He must've...

But before I could make an even bigger ass of myself by waking him up with shouted accusations, a flash of hazy memory stopped me. I'd woken in the night, plagued with the boiling heat under my skin I couldn't seem to shake. Then I'd tumbled out of my bed, looking for water. I'd shuffled around the darkened cave until I found a pack and grabbed the thermos.

In my half-asleep stupor, I'd assumed it was my pack. But I'd lost my pack in the river. That had to mean... My gaze trailed past the nipple staring me down to Jalen's bag, lying on the floor within reach, the top gaping open.

Oh god... I didn't do this to myself, did I?

I must've slipped into his bed by mistake. How stupid could I be?

Panic clawed at my chest. *I need to get out of here—now.*

After I peeked at his face, a little of the frenzied fear receded. He was still asleep. Jalen was sprawled on his back with both of his arms folded beneath his head like a pillow and me pressed against his side. If I kept my cool, I could sneak away with no one the wiser.

Keeping my movements slow and measured, I rolled away. Cool morning air chilled my skin instantly, making me shiver for another reason.

I'm practically naked! I popped to my feet and snagged my skinsuit from where it was hanging, dressing in about two seconds flat. Then, sucking in a breath, I turned, half-expecting him to be lying there, watching me with a smirk.

The breath escaped in a huge, relieved whoosh. Still asleep.

That could've been so much worse...

My agitated pulse rattled in my chest like an engine with a misaligned motor. I needed some space. And since daylight was bleeding through the cave, I decided to grab some fresh air while I was at it.

After shoving open the boulder door, I escaped into the jungle. I stopped myself before going too far. It wouldn't be smart to get lost. Still, I felt a bit better with some distance between us, though that weird sensation of my insides roasting started again as soon as I walked a few feet into the trees.

The neat line of thread that Jalen had stitched in my skinsuit stared up at me. Guess that wasn't the problem after all.

Was I getting sick? Could it explain why I'd been out of it enough to climb into the wrong bed?

Honestly, I had no clue. But there was someone who might... I just hoped she was awake at this hour.

Tapping my neck, I activated my comms implant and waited.

"Ren?" Karsen's voice answered groggily. "That you?"

"Hey, sorry if I woke you."

A yawn echoed in my ears. "It's okay. I needed to wake up soon and check on Arda, anyway."

"How's she doing?"

"She was much better yesterday, with only a few scattered episodes of hallucinations. I suspect the worst has passed by now."

"That's good." I sighed.

"Something else bothering you?"

I pinched my eyes closed, silently working up the courage to spill the whole crazy story. "I think I'm coming down with something."

Karsen slipped into full doctor mode, her voice losing all sleepiness. "I'm sorry to hear that. Describe your symptoms for me and let's see what we can do to help you feel better."

"I keep feeling hot. Like boiling hot under my skin."

"Okay. What else? Any coughing or congestion?"

"No, none of that. It's not like any cold I've had before. It's mostly just the heat."

She fell silent for a moment. "Hm. If that's all, then I suspect you're feeling the effects of hiking through a sweltering jungle for two days straight. You're bound to be dehydrated. Make sure you drink plenty of water and rest whenever you have the chance. Unless there's something else?"

Ugh... I really didn't want to go there. "Well, there was one weird thing that happened last night."

"Go on."

"I kind of... sleepwalked."

"Interesting. How do you know it happened? Did Jalen see you in the act and tell you about it?"

"Not exactly." I winced. "I remembered it happening vaguely, after I woke up this morning—in the wrong bed."

"Ren..." The way she said my name made me certain Kar was trying her best not to laugh. "Did you sleepwalk into the hottie's bed?"

"It's not funny," I hissed. "I was practically naked."

"That doesn't sound like a problem to me." She did laugh then, and the sound seriously grated on my frayed nerves.

"Damn it, Kar! I'm freaking out over here!"

"Sorry." She cleared her throat. "It's just that most sleepwalkers have no idea they're sleepwalking. The fact that you do leads me to believe that your subconscious mind is trying to tell you something with these symptoms that your conscious mind is ignoring."

God, I'm afraid to ask. "Yeah? And what's that?"

"Simple. That man is a freaking snack you want to take a bite out of."

I gagged dramatically. "Do you know me at all, Kar? Come on! There has to be another explanation..." But my attempt to deflect sounded lame, even to my own ears.

Fact was, he was a snack. And from the thoughts pinging through my brain while bathing last night, it seemed I was feeling a bit peckish...

"There's one fool-proof way to figure out if my theory is true."

"What is it?" At this point, I was desperate enough to try anything.

"The next time you end up in his bed by mistake, take a ride on his pogo sticks. See if your symptoms disappear."

But not that. "Ugh, really?"

Karsen laughed again. "Yes, really. An active sex life can benefit many aspects of your overall health and well-being. If it makes you feel better, consider it doctor's orders."

"Eww, Kar. Please tell me you didn't just say that."

"Live a little, Ren. Or at least think about it."

She couldn't be serious. There was no way—

"I gotta go," Karsen said. "I told Arda I'd meet her for breakfast."

"Okay. Tell her I said hi."

"Will do. Later."

Karsen's advice reverberated in my skull, but no matter how many times it repeated, I couldn't wrap my head around it—or her *orders*. Sure, Jalen was attractive. Really fucking sexy, if I was being completely honest with myself. But I'd been around hot guys before, and this weird heat under my skin had never happened until now.

There was more going on, and fucking Jalen wouldn't magically make everything better. Right?

16

Sunlight

Jalen

I reclined on my mat, staying still and quiet long after the boulder had swung open. I'd barely slept, especially after Ren paid me a visit in the middle of the night.

Harlx's ghost... That had been an exercise in control I wasn't expecting. My cousin's demand had played in my ears on repeat all night long. *Keep your hands to yourself. Keep your hands to yourself.* The next time I saw Rhelt, I owed him a swift punch to the groin for the pain he'd caused me.

I'd lain there unmoving while Ren slept, after she'd crawled into my bed and plastered her naked flesh against me. All I'd wanted was to roll her over and make her mine. But I couldn't quiet the whispered warning echoing in the depths of my mind. The one saying that she was acting out of character. The female who insisted I turn my back *and* close my eyes while she was wrapped in a towel wasn't the same female who'd brazenly climb in a male's bed while only wearing that tiny scrap of—

No... I had to stop picturing it. To stop remembering how she'd felt, so warm and soft, pressed against me. Otherwise, I'd be stuck lying here all morning, willing my arousal to subside.

It was a good thing I'd listened to that voice. If Ren's reaction when she woke and hastily scrambled off me was anything to judge by, she hadn't meant to climb into my bed at all.

I'd been careful to keep still, not letting on to the fact that I was awake and aware of her presence. She clearly felt awkward about it. And I wasn't in the habit of making anyone feel worse. Especially not her. If she gave me the chance, I'd love to make her feel amazing.

There I went again. *Stop it, Jalen. She's not for you.* Perhaps if I told myself that enough, it would start to ring true.

I couldn't help wondering why Ren was so unwilling to be touched. And if she was seeking out physical contact in her sleep, did that mean on some level she was aching for connection?

Honestly, after three long years on my own, those few hours with Ren lying against me had been like the answer to an unspoken prayer. It was part of the reason I hadn't slept much. Not only from the undeniable attraction I fought so hard to tamp down—but because I didn't want it to end.

It was kind of pathetic when I thought about it. I was so starved for affection I'd hoarded her unintended embrace like a fiend with his favorite drug. Even when I'd felt the urge to scratch an itch or roll over, I'd ignored it, desperate for a few more stolen moments.

Was it just wishful thinking to hope that she secretly craved a moment of connection with me too?

I finally rose from my mat and gathered my things. We had another long day of hiking ahead of us, and it was time to get started.

I emerged from the cave into the jungle and spotted Ren pacing between two trees. "Good morning."

She flinched, jumping enough that her head bumped into a low branch, sending a shower of pollen into the air. The shimmering flecks of gold spread around her in a halo, making her ever-present beauty shine ethereally in the morning sunlight.

"What?" she snapped.

Great. I must've been staring like an idiot. "N-nothing. Just thought we'd eat breakfast while we walk. I got a later start than I'd like."

Her gaze darted to the forest floor briefly before it rose, examining my face. "Did you sleep well?"

I grinned inanely. "Oh yes. Best sleep I've had in ages. I was dead to the world. Dead to the entire universe. Like a corpse, even. You could've slapped me and I still wouldn't have woken up." My jaw snapped closed, stopping my rambling. I dug in my pack, needing to distract her from my stupidity. "Here. Want some haldi bread?"

She inched close enough to snatch the bread out of my hand, then retreated a step. "Not that I don't like this stuff, but is it all you brought?" She punctuated the question with a bite so big I was surprised she didn't need to unhinge her jaw to fit it all in.

"It's the only thing I had at home that I knew would keep while we were out in the heat." I jerked my head toward the path and started moving, hoping she'd take the hint and follow. "If you want more variety, we can pick some fruit. And we can forage enough greens to make a salad."

She shrugged. "Sounds good to me."

As the morning wore on, the awkwardness slowly receded as I pointed out dozens of edible plants along our route. Ren seemed content to listen to me spout off facts about how to grow each plant and which meals they tasted best in.

"What's that one?" Her nose wrinkled as I plucked an oblong root vegetable out of the soil just as the sun reached its zenith.

I lifted it with a smile. "This is biteroot." I dusted it off before quickly discarding the outer layer and offering her a small piece. "They're easy to locate. Look for reddish-yellow stalks and pull them out."

She chewed thoughtfully. "Huh. Reminds me of an onion, but sweeter." She eyed the leaves that I'd pulled off while cleaning the biteroot. "Those are pretty."

"We have a use for these too." I crumbled a biteroot leaf between my fingers, then rubbed the plant across a tree trunk, smearing a bright dollop of orange-red across it.

"Let me guess, clothing dyes?"

"Among other things..." I led the way further down the trail, listing several different uses. But then, I sensed something was wrong. Ren's pace slowed, and her face drained of color.

"I think we should take a break." I gestured to a downed log on the side of the path. "Sit down."

She followed without complaint, releasing a big sigh as she sank beside me. Since the log wasn't very big, we were forced to sit shoulder to shoulder. I chewed the inside of my cheek, worried she'd pop back to her feet when she realized how close we were.

Instead, she leaned her head against my shoulder. "Can I have some water?"

"Certainly." I handed her the thermos, my heart pounding. "Are you feeling okay, Ren?"

She drained most of the water before answering. "Yeah. I just got really hot for a second. I'm starting to feel better now that I'm sitting down." She passed the thermos back and seemed to belatedly realize how close we were sitting. She lifted her head and slid as far away as the log allowed, which still left her close enough that our elbows might bump if we weren't careful.

"I'm glad you're feeling better. Why don't we break for lunch while we're here?"

"Okay. I could eat."

I grinned. "Why do I get the feeling you're always in the mood to eat?" I set my pack on the ground and rummaged inside, pulling out the plants we'd foraged and setting them atop a flat round leaf I snagged off a nearby tawl bush.

Her nose wrinkled. "Probably because it's true. I've always had a healthy appetite. High metabolism, I guess. Though sometimes when I'm in the zone at work, I miss a meal or two."

"Hm. Well, I'll make sure you don't miss any meals while we're together. We need to keep our strength up for the hike." I finished chopping everything and heaped it in a pile. "What do you think?"

Ren glanced at the salad with a crooked smile. "It's weird I'm about to eat something that didn't come from a food processor or a restaurant."

I pulled a disgusted face. "That's all you're eating?"

She rolled her eyes. "What would you know about it? I don't see a bunch of food processors lying around the jungle."

"I've tried enough food-processed meals to realize they're no re-placement for the real thing. Like those puny bars of sadness you tried pawning off on me."

"Hey!" She shoved my shoulder, nearly making me drop the salad. "I didn't have to share, you know."

I dragged the tawl leaf close to my chest. "Perhaps I shouldn't share either."

Her face contorted into a look of pure outrage. "Don't you dare!"

Chuckles rumbled out of my chest. "Just kidding. I don't need you gnawing my arm off."

"Please. Like I would eat something so heinous."

"Heinous... I don't know that word either." Which was true, although it was pretty clear from the snarl on her lip it wasn't complimentary. "Is that what you say when something looks much too good to eat?"

"You guessed it," she deadpanned.

I set the tawl leaf on my lap but waved Ren away when she leaned closer. "Hold on," I insisted when the action earned me a scowl. "It's missing one last finishing touch." I plucked a ripe haldi fruit from my bag.

"Are we having a side of fruit with our salad?" Ren asked.

"Haldi's not the tastiest without cooking. But the juice makes a decent dressing in a pinch." I sliced into the striped flesh, then squeezed both halves over the salad. Then I picked up the tawl leaf and plopped it on Ren's lap. "Go on. Try it."

Ren tentatively lifted some greens into her mouth as I tossed the squished haldi into the jungle. "Mmm." My blood turned molten as her moan echoed in my ears. "Oh my god! That's really good."

I cleared my throat. "Glad you like it."

She scarfed another bite down. I watched her delicate throat work while I licked the sticky haldi juice off my fingers.

Ren swallowed and said, "Aren't you going to have—" She froze as her gaze lifted and caught me sucking the last of the juice off my thumb.

I pulled it out of my mouth with an audible pop. "Have as much as you want. I'll finish it... if you save me some."

Ren's cheeks flushed, and her gaze returned to her lap. She finished about half, then passed the leaf to me.

"You're full?"

She nodded. "Yeah. Thanks."

I passed her the thermos before tucking in. I even had to bite back my own moan. I don't know why—since salads like this were a staple in my diet—but for some reason, this particular dish hit the spot in a way I wasn't expecting.

After I finished, I threw the leaf into the trees and drained what was left of the water. Luckily, there was a small settlement close by. I wagered we could pass through and refill with one of their wells.

Dionions were usually kind to travelers, especially other Dionions. I couldn't be certain they wouldn't look at Ren with suspicion. After all, there was a history of poaching in the jungle that many locals weren't keen to forget. But I suspected as long as Ren was with me, they'd accept her easily enough.

"Ready to get back on the trail?" I asked.

"Sure." Ren stood, and I followed suit.

"Good news is we should reach—" My statement cut off with a gasp as Ren collapsed. I lunged forward, catching her with a grunt before she smacked into the forest floor.

My stomach plummeted as I gently laid her down and kneeled beside her. "Ren? Are you okay?"

I patted her cheek gently, but she didn't wake. And to make matters worse, with my palm pressed to her face, it was impossible to ignore how unnaturally warm her skin was.

She kept saying she was hot. I should've paid more attention to her symptoms.

What's wrong with her?

Panic set in, and terrible images flooded my mind, like her breathing slowing and fading away to nothing as the color leeched out of her skin. Then her face flushing beet red and sweat seeping out of her pores as she overheated.

Shoving the awful premonitions aside, I stood and scooped her into my arms. I refused to sit there and do nothing. Ren was in trouble, and I wouldn't rest until I figured out why—and how to fix it.

Jalen

I wrung my hands inside the most garishly decorated cabin I'd ever had the displeasure of visiting. Vomit-green walls dotted with abstract paintings in clashing colors assaulted my eyes. Yet I was willing to put up with the nauseating sight because the house belonged to one of the most skilled healers on Dionus.

Asani might have the design sense of a color-blind tike, but she knew her craft. And right now, she was the best chance I had at discovering what had made Ren collapse.

I'd rushed into the village, barely pausing until I made it to Asani's door. She'd welcomed me in, then shuttered herself and Ren in a side room while she completed the examination. Only the knowledge that Ren would definitely not appreciate me sneaking peeks at her while Asani checked her everywhere kept me from demanding to stay at her side.

What was taking so long?

The door slid open a few moments later. Asani blinked at me, her wrinkled lips pursing into a displeased glower. "You should've brought her somewhere sooner, young one."

I bristled but refrained from correcting her. As a male in my early thirties, I hadn't been called young one in almost a decade—but I supposed Asani, who must be in her seventies by now, got away with calling out nearly everyone for being young. "I've barely known her for two days," I grumbled.

"She's in this state after two days?" Asani looked me up and down. "That's good. Means a strong connection. Your harmonies are in peak alignment."

My throat went dry. "What?"

Asani walked closer with her finger outstretched. "Don't be deliberately obtuse, young one. You're not so inexperienced you can't see what this is."

"No." I shook my head gravely and stared at the floorboards—which were the ugliest shade of brown imaginable. "I'm certain you've heard what happened to me... before." I didn't need to go into the details. As huge as our planet was, news and, more importantly, gossip, hopped from one place to another like fire through dry brush.

That finger of hers reached me first, and she used it to her advantage, poking me between my neck and shoulder in some weird spot that hurt so badly I yelped. "Doesn't matter what did or didn't happen in the past. Are you blind?"

I rubbed myself with a scowl. "No."

"Then you know what that means. There's only one way to stop what's ailing her." She wagged her finger at me again. "Don't make me point that out, too."

She lunged for me, and I backed away, my hands falling instinctively to cradle my groin. "B-but... I thought..."

"You're mates," Asani announced bluntly. "She won't stop feeling like she needs to cool off until you complete the bond."

I shouldn't have been shocked. I'd lived on Dionus my whole life. Seen thousands of couples affected by the heat. But nonetheless, Asani's words rocked me to my core. "But... she's Terran."

"Yes. I suspect that may be another reason she's been affected so severely." She cocked her head. "Won't be long now before it creeps up on you too."

Come to mention it, I had been feeling warm since carrying Ren here. I'd tried to convince myself it was from walking so far with a full-grown female in my arms. But in hindsight... Asani might be on to something.

"So it has started..." Asani leaned in. "You want my advice? Just bed her and be done with it. You'll both start feeling better once you surrender to fate."

My eyes pinched closed, and I rubbed the bridge of my nose. I tried to picture myself marching into Asani's spare room and telling Ren to spread her legs—for her own good, of course. I'd likely earn a swift kick between mine, and rightfully so.

No, this needed to be handled much more delicately. With Ren's aversion to touch, and my less-than-savory past, there was a lot we needed to talk about before any mating transpired.

"I'm afraid it's a tad more complicated in this case."

"Hm... thought it might be. I'll wake her and prepare a liquid dose of blockers. They'll begin working swiftly, easing most of her symptoms. She'll need to follow up with tablets." She headed for a cabinet oddly decorated with polka dots on one section and a starburst pattern on the rest. After rummaging in the drawer, she slammed it closed and said, "Here. Take these. Have her swallow one in the morning at first light and one at dusk." She thrust a rattling bottle at my chest. "You'll need to do the same once your symptoms become more pronounced."

"Thank you." I clutched the bottle to my chest.

"Those are only a temporary solution. Sooner or later, you need to complete the bond."

I gulped, my mind whirling as I tried to digest her words. "I know."

Ren was my mate. *How in Harlx's name am I going to tell her?*

17

Snake Oil

Ren

Something cool and damp pressed against my forehead, and my eyes fluttered open. My brow furrowed. "Where am I?" The last thing I remembered was eating salad with Jalen. How did I end up in a room decorated in the ugliest wallpaper ever invented? It was brown with bright-orange accents that I suspected were meant to be flowers—but which looked more like a certain part of female anatomy.

"Good, you're finally waking," a woman said.

I turned my neck slowly, spotting an old Dionion, her blue hair streaked liberally with gray, holding a washcloth against my head. "Who are you? What happened to me?" I was sprawled flat on my back on a raised platform in the center of a small room, allowing the lady to putter around beside me while I rested at waist level.

"There, there, young one. All will be well in time." She lifted the cloth, dipping it into a basin.

I attempted to sit up, but all that earned me was a wave of dizziness. Added to the heat cooking me from the inside out, I had never felt so strange in my life.

Who was this lady? From the gentle way she took care of me, and the kindness in her eyes, I suspected she wasn't a threat. But why wasn't she answering my questions?

Once I didn't feel like I was about to faint, I tried again. "I don't understand what's happening. How did I get here? Where is Jalen?"

The woman's brows dipped and her lips pursed as I spoke until the last word. "Ah, of course. I'll bring your harmonic." She patted my shoulder with a wrinkled hand and marched across the room toward the door. "Stay right there."

What did she say she was getting? A harmonica?

"Seems like I don't have much choice." A little voice in my mind begged me to get up, but there was no way I'd get far if lifting my head made me so dizzy I had to immediately lie back down.

The door swung open soon after, and Jalen rushed in. "Ren? You're awake."

"Hey, there you are." I attempted a smile, but I suspect it looked more like a grimace. "What's going on? How did I get here? That lady wouldn't tell me anything."

"Sorry about that. Asani doesn't have a translator implant."

"Oh." That explained it. I could understand her, but she couldn't understand me. "Who is she?"

"A healer. You collapsed in the jungle and I brought you here."

Asani strolled back in, a small cup in her hands. "After we get some liquid in her, she'll be up on her feet." She faced Jalen. "Help her sit up, young one."

Jalen slid in behind me, gently lifting my shoulders until I was upright. He stayed there, supporting my upper body by resting it against his chest. The position was far too intimate for my liking, but desperate times...

"Drink this." Asani lifted the cup to my lips.

I sipped dutifully, only to twist away when the wretched liquid accosted my taste buds. There were simply no words to describe it, although putrid came close. I swallowed the first mouthful reflexively, but there was no way in hell I was finishing the rest. "Ugh, what was that?"

Asani waved the cup in front of me. "You must finish it."

Jalen winced. "It's medicine. You should listen to her."

"Nope. Not happening. She's trying to poison me."

Vibrations tickled my back as a startled laugh rumbled in Jalen's chest. "I promise she's not poisoning you."

"You don't know that. She could be losing her mind. Who decorates their room with vaginas?"

His gaze darted to the weird "flowers" on the wall and more laughter spilled out of him.

I didn't join in. "I'm glad you find this hilarious, but I don't want a crazy woman doctoring me! Hell, she told me she was bringing me a harmonica when she went to get you."

Jalen stiffened.

"You think I'm right, don't you?" I could tell the last little factoid struck a nerve. "Let me call Karsen. She's a doctor too. One I know for sure is sane. I want a second opinion before I drink that"—I grimaced at the cup—"disgusting snake oil."

Asani picked that moment to dart in, trying to pour the poison down my mouth while it was partially open in an outraged sneer. I slammed my lips shut at the last instant and glared at her with murder in my eyes.

"Make your harmonic drink," Asani barked at Jalen.

There she goes with that nonsense again! I refused to open my mouth and give the old lady another opportunity to drown me, but I aimed a pointed stare at Jalen, lifting my brows as if to say, *See? The bitch is crazy.*

Jalen sighed wearily. "Ren, Asani isn't trying to harm you. She's been a healer for her entire life, and I trust her completely."

I covered my mouth, making sure Asani didn't try a sneak attack while I spoke. "If that's the case, then *you* drink it."

"If I drink the medicine, then you will too?"

Maybe I just craved company in my misery. "Yes."

Jalen snagged the cup from Asani and drained it in a few swift gulps. "Harlx's beard! That was awful." My back shook as a full-body shudder ripped through him.

"See?" I spit out.

Asani threw up her hands before grabbing the empty cup. "I'll bring more," she grumbled as she shuffled through the door.

"Fuck..." *I can't believe he drank that.* "I take it back. I'd rather be dead."

"No way. You agreed." Jalen chuckled. "Just get it over quick. Truly, it wasn't that bad."

Of course Mr. Positive would say so... I craned my neck sideways, glaring at him. Only... I hadn't realized how close we were. Or how beautiful his green eyes would be up close and filled with mirth. I swallowed as we locked gazes, my heart pounding.

Jalen brushed a stray lock of hair off my forehead. "Be honest now. You wouldn't rather be dead, would you?"

My breath caught, and the next words that escaped my throat came out in a husky murmur. "No. I-I don't know why I said that..."

"Mmm. I thought so." He inched closer, his gaze falling to my mouth.

And I just sat there, stunned, my breath getting shallower with every inhale. *Is he going to kiss me? Do I want him to?*

The door slammed open, and Jalen jerked back. I flipped forward so fast another blast of dizziness hit me.

Fuck... Maybe I *did* need to drink that vile medicine. If it stopped the dizziness and the overwhelming sensation of lava boiling my veins, then it would be worth it.

Asani hustled over with the cup outstretched.

"Fine. I'll drink it." But before grabbing the cup, I pinched my nose closed. Then I poured the awful concoction down my throat, willing myself not to gag.

"Good," Asani praised. "You ought to start feeling better momentarily, young one. Please, rest here until you're steady on your feet." She turned to Jalen. "Remember my instructions, yes?" She ducked out of the room, leaving me and Jalen alone.

"What was that all about? What instructions?"

"Hm?" Jalen patted his vest. "Oh, she gave me more medicine to take with us."

"Oh, hell no. I'm not drinking that again."

"Relax. The rest is in tablet form."

"They make that crap in tablets? Why couldn't I just take that instead?"

"It would've taken a lot longer to begin working."

I scoffed. "I would've waited."

"But isn't it nice to have it over and done with?" He backed away but kept a hand on my shoulder. "Think you can sit on your own yet?"

I stiffened my spine and found that I could handle the task without wobbling. "Yeah. I think that stuff is working. I feel a lot cooler, too." A shadow of the heat boiling my insides was still present, but most of it had subsided. "Guess she wasn't trying to poison me after all."

"See? I told you we could trust her."

I flicked my legs over the edge of the raised cot. "Hm. Well, I still maintain that anyone who'd look at that monstrosity every day is at least a little bit crazy." I nodded to the wallpaper.

Jalen grinned, a devilish glint in his eyes that made me feel a bit dizzy again. "This is nothing. Wait until you see the rest of the house."

Ren

Less than an hour later, after gawking at one of the weirdest living rooms in the universe, we bid goodbye to Asani and headed outside.

I squinted at the sun. Twilight wasn't far off. "How long was I out?"

Jalen shrugged. "Most of the afternoon."

"Yikes. I hope that doesn't put us behind schedule."

"It's all right. We can make up some time before full night." He cocked a brow. "Unless you'd rather stay in the village tonight? I'm certain I could find someone willing to lend us a room."

"No. I rested enough already. Unless... are you tired?" Sure, I'd been passed out for half of the day, but Jalen must have exerted a lot of energy carrying me out of the jungle.

On the other hand, the village wasn't much to look at. Just a few scraggly cabins tucked into a clearing. And if the rest of the locals hadn't bothered to get a translator, it'd be a pain trying to communicate with them.

"No worries. I'm not tired yet."

"All right. Let's go."

We set off down a path leading into the trees. It wasn't long before we ran into something that made the skin on my arms prickle. An enormous wall blocked our path forward, virtually identical to the one that had bordered Jalen's cabin, only three times bigger.

"How are we supposed to get around that?" More importantly, did we even want to cross it? They wouldn't have built a wall that size unless there was something on the other side they *really* didn't want passing through.

"There's a gate ahead. I know the code," Jalen said.

"Okay... Can I just ask, what is that wall keeping out?"

"This is dradhowler territory, remember?"

"Oh. Right." The big beasties Arda had told me about. "And how are we supposed to keep them away from us again?"

He sent me a reassuring smile. "As long as we're under shelter before full dark, they won't be a problem. Don't worry. The spot I was telling you about won't take nearly that long to reach."

"If you say so." The words came out confidently enough, but I almost chickened out and told him I *would* like to spend the night in the village after all. But then a chime distracted me from my cowardly thoughts. "Someone's ringing me on my comms implant."

"Answer it. I'll open the gate."

As Jalen strode out of earshot, I slapped my neck. "Hey, what's up?"

"Ren, how are you hanging in there with the hot guide?"

"Arda." I grinned, happy to hear her sounding like herself again. "I'm doing okay. How about you? Did you break Lux's heart yet by admitting you're into humping plants now?"

She scoffed. "Please. If I really wanted to get into plant husbandry, he'd be the first one hauling a tree inside the *Verne* and figuring out how to make it the third in our weird little menage."

Laughter bubbled out of me, and Jalen turned back with a crooked grin when he heard it. I shifted sideways, not wanting his distracting smile to be all I could see. "Um, so you're back to normal?"

"Yeah. Ankle's good as new. Still have a killer headache. Doesn't help that Smudge is still howling about how horny she is every chance she gets. I swear, sometimes I can hear her yowling inside my head. I even heard it when I went outside to check the landing gear earlier. Guess those are just auditory flashbacks, though."

"If it makes you feel better, Dionus doesn't like me much better."

"Fuck." Arda's voice grew concerned. "What happened?"

I shared a shortened account of the last few hours, along with a description of Asani's home that had her roaring with laughter. By the time I'd finished, we'd made it through the gate and a short distance down the trail.

"Wow. That's rough. I'm glad the healer forced you to choke down the medicine in the end. Did she say what caused your symptoms? Knowing my luck, I better keep an eye out while I'm exploring or I'll be the next one burning up."

"She didn't. Or maybe I was too out of it when she explained."

"Well, if you find out, let me know." Arda chuckled. "Vagina wallpaper. Wish I'd seen that."

I shivered. "Trust me, you really don't. I'll be having nightmares about that room for weeks."

A huge yawn echoed in my ears.

"Feeling tired?" I asked.

"Still catching up from the sleepless night while I was hallucinating. I didn't realize that stuff would keep me wired for hours on end."

"I'll sign off, then, so you can get some rest."

"All right. But before you go... thanks, Ren. I know you were the last one of us who should be stuck out there with some rando considering—"

"It's fine." I glanced ahead, making sure Jalen was still far enough away that he couldn't hear me. Even so, I lowered my voice. "I actually think he might be one of the rare decent men in the universe."

"Nice. I'm glad he's not some big weirdo like we were worried about."

"Yeah, me too. Later, Capt."

As I deactivated my implant, I stole another look ahead. It was strange to realize, but what I'd admitted to Arda—mainly hoping to set her at ease—wasn't even a lie.

Jalen might annoy me to no end with his endless positivity, but he'd helped me again today. I had no doubt if he hadn't been around to carry me out of the jungle, I'd still be lying on the ground, passed out and overheated. That made it twice now that he'd saved my life.

Maybe he really is one of the good ones...

18

Full Dark

Jalen

The sun eased its way toward the horizon, lengthening the shadows shading the overgrown footpath. We'd made good time that afternoon despite finding a few spots that were so densely packed with vegetation I'd had to dig out my machete for the first time. Luckily, it wouldn't be long until we reached our campsite for the night.

"You still hanging in there?" I tilted my head, eyeing Ren for any signs of fatigue.

"I'm good." She slapped her neck. "But I might need some more of that insect repellent."

I swung the heavy pack off my back. "The bugs come out in force around twilight. Here."

"Thanks." She slowed to a stop and twisted the top off the ointment bottle. "Mosquitos back on Earth like to come out at twilight, too. I wonder if this stuff would work for them?"

I shrugged. "It might."

"If it does, you could make a killing manufacturing this as an export." She glanced up at my face and her eyes widened. "Something wrong?"

I forced the look of displeasure off my face, though I couldn't completely hide my cool tone. "Dionions don't have any interest in the export business."

She twisted her lips. "Was just a suggestion."

With a sigh, I explained, "Dionus was once invaded for our natural resources. The invaders had no respect for the jungle, even causing the extinction of an endangered species that lived in only one small area. We knew back then that we needed to protect the bounty of our planet."

"That's really sad. And I kind of get it." She shook the ointment at me. "But this stuff has the potential to save a lot of lives. Diseases spread by mosquitoes kill thousands of Terrans each year. Mostly the poor, who don't have access to med-bots."

"Sounds like you already have technology that cures those diseases. Why don't you share that with the ones in need?"

Ren's lips pursed. "I don't know. I guess some of it is greed from the companies that manufacture the equipment. They value their profits more than making the tech available to everyone."

"There's no guarantee this ointment wouldn't end up the same." I took the tube back from her. "Someone with power could hoard it. Then more would come, hunting for the secret. They'd tear down the jungle in their ignorance."

"Huh. I didn't consider it from that angle." She started walking again but only made it two steps before stopping abruptly. "Jalen, look!"

I glanced off the path where she pointed. "Another rider."

She clapped her hands together, and her eyes sparkled. "I might be able to fix this one!"

I couldn't say no when the excitement pouring off of her was this palpable. "Let's check it out."

She barreled off the path, crunching through the underbrush, her gaze glued to the rusted machine. "Give me your pack. I need my tools and the spare parts."

I handed the bag over and leaned against a tree while she popped the hood. "Will this take long?" I glanced at the sky, my brows dipping.

"Hopefully not. Won't know for sure until I test a few things." With that, she proceeded to ignore me like I wasn't there.

It wasn't long before I realized I wasn't needed. "Ren." She didn't look up or acknowledge me. "Hey, Ren."

"Hm?"

"While you're working, I'm going to hike up the trail to our camp-site. Get everything set up for the night. That all right with you?"

She nodded absentmindedly, her hands still moving within the old vehicle. "Okay."

Was it foolish leaving her alone when she was deaf to the world? I doubted it. Travelers had rarely ventured through this stretch of jungle back when I'd frequented these trails. And judging by how overgrown the footpath was, that was still the case.

We still had a couple hours before full night descended and the real danger arrived. Dradhowlers weren't an animal you wanted to cross—ever.

I just hoped that when we needed to head in for the night, I'd be able to drag Ren away from her new toy.

Jalen

A dull ache settled in my shoulder blades as I trudged down the trail to where I'd left Ren. I'd been forced to clear more brush on the way to the cave, including a particularly stubborn patch of weeds laced with thick vines.

Now the long day began to compound with the lack of sleep I'd gotten last night, making yawns split my lips frequently. Two moons graced the sky, lighting the way nicely, but in a few moments, the larger moon would set, washing the trees in near darkness. Then less than an hour later, the second would follow, bringing on full night.

The moons orbited Dionus at varying orbits, which meant full night didn't always come at the same time. Some nights, one moon or another graced the sky the entire evening. Unfortunately, tonight was one of the rare nights when full dark lasted most of the night.

Luckily, the moons' path was predictable. I'd memorized them long ago, same as most Dionions with a fondness for travel.

A bit of my tiredness washed away when I rounded a corner and spotted Ren ahead, still busy tinkering with the rider's engine. "You ready to go?"

"I need a few more minutes."

Great... this will be fun. "I'm sorry, but we have to head inside now."

Ren scowled. "But I'm almost done." She brightened. "At first, I thought this was a lost cause, like the last one. I'd almost given up and scrapped it for parts when I realized—"

Though I hated to stop her when she was speaking so animatedly, I had to. "That's great, but if we don't go inside, we'll be in danger. Remember the dradhowlers."

"How far is our campsite? I don't mind jogging—"

Harlx's bane! She just wasn't getting it. "Ren, get your pretty ass moving or I'll toss you over my shoulder and carry you to safety."

Her jaw dropped for a split second before her expression shifted to a glare. "Are you fucking kidding me right now?"

I advanced on her, stopping just shy of her personal space when she retreated a step warily. "I'm not joking. This is serious, Ren. The rider is worthless if we're torn apart by a dradhowler before we can use it."

The universe picked the perfect time to highlight the gravity of my words. Just then, the first moon set completely, washing the forest in deepening shadows.

She sighed. "Fine. I guess you're right."

I scooped my pack off the ground, thankful she'd kept her tools contained within it. "Come on." I stretched out a hand, which Ren ignored, electing to pick her way through the underbrush unaided.

We hiked in silence, with Ren tossing icy glares at me every few steps. I didn't bother trying to thaw her disdain. She'd get over it eventually—I hoped.

Perhaps it wasn't the smartest move to threaten a female who hated to be touched with throwing her over my shoulder. But I had to do something. She'd been determined to keep working, even when she'd be endangering herself.

She kept up the silent treatment all the way to the cave. Once we were in and the door firmly closed behind us, the tension in my shoulders finally subsided.

Ren glanced around the cave, which was pretty similar to the last one we'd stayed in, but her gaze zeroed in on the pool before long.

"Why don't you wash first?" I suggested. "You must want to clean that grease off your hands."

She thrust out a palm expectantly. "Fine. Towel and soap."

Guess the short-clipped sentences are a step up from complete silence. "Here you go." I handed them to her with a smile—one she didn't return.

As she spun on her heel and disappeared behind the screen, I sighed. It seemed Ren still wasn't ready to forgive me for barking at her earlier. But I might know one way to get back on her good side... Quietly, I slid out of the boulder door and took off running.

19

Relax

Ren

Sloshing echoed around me as I furiously scrubbed myself in the cave's pool. The nerve of that man! At least he had the sense not to start his dumb humming.

Jalen's voice reverberated in my ears, that stupid order of his playing on repeat. *He's lucky he didn't try to throw me over his shoulder. I would've...* Well, I probably wouldn't have done anything other than flail around like a dead fish. Jalen was way bigger and stronger than I would ever be. I'm sure he would've had no trouble manhandling me. A shiver spread through my belly, and I wasn't entirely convinced it was only from my righteous indignation.

I climbed out of the tub and dried off. My upper lip curled as I studied my lone skinsuit and pair of panties. Both could use a good washing—the skinsuit especially, after the work I'd done on the rider. Several new stains marred the chest and arms, darkening the navy-blue fabric to near black.

I settled for handwashing the panties and hanging them to dry, and slipped into the skinsuit without them. Hopefully, they'd be dry in the morning. I refused to spend another night sleeping in the nude. Not after that weird sleepwalking incident last night. Washing my skinsuit would have to wait.

I wrenched the screen back and stormed into the cave, prepared to shower Jalen with more disdain... except he was nowhere to be seen.

"Jalen?" My pulse sped. It wasn't like there was anywhere to hide. That could only mean one thing. He must've gone outside.

Why in the universe would he go out there after he'd insisted on dragging me in? I strode for the door, intending to push it open, but before my fingers pressed against the rock, a blood-curdling howl rent the air somewhere nearby.

"Holy fuck!" Terror seized me, rooting my feet to the floor. The roar sounded like what you'd get if a lion and a dragon had a baby, with a little wolf thrown in. Whatever creature had made that sound had to be terrifying... Anyone with half a brain would stay as far away from it as possible.

Guess my brain hadn't gotten the memo. As if it had a mind of its own, my hand darted out and shoved the boulder door open.

"Jalen!" I yelled into the dark. The barest sliver of a lone moon hung over the horizon, providing only the scantest hint of light. I squinted, praying one of the shadows would move. And that it didn't belong to whatever creature had produced that dreadful howl.

Nothing.

My heart hammered loudly in my ears as I stepped outside. "Jalen, where are you?"

"Ren? What are you doing? Go back inside!"

Relief pulsed through me so swiftly I didn't even scowl at his agitated demand. "Thank god! What were you thinking going back out?"

As Jalen hurried forward, grunting, the answer to my question became clear. He hadn't returned empty-handed. He clenched a length of rope in his fists, dragging the rider behind him. "Get inside, would you? You're blocking the entrance."

Another howl somewhere in the trees made me flinch. Then I hopped into motion, backing away into the cave with my mouth agape. "You went back for the rider?"

"That obvious, huh?" With a grin, he pulled the machine in the last small stretch and shoved the door in place.

My speeding pulse finally slowed. As the panic subsided, annoyance rose to replace it. I strode forward and punched Jalen in the shoulder. "Are you fucked in the head? Why did you scare me like that?"

"Hey!" His smile fell, and he rubbed the spot with a frown. "I thought you'd be happy. You wanted more time with the rider. Now you have all night."

I planted my hands on my hips. "And what if you'd gotten eaten by a dradhowler? Where would that leave me? I'd be stuck without a guide. I don't know anything about this stupid planet, remember?" And yeah, I'd be pretty devastated that one of the few good men in the universe was gone, but I wasn't exactly in the mood to hand out compliments.

Jalen stared at the floor for a second before lifting his gaze to mine. "I knew if I ran, I'd make it back in time. I thought you'd still be in the pool, and the rider would be a pleasant surprise when you got out. It may have been stupid to chance it, but I wanted to do something nice after I yelled at you earlier."

Fuck... If I hadn't been so pouty on the hike to the cave, he wouldn't have felt compelled to put himself in danger to please me. "It *is* a nice surprise," I conceded, forcing a smile. "Just don't pull that kind of stunt again, okay?"

"I won't. Promise." Jalen dragged a hand across his sweaty brow. "You mind if I take a turn in the tub?"

I shook my head. "Go for it."

As I watched Jalen wearily trudge toward the tub, my stomach twisted. I wanted to stay angry with him. Hell, deep down, I was still a little angry. I mean, who runs out in a monster-infested jungle to make amends? That was crazy...

But another part of me was stunned. When had anyone ever cared enough about me to do something crazy? Sure, I had Arda and Karsen. Zenda too. But they'd never put their life on the line to make me happy. My foster brother, Demi—he'd come close once. That had been a totally different situation, though.

With a sigh, I grabbed Jalen's pack and started digging out my tools. Might as well make the best out of the opportunity, now that I had it. Soon I was elbow-deep inside the engine again, trying not to think about what Jalen was doing on the other side of that screen.

Yet, try as I might, I couldn't get over what he'd done. Did my opinion matter so much to Jalen that he'd go to such extremes to put a smile on my face? Or was I making a big deal out of nothing? Maybe he made a habit out of doing crazy things for other people.

Yeah... that was probably it. I was just used to men being shitty, so it seemed bonkers when they acted nice.

"Fuck!" In my distracted state, I made a stupid mistake, splashing oil across my forearms.

"You okay out there?" Jalen asked.

"I just made a mess. Let me know when you're out of there. I'm gonna need the tub again." Luckily, I'd had my sleeves rolled up, so I hadn't completely destroyed my skinsuit.

"Harlx's bones! I just got in." Jalen clicked his tongue. "I don't mind sharing if it means I can relax here for a while longer."

Is he serious?

I couldn't wash while he was in there—naked.

But then I spotted a light flash behind the screen, and the unmistakable scent of smoke filled the cave. Seemed he had no intention of getting out soon. And my arms were starting to itch...

I slammed the hood closed. "Fine. I'm coming over. You better not be hogging the soap." I'd keep my eyes averted. Nothing to worry about.

Jalen chuckled. "It's all yours."

Inching the screen back, I slipped inside, keeping my gaze trained on my feet. "Where is it?" I squeaked.

"On the ledge. You'd see it if you weren't so interested in your boots."

My gaze flashed up in an instinctual glare. *Holy mother of muscles...* It was a chore maintaining my sneer with miles of wet bronze skin on display, yet somehow, I managed. "I didn't come here to be teased." I snatched the soap off the ledge and leaned over the edge, plunging my arms into the water up to the elbow.

A cloud of fragrant smoke wafted around me. "You don't have to stay out there. Plenty of room for us both."

Is he deliberately trying to make me blush? Even if he wasn't, I could sense from my burning cheeks my face was currently crimson. "I'm good where I am." Jalen's relaxed laughter filled the space—that and more smoke. "Why are you smoking? There are no plants in here to hypnotize."

"I don't need a tawl bush to enjoy a burner. Besides, it helps me sleep." A sharp intake let me know he'd taken another drag, but I didn't look up from my task. "Does it bother you?"

"Just making conversation."

"Thought you were against talking while bathing?"

I just needed something to distract myself from how insanely awkward this was. Didn't help that my perverted brain kept begging me for a peek at more than just his chest. Nope... *I'm not gonna look. Shut it down, Ren.*

"Perhaps you should reconsider hopping in. You look... tense." I didn't need to see his face to know he was smiling.

"I'm plenty relaxed."

"If you say so," he drawled. "No worries. There are countless caves with pools in this part of the jungle. Next time, perhaps."

My blood boiled, causing another flash of heat to smolder beneath my skin. Only this time, I doubted it was the sickness causing it. I'd had about enough of his stupid invites. Luckily, I'd finally scrubbed my arms clean.

I straightened, helped myself to Jalen's towel, and turned to go.

"Pull that screen closed when you leave, would you? I think you've had enough of a show."

I froze, my shoulders stiffening. The prick! I hadn't looked. Not once. Well, except for that one glare that barely even counted... I needed to say something cutting. Some comeback that would make him cower in the tub and his balls wither to dust.

Seconds ticked by, and my brain might as well have been on vacation. It was like I was the one puffing on that—wait...

I spun on my heel and prowled toward Jalen, a smirk on my lips.

He grinned lazily as our gazes locked. "Did you change your mind? Invitation stands—hey!" His smile vanished as I plucked his joint out of his fingers.

Lifting it to my lips, I backed away, holding his gaze as warm smoke filled my lungs. "What?" A cloud wafted around my mouth as I expertly exhaled while I spoke. "Thought you wanted me to relax?" I let the words linger as I whipped around and pulled the screen closed, taking my stolen stash along with me.

I'd hoped it would infuriate him. Or at the least, mildly piss him off. But as Jalen's delighted laughter followed me into the cave, I realized it would take a lot more than stealing his weed to ruffle Mr. Sunshine's feathers.

Oh well... At least my dinner's gonna taste great tonight.

20

Mounted

Ren

Every cell in my body prickled with flames, only this time, the fire didn't bother me. It pulsed through my veins, the molten heat burrowing all the way to my core. I throbbed. I ached. The sensation at once thrilling and deeply unsatisfying, forcing me to move. My hips rocked, finding purchase in the dark.

God, that felt *amazing*… I rocked again and again, riding the wave of pleasure. But just as it edged toward the point of no return, a low moan echoed in my ears. One far too low and rumbly to ever come out of me.

What the hell?

I blinked my eyes open, wondering what had ruined my dream. It wasn't the first time I'd awoken with a pillow crammed between my legs, my body working off some tension as I lingered between sleep and wakefulness.

Only I wasn't in my bed back on the *Verne*. And that sure as shit wasn't a pillow!

This time I wasn't plastered to Jalen's side. I'd not only sleepwalked into his bed—again—but I'd *mounted* him in my sleep. My heart pounded as I lay there frozen with my cheek pressed to his chest and his hard length between my thighs.

I scrambled off Jalen, cursing my rotten luck. Luckily, this time I wasn't half-naked. And someone up above must've taken pity on me, because even with me stumbling off his lap, Jalen's eyes stayed miraculously shut.

Once again, I retreated to the safety of the brightly lit morning jungle.

What the fuck is wrong with me?

One occurrence of sleepwalking I could almost understand. I'd been racked with those flashes of heat, so I was clearly crazed with a fever or something. But last night before bed, I'd swallowed one of the tablets Asani had given me and fell asleep feeling fine—on my own pallet. So why did I wake up mid-hump in his?

I dragged a few deep breaths into my lungs and waited for my hands to stop shaking. Then I slapped my neck and activated my comms implant, sending a call to the *Verne*.

Maybe Arda would know what to do. Hell, if I begged her nicely, I might even talk her into chancing a flight in the no-go zone to scoop me up. Assaulting unsuspecting aliens while they slept counted as an emergency, didn't it?

Within moments, the comms connected. "Hello?"

"Arda?" My stomach dropped. Even with just that single word, I sensed something was off. "What's wrong?"

She sighed deeply. "I fucked up, Ren... I lost Smudge."

"Oh shit. How did that happen?" Lux had to be devastated. And judging by the way her voice warbled, Arda was too.

"I was working in the docking bay around sunset last night when I heard something scratching the hull. Smudge must've snuck in there without me realizing it. When I opened the hatch, she darted out and disappeared into the jungle."

"God, I'm so sorry." I wasn't normally one for physical contact, but at that moment I wished more than anything I could've given her a hug. "She's still out there?"

"Yes. It's honestly been insane over here." She sniffled. "Lux stormed out after her as soon as the sun went down and refused to come in. I've been up all night, worried sick about them both."

My eyes widened. "Even with the dradhowlers?"

Arda's voice broke. "Yeah. He just got back empty-handed. If the damn sun wasn't out to kill him, he'd still be out there. Me and Kar are heading out now to take over the search."

"You'll find her. She's gotta be out there somewhere." The words felt like a lie as they left my lips. Smudge wasn't a predator. She wouldn't stand a chance against a dradhowler, or anything else that tried to eat her.

"I hope so." Arda sniffled again. "I don't know what Lux will do if we don't find her. She's his baby..."

I'd never had a pet of my own, but I'd seen how much Lux loved that ugly little critter. If they didn't find her, he'd probably be depressed for months. "I'm so sorry. I wish I was there to help."

"It's all right. You're already helping by handling this mission." A humorless laugh escaped her. "You wanna know what's the worst part of all this?"

"What?"

"The stupid scratching I heard. There was nothing out there when I looked. It was just another damn auditory hallucination."

"Fucking hell..." Jalen had said she'd have flashbacks, but I never suspected they would lead to this.

"I'm just glad you're out there and not me. I'd have gotten myself killed by now."

My heart sank. Arda was depending on me. And here I was, ready to throw in the towel.

Arda cleared her throat. "How's it on your end? Please tell me things are going better for you than they are over here."

Here was my chance. I could spill everything. Beg her to come get me and for us to hightail it off this cursed planet. She'd do it. Just like when I'd begged her to speed away from Oraxis Station... but then she couldn't go hunting for Smudge.

"I'm fine. I was only calling to check in. I even found an abandoned transport in the jungle that I'm close to repairing. If I can manage it, we might return before schedule."

Arda exhaled, the sound laced with relief. "That's fantastic, Ren! At least things are looking up for one of us."

"They will for you too. You'll find her. I know you will." Honestly, I had a feeling she'd be shit out of luck, but she didn't need to hear my doubts right now. Besides, Arda made a habit out of doing impossible things. If anyone had the tenacity to find an escaped critter in an unfamiliar jungle, it would be her.

"Thanks," she answered brightly. Maybe my pep talk helped. "I better go. Smudge ain't gonna find herself."

"Good luck!"

I ended the call, feeling more embarrassed than I had when I'd made it. There was no chance of rescue now. Frankly, after hearing about Smudge's disappearance, it made my problem seem insignificant.

So I woke up straddling a hot alien... At least I wasn't alone in a jungle teeming with poisonous plants and predators ready to tear me to pieces.

I just had to put on my big girl panties—and come to think of it, my actual panties, which ought to be dry by now—and fix that rider.

With that decision fresh in my mind, I reentered the cave.

"There you are." Jalen smiled. "I was about to look for you. Do you want some breakfast before we head out?" He gestured to a blanket laid out with fruit and haldi bread, picnic style.

"Um, sure. Thanks." I gulped, advancing slowly. "Did you sleep okay?" My pulse raced, and I carefully examined his face. If he said anything about this morning, I might have to run off into the jungle too.

His smile didn't slip in the slightest. "I did. I told you those burners do the trick. Bet you slept well too, huh?"

I bent and snagged a piece of bread. "Um, guess you could say so."

Instead of sitting, Jalen strolled to the door.

"Where are you going?"

He turned back with a grin. "Just need a break in the trees before I eat. Be right back."

At least he was acting normal. As the door slammed closed, I ducked behind the screen and slipped into my panties. By the time Jalen returned, I'd popped the rider's hood and was hard at work.

A loud crunch made me flinch. I glanced over my shoulder and spotted him behind me, chewing on a fruit that looked like a mix between a mango and an apple. "Do you have to do that in my ear?"

"You still think you can fix that?" He took another loud bite, his eyes glittering as my scowl deepened.

"I don't think I can." I whipped back and continued the repairs. "I know I can."

I expected him to put up a fuss. Or bark another order about how we need to go—now. But he just said, "I'll start packing while you work."

I forced his confusing about-face out of my mind and concentrated on the repairs. It was actually kind of funny, but in a way, I could credit Jalen for what I was currently trying. I'd come to a bit of an impasse last night, and I wasn't sure what direction to take. Once I'd smoked that stolen joint, the answer appeared to me in a flash of inspiration.

Maybe I'd have thought of it without the weed, but maybe not. Either way, as I replaced the last part and slammed the hood closed, my skin thrummed with anticipation. Even before I climbed on the rider and started the engine, I *knew* it would work.

Jalen turned to watch, the sheet he'd laid out for breakfast half-folded in his hands.

I inhaled and pushed the ignition.

The engine kicked on, and the rider lifted about a foot off the ground, the steady pulse of the motor thrumming beneath me with a slight vibration. Since the rider was basically a motorcycle without the wheels, that sensation landed in a very distracting place.

Fuck... That's gonna be hard to ignore.

I squirmed in place, but at the same time, a wide grin split my cheeks. I'd done it!

"Great work." Jalen set the blanket down and strode closer. "There's only one problem."

I frowned. "What problem?"

"I think it will be a tight squeeze fitting us both on there."

My breath caught in my throat as I glanced at the empty space behind me. Fuck... He was right. There was no way we were cramming on there without being plastered together the entire time.

I was about to spend the day with what was essentially a low-powered vibe rubbing against my crotch, with Jalen pressed indecently against me. And it wasn't like I could back out now. Not after I'd spent hours of my life fixing the damn thing, and Jalen risked his skin to lug it inside the cave.

How the hell did I get myself into this mess?

21

Riding Bitch

Jalen

I fought not to chuckle as it dawned on Ren that we'd be pressed together. It was clear she hadn't noticed until now exactly how little space there was on the rider's seat.

Me? I'd realized it almost immediately. Perhaps I should've mentioned it earlier, but it was kind of fun watching her horrified expression shift to one of reluctant acceptance.

It was odd seeing that reaction after what happened this morning. Once again, I'd barely slept a wink—despite the lie I'd fed her earlier. She'd crawled into my blankets in the dead of night and snuggled against me with the cutest sigh of contentment that made my heart ache. It was like her gruff exterior had washed away, leaving behind a warm, snuggly female who just wanted to be held through the night. After hearing that sigh, there was no way I could wake her and force her to leave.

I'd finally managed to drift off sometime before dawn, only to wake with a start when she rolled atop me and started grinding that perfect ass of hers like her life depended on it. I bit my tongue through all of it—until she did this swirling move with her hips that forced a moan out of my throat.

I'd never wished I'd been mute in my entire life—but in that moment I would've happily torn out my tongue to keep her going.

Instead, she hopped off me like my cocks were afire. And now this. She had to be sweating under that rumpled skinsuit of hers.

A muscle in her jaw ticked. "It's fine. We'll make it work."

"You're certain? I could run alongside you." That wouldn't be much fun, but I'd do it to wipe the frown off her face.

"Don't be ridiculous. Open the door. Let's get out of here."

"All right. As you wish." I pushed the door open and picked up my bag, but paused before slinging it on my back. "Do you want me to drive?" I'd never operated anything like that before, but it couldn't be too hard to figure out.

She scoffed. "Nope. You're riding bitch."

"I'm what?"

A tiny smirk painted her lips. "Just a Terran expression. Means you're in the back."

"I'll have to remember that." I grinned and strapped my pack on.

For some reason, that comment earned me a snicker. But once I approached the rider, the mirth faded from Ren's eyes.

"Don't worry. Promise I won't crush you." I carefully climbed on, making certain not to jostle her too much, though I couldn't avoid touching her completely. It simply wasn't possible with the space we were working with. The best I could do was to keep my chest lightly pressed against her back.

But then my ass hit the seat, and I choked down a yelp. "That's an interesting sensation."

Ren groaned. "Don't remind me." She squirmed, jostling me in a way that immediately brought memories of that morning to mind.

Calm down, I warned myself, though it was pretty clear that my body wasn't inclined to listen.

I tilted my pelvis back as best as I could, but there was only so far I could move. I nearly hopped off and told her I would be okay with running, until she took off like a shot.

The momentum slammed me into her back, and my hands shot out, grabbing her hips. But after barely a moment, she stopped.

"You need to close that, don't you?"

I wrenched open eyes that had slammed closed in fear. "Yes." I jumped down and locked the cave. Then I turned back, seriously reconsidering my decision.

"What are you waiting for, bitch?"

There was that smirk again. I couldn't help lighting up at the sight of it. "Coming."

Jalen

A few hours later, I grinned as the wind blew through my long blue hair. I'd been apprehensive at the start—who wouldn't while straddling a vehicle that moved about twice as fast as they could run—but it hadn't taken me long to get used to the speed.

Ren was an expert driver, dodging trees easily and hovering perfectly in line with the jungle footpaths. And since the rider didn't have wheels, there was no need to chop any underbrush. We flew atop it, making such good time we passed the campsite I'd planned to stop at that night around midday.

Of course, having Ren pressed against me hadn't exactly been ideal. I kept a running commentary in my head, replaying boring moments from my life, and even some disgusting ones, to keep myself from getting too excited by her proximity. Even so, it was a struggle I hadn't conquered completely. Between the constant vibration and her curvy behind rubbing against me, I'd spent most of the day half-hard.

So far, Ren hadn't noticed. Or if she had, she hadn't said anything. In fact, she hadn't said much of anything at all. The whole ride, she'd been remarkably... distant.

What happened to the ease I'd fought to develop over the last few days? Would she ever be ready to give me a chance?

No. She would. She had to. It was fate.

The self-assurance calmed me slightly. Enough that I began absent-mindedly humming as we drove, a small smile on my lips.

Ren peeked at me in the side mirror. "What's got you so happy?"

My grin widened. "What's not to like? We're making great time. I have a pretty female with me. This has been a fantastic day so far."

I glanced at the mirror and spotted her cheeks pinking. But Ren didn't bother replying. Her gaze stayed locked on the road, like the scenery was so thrilling she couldn't bear to look away.

Don't be stupid. It's all the same trees, over and over.

Or she was just back to being distant again.

I sighed. Perhaps Rhelt was right. I shouldn't be touching her.

It was clear there was something stopping Ren from connecting with me. Would she ever feel comfortable enough to share?

If what Asani said was true, she should be drawn to me the same way I was drawn to her. But—at least while she was awake—she wanted nothing to do with me. Even now, each time I adjusted my grip on her waist, she stiffened.

How am I supposed to show her we're meant to be together if she won't let me touch her?

Even if we did somehow make things work, would that be wise? My stomach churned. What would Rhelt say when he discovered Ren and I were mates? Would he understand, or follow through with his threats to lock me back up—for good this time...

The rider slowed. I shoved aside my perplexing thoughts and asked, "What is it?"

Ren peered into the forest. "I just spotted something... unusual." She reversed the rider unexpectedly, which made the rider's hum change slightly as her ass rubbed against me. And my dicks responded, thickening in my shorts.

I gritted my teeth and chanted in my head, *Garbage. Hot steaming piles of garbage left out in the sun.*

By the time I'd calmed enough to return my attention to the scenery, Ren had stopped the rider and hopped off. "What is that?"

I followed her gaze into the trees. "Those are some of the rarest plants you'll find on Dionus. We call them ellbright."

"They're gorgeous." Ren's eyes lit with wonder as she strode closer to the vibrant blooms. The petals were two-toned, either yellow and pink or purple and blue, and lit with an inner glow that almost made them appear neon, even in the shade.

I hopped off the rider and followed her, paying more attention to her face than the flowers. "There's a legend about ellbright."

She lifted a brow. "Really?"

"Mm-hmm."

"Are you planning to tell me?"

Leaning against a tree, I explained, "You may have heard me mention Harlx a time or two."

"That the name you're always using like a curse?" She leaned forward, her hand outstretched, but before she brushed a blossom, she asked, "Wait... I'm not gonna hallucinate if I touch these, will I?"

I chuckled. "No, you won't. And yes, Harlx's name is often called on as an oath by Dionions, or sometimes a prayer. He's our god of the cosmos."

"Okay..." She tentatively stroked one of the pink-and-yellow petals. "What does good old Harlx have to do with these?"

"The story says that one day, Aarus, the god of ellios—our underworld—stole Harlx's true love, the fair maiden Umera."

"Oh boy. Bet he wasn't too happy about that."

I grinned. "Of course not. But Harlx wasn't a fool. He knew if he retaliated with violence, it would start a war to end all wars. And that if the heavens and the underworld fought, it would cause chaos to fall over all of Dionus."

Ren moved on to one of the purple-and-blue buds, lightly tracing the bright petals with her fingertips. "So what did he do?"

"He used what he knew about Aarus to his advantage. After living in the underworld for so long, Aarus craved beauty. That's why he took Umera."

"Since she was so fair... I get it."

I pushed off the tree and strolled closer. "Harlx created ellbright that day. He brought them to the underworld and promised Aarus that they would always bloom in the dark."

Ren frowned. "Do they?"

I nodded. "The ellbright only bloom during a night when it's full dark. Once the sun rises, they'll continue to flower if they're in the shade. But the moment the sun touches them, the petals wither away."

"That's pretty cool." Ren straightened. "So did it work? Did Harlx get Umera back?"

"What do you think?" I asked.

"He went searching for her in hell..." She wiggled her brows. "I bet she didn't stay a maiden for much longer after that grand gesture."

I barked out a laugh. "And you would be right. At least, according to legend."

She smiled at me softly before reaching out again to caress a petal. "I like that story. Explains a lot about you, actually."

"Oh? How so?"

Ren's hand fell to her side. "Just that with a legend like that, I can see why you're not the barbarians the rest of the universe thinks you are. If you value intelligence over violence, that's pretty damn civilized in my book."

I puffed up my chest. "We're extremely intelligent, I'll give you that."

Ren rolled her eyes. "And so modest, too." She turned, likely intending to head back to the rider, but as she did, I spotted something behind her that made my skin prickle. She must've noticed some sign of distress on my face. "What is it?"

I stalked forward, brushing aside the ellbright Ren had been touching and ducking behind it. "Harlx's bones!" Normally, ellbright sprung up like weeds to fill entire clearings. But not here. A dozen holes marred the ground, and as a planter, I could tell whoever tore the plants out did so carelessly.

Ren appeared at my elbow with a gasp. "Who did this?" With widened eyes, she stared at the disturbed dirt littered with broken roots. "I thought it was against the law to destroy anything in the jungle."

An awful churning tore at my gut. "It is. I highly doubt this was done by a Dionion."

"What does that mean?" She blinked, meeting my gaze.

I drew in a deep breath. "We might have some dangerous company to worry about."

22

Come and Get It

Ren

The sun sank into the trees as I parked the rider beside a cave. As the engine shut down and that damned vibration finally cut off, I sighed heavily. Between that, Jalen's big hands wrapped around my waist, and his cocks rubbing against my ass, today had been one long edging session, leaving me so damn horny I could scream.

Jalen climbed off first and turned to me with a smile. "Need a hand?" He offered me his, but I left him hanging.

I could tell from the way his grin faded around the edges he wasn't too pleased. But I was all touched out. I couldn't handle another second of contact. Not unless it ended with an orgasm, and *that* sure as shit wasn't about to happen.

"Come on." Jalen led the way to the boulder door. "Bet you're hungry after all that driving."

My gaze fell to his ass as he strolled ahead of me. *Hungry enough to take a bite out of that—Fuck.* I clenched my jaw, trying to ignore the heat pulsing relentlessly in my core. I needed to relieve some of this tension. But how could I do that when I had no privacy?

After we headed inside, entering another cave set up like the others we'd visited, Jalen pulled some food from his pack. I snagged a piece of haldi bread and crammed an enormous bite into my mouth.

"Guess I was right." Jalen chuckled while rolling his neck. "Mind if I hop in the tub first tonight?"

I waved a hand. "Have at it."

"You know"—he spun around as he approached the folded screen and met my gaze—"it is big enough to share."

Ugh... this again. "No thanks." Maybe while he was in there, I could even take care of that little problem between my legs. Yeah, I'd dismissed the idea a few days ago, but right now, I was desperate. I'd just have to be really, really quiet. Cram a pillow in my mouth or something...

"Suit yourself." Jalen grabbed the screen and unfolded it slowly. "Um... small problem."

"What is it?"

"I think they made this one a hair too short."

My stomach sank as I examined the screen. When unfolded, it covered the pool about three quarters of the way. Guess my plan was foiled. No way was I gonna rub one out if there was a chance he could see.

Molten lava burst through my veins as an image coalesced in my head. Jalen's green eyes watching me while I... No! I had to stop. There would be no relief tonight. *Just deal with it, Ren.* "It's fine. Stay on the side that's covered. I'll sit where I can't see."

"Sounds good." Jalen disappeared behind the screen, and my body tensed as fabric fluttered and then slapped the floor. Next, water splashed, and my brain conjured a new set of images to drive me mad.

Jalen naked and wet. Those big hands that spent all day wrapped around my waist, smoothing soap over his muscled flesh. Would he start at the top and work his way down? Or maybe he'd go straight for the kill, so keyed up from that ride he couldn't wait to take matters into his own hands.

Carefree humming filled the cave a heartbeat later, making my blood boil.

"Can you *please* not?" I blurted.

Jalen replied breezily, "Would you rather talk? I can tell you another legend, if you'd like."

Would I like that? No. What I'd like wasn't on the menu. Frankly, the fact that he was sitting there, so unaffected by the teasing touches we'd endured all day, really grated on my nerves. "No, I don't want to listen to a story," I stated harshly.

"What's wrong?" he asked.

"What's *wrong*?" I stood, dragging a hand through my hair as I paced. "I don't get how you can be so cool and calm, while I'm over here—" I slammed my lips shut, belatedly realizing what I'd almost just admitted to.

Water sloshed, and Jalen appeared in the open space the screen couldn't cover. My traitorous gaze shot to him, taking in every sexy wet inch of his chest that was visible above the lip of the tub before I averted my eyes.

"Nothing. Forget I said anything."

"Does this have anything to do with what happened this morning?" His voice dropped an octave before he finished speaking, and my heart dropped with it.

"Wh-what are you—"

"I was awake, Ren. Did you truly think I could sleep with you riding me like that?"

Oh fucking hell. My cheeks burned, and my mouth felt dryer than the Sahara. "I-I was dreaming. I didn't do it on purpose."

"I understand. That's why I didn't say anything."

"But you're saying something now." Our gazes locked and my skin tingled.

A cocky smile crossed his face before his brows dipped. "I am. Because I have a problem I need your help fixing."

"What problem?"

"I'm tired. After two nights with you crawling into my bed in the dead of night, I've barely slept."

Oh god... he knows about both *nights.* That meant he remembered me pressed against him in just my panties. My breath grew shallow, and I backed up a pace, unable to tear my gaze off him.

"I was thinking, you should finish what you started this morning. Then I won't have my sleep interrupted again."

Is he seriously inviting me to ride him? My eyes widened until they felt like they might fall out of my skull. "Are you crazy? I'm not doing that."

Jalen chuckled and tilted his head. "Why not? You clearly want to."

He was right... but that didn't mean I was going to listen. We were out here all alone. And just because I wanted to get off didn't mean I wanted to fuck. If I climbed into that pool, he'd expect sex. But I wasn't ready... I might never be.

"And you're just going to what... sit there and let me use you like my own personal toy?" I crossed my arms. "No. I don't buy it. You'll take it further than I want to go, and I won't—" I cut myself off before I finished laying my old insecurities bare.

My refusal didn't seem to faze Jalen in the slightest. "If that's what you want, then yes." He grinned and pushed away from the tub's edge, then settled with his back resting against the wall. Then he folded his arms, tucking his hands under his head. "I promise I won't do anything you don't want me to."

Could I trust him? He'd never given me a reason not to. The man had saved my life—twice. But this seemed insane. Then again, if he was awake last night, and the night before, he knew how to control himself. If he hadn't taken advantage of me then, he wouldn't now... right?

"Would it help if I pretend I'm asleep?" Jalen grinned lazily, then closed his eyes. "You seem to like me well enough then..." he trailed off, and I thought I caught a hint of vulnerability in his voice.

"I like you when you're awake too," I muttered.

"Good to know." His smile lengthened, but he didn't open his eyes. He lounged there, looking relaxed and so damn sexy my fingers itched to touch him. "I'll hang here for a bit." He swallowed, and I licked my lips as I watched his Adam's apple bob up and down. "If you want it, come and get it."

I hovered there, my pulse pumping like a piston. Could I seriously climb in there and rub myself off on his lap? *Fuck, I really want to do this...* As the realization stole over me, I lifted a hand to my neck. My fingertips closed around my zipper and tugged.

Maybe this was insane. Maybe I was fucked in the head to attempt it, considering my history. But I couldn't deny myself any longer. Not while he was sitting there, looking so damn fine, and my pussy was on fire.

I at least had the sense to keep my panties on. With that barrier in place, things wouldn't go too far. I pulled the rest of my clothes off as quietly as I could and padded toward the tub on bare feet.

Jalen had started humming again, so he didn't seem to notice what I was doing until my toes hit the water. "Ren... Come here." His voice turned gravelly, and it did crazy things to my already soaking cleft.

I hissed as the water drenched my panties, and again when it glided over my hard nipples.

Jalen shifted, drawing my attention to the rest of his body below the water. The clear liquid did little to hide him, and a tiny gasp escaped me as I drank in his stacked abs, brawny thighs, and two hard cocks pointing straight up.

I'd never seen a man with two dicks before. They were stacked one atop the other, not side by side, both so thick and long a frown creased my brow. It'd be a tight fit, that was for sure. Luckily, I'd already decided the panties were staying on, so it wasn't something I had to worry about.

Jalen's chest heaved as he choked out, "What's the holdup?"

"Just... looking."

He chuckled softly. "You like what you see?"

Fuck... "I-I... Uh—"

"It's okay. You don't need to answer that." He licked his lips. "Can I look too?"

I tore my gaze off his cocks and lifted it to his face. He still had his lids pinched closed. My stomach flipped. I wasn't sure if I should say yes. But the fact that he respected me enough to seek my consent calmed something deep within me. "Yes," I whispered.

His eyes slowly opened, first focusing on my face intently, like he was hunting for something. After a long moment, his gaze trailed lower, and it was almost as if I could feel it tracing over me. My nipples pebbled into stone, and my pulse strummed a steady beat between my thighs.

"Beautiful." His green eyes shot back to mine. "I already knew it, but seeing you like this—" His gaze slipped back down, trailing over every inch of me beneath the water. "I want you so bad, Ren."

I gulped. "I thought this was about what I want."

"It is." He grinned. "You can have everything you want." He re-clined his head a little more, pressing his back into the wall and puffing out his chest. "Come take it."

I cautiously stepped closer. "And when I'm done... what then?"

"Then we both go to bed," he replied without hesitation.

"What if you're not... satisfied?"

Jalen chuckled. "Not satisfied? Seeing you like this... I'm already ecstatic. You can leave right now and I'll ride on this high for weeks." He kept staring at me as he spoke, his greedy gaze devouring every inch like he was mesmerized.

And honestly, having his eyes on me felt... *incredible*. I'd never been particularly proud of my body. I was too skinny and flat-chested for that. But with Jalen, it felt different. Like he'd happily worship every inch of my skin if I let him.

Not tonight. I wasn't kidding about not being ready. The thought of a guy's hands on me—even Jalen's—made me more nervous than I cared to admit.

But I wasn't ready to call it a night. I took another step forward in the pool, stopping so close he could reach out and grab me if he wanted to. Clearing my throat, I said, "Promise you'll stay just like that. No hands."

Jalen smiled. "I promise. Believe me, Ren, I know exactly how to keep my hands to myself."

23

Worth Waiting For

Jalen

I stared at the vision before me, my heart pounding like the drums at a village bonfire. *Is this actually about to happen?* I kept my hands pinned behind my head, desperate to keep her from changing her mind.

I'd almost choked on my tongue when I heard the water splashing. Yes, I'd hoped she'd accept my indecent offer, but I hadn't actually believed that she would. Now it looked like my wish was about to come true.

Well, with conditions...

I wasn't entirely certain why she insisted on me keeping my hands off, but I had my suspicions. If my guess was correct, then it could explain a lot. Like why she was so prickly when we first met, and why she didn't like being touched.

The thought had popped into my head the moment she brought up *things going too far*. Why would she be worried about that, unless at some point in her past, she'd lived through it? It made my stomach churn like mad, but I couldn't help worrying it was true.

Since then, I'd been careful to not say anything that would make her doubt my intentions. I let her know she was running the show, and I had no plans to step out of line. Fact was, even without her clueing me in to her worries, I'd been taught to respect others' bodily autonomy. Everyone on Dionus had.

It made me sick to think that wasn't the case for her. I wanted to find whatever fool had wronged her and tear him to pieces. But my anger wasn't called for, so I shoved it aside and forced myself into the moment.

Harlx's bane... She's perfect. I was dying to touch her. To run my tongue across her hard nipples and listen to her moans. I wanted to rip those tiny panties off her legs and sink my fingers into her heat. To squeeze her tight ass as she bounced on my—

Not happening, Jalen. Take what she's willing to give.

I leaned back and contented myself with looking at every flawless inch. She was all lean lines and elegant curves, with heady desire shining in her eyes that had my pulse thudding furiously. I wished more than anything she'd let me see all of her, but I bit my tongue when the demand tried to force its way out of my throat.

If she needed that puny scrap of fabric to make her comfortable, then she deserved to keep it. Just seeing her like this made me the luckiest male in the universe.

She reached out tentatively, aiming for my shoulder, but before her fingers connected, she met my gaze and asked, "Can I... touch you?"

"Please." My voice was so strained I barely recognized it.

Her eyes raked over my chest as her fingers dusted my skin. I sucked in a shaky breath and shuddered, my skin tingling. A tiny grin lit her lips, and she drifted closer, one of her legs brushing against mine beneath the water.

"That's perfect, Ren," I praised. Her gaze slid to my mouth, and I gifted her a smile as she trailed a teasing touch over my chest. "Take what you want. You can have it all."

Her other hand gripped my shoulder. She bit her lip as she settled on one knee beside my hip. Then she slowly swung the other over, straddling my waist. She hovered there, lifting her chest out of the water.

I stared at her breasts and my mouth went dry. What I wouldn't give to lean forward and capture those delicious peaks in my mouth... The urge slammed into me hard, but I pushed it aside violently. She was right. This was about what *she* wanted, not me.

Still, I wasn't one to keep quiet. "I need this, Ren. You had me hard all day. I could barely stop myself from spilling in my shorts every time your ass rubbed against me on that ride."

Her eyes widened, and she smirked. "Yeah?" Then she sank onto my lap, and I groaned so loud waves of vibration thrummed through my chest.

That felt *amazing*. She applied pressure with her panty-covered mound, just holding there with my top cock pressed against her. I looked down, and my dicks throbbed at the sight of that pink scrap of fabric wrapped around my length.

Ren blew out a thready breath, drawing my attention to her face. Her cheeks were flush, her eyes half-lidded. "I was going crazy today too," she admitted softly.

"I bet. Did you like having the rider humming beneath you?"

She shook her head. "It was so bad. I could've crashed."

"That's nothing." I concentrated, willing my body to listen. Ah... there.

Ren gasped, and her eyes rolled back, eyelashes fluttering. "A-are you—" She gulped. "Are your cocks *vibrating*?" she asked incredulously.

I nodded slowly, keeping the pulse going. "You didn't do much research on Dionions before you came here, did you? When the males of a species need to prep their females for double penetration, it helps to have a few tricks up their sleeve. Probably why we evolved the ability to do this."

"Oh god." Ren shuddered and quaked. And she hadn't even started moving her hips yet.

Carefully, I asked, "Does that frighten you?"

She gasped. "What?"

I glanced down. "That I have two cocks instead of one."

Ren moaned, the sound so full of lust it made me crave her even more.

"Should I take that as a no?" I grinned, lifting my gaze to hers.

She panted as she met my eyes. "That doesn't scare me."

"Good." I stared back at her, willing her to hear my sincerity. "You never have to be afraid of me, Ren. I want to make you feel good."

"This"—her head fell back and her hands tightened on my shoulders—"feels pretty amazing already."

"That's how I felt this morning with you riding me."

Her cheeks flushed, but she leaned forward, meeting my gaze. "You mean like this?" Her hips started moving just like they had that morning, only now it was so much more *intense*.

Now, I knew it was me she was thinking about, and not some random dream. I didn't have to force my eyes closed and pretend to be asleep. I could feel her nails dig into my shoulders and listen to the soft breathy moans echoing in her throat. I groaned again, unable to contain the cry of pleasure.

"Jalen..." she breathed. "I'm close."

"That's right. Take it, Ren. I want to watch you come."

She shuddered, her eyes falling closed.

"Eyes on me," I insisted before I could stop myself.

She froze, and my stomach twisted.

Why did I say that? Idiot... She's supposed to be in charge.

But then her eyes popped open and connected with mine at the same moment her hips twisted. She rolled them in the same sensual pattern that forced a moan out of me that morning. It worked again. I growled, my fingers itching to clamp down on her hips. But I had the sense to shut down that urge, at least.

"Jalen. I'm... I'm coming!" She gasped and bucked, riding me through her orgasm. I watched her with hungry eyes, keeping completely still. I knew if I moved at all, it would be over. I wouldn't be able to stop myself from making her mine.

Instead, I memorized every moan. I raked my gaze over her heaving chest and reveled in the way her thighs clenched around me and her legs quivered. And through it all, I kept up a steady vibration with my cocks until she squirmed on my lap like she'd had enough while fighting to catch her breath.

Finally, I moved my hands, thankful they hadn't fallen asleep. I gently lifted her off my lap and set her beside me. Then I stood and held out a hand.

Her gaze locked on my still-hard dicks, which twitched under the scrutiny. "Are you—"

"Ready for bed? Yes." I twisted my hips away and lowered my hand more. "Do you want me to leave you in here to wash, or are you getting out?"

She bit her lip and sank down until the water hit her chin. "Washing would be nice, I suppose."

I grinned. It was cute that she was acting shy now. I'd have thought after that, she wouldn't need to feel shy around me ever again. It was pretty clear I was obsessed with her. She had to realize that now, didn't she?

She probably just wanted to wash her panties again. I hadn't missed them hanging out to dry last night. "All right. I'll leave you to it. I need to grab something to eat."

"Wait." Ren peeked at my face nervously before gesturing to my crotch. "You aren't going to do something about that? Did you want me to..."

It was pretty clear what she was alluding to. And if I was being perfectly honest, I was dying to feel her soft fingers wrapped around me. But I could tell from the crease between her brows that she wasn't comfortable touching me yet. So I said, "This was for you, Ren. Remember? Don't worry about me."

With that, I climbed out of the tub and wrapped a towel around my waist. I refused to rush her into something she wasn't ready for. Especially not if what I suspected turned out to be true. That was the last thing Ren needed.

I could wait. *She's worth waiting for.*

Jalen

I woke the next morning with a sleepy female snuggled against me, refreshed and ready to take on the day. *That's a pleasant change.* For once, Ren wasn't leaping out of bed, horrified to realize where she'd ended up in the night. And I'd actually gotten a decent amount of sleep, too.

She'd balked when she'd climbed out of the tub and realized I'd shoved two pallets together. But when I reminded her about my lack of sleep, she relented. She'd kept to her side at first until her breathing evened. Then, in her unconscious state, she'd rolled closer, not stopping until we were lying flush.

I wasn't complaining. Snuggling with Ren was beginning to feel… right.

She stretched beside me, an enormous yawn splitting her cheeks before her eyes opened.

"Good morning," I said softly.

Ren blinked, and her cheeks pinked. "Morning."

I smiled, wishing I could reach out and drag her lips to mine. *Not yet.* "Sleep well?"

She nodded, shifting to sit. "Have you been awake long?"

"No. I was just talking myself into climbing out of these warm blankets."

She chuckled. "I hate that too."

"Could've fooled me. You jumped out quick enough the last couple days."

"Hey!" She scowled. "You would, too, if you sleepwalked into a strange man's bed."

"A male, perhaps. If it were your bed, I'd stay right where I was."

Ren's flush deepened. She flicked the blankets off both of us. "Well, bad news for you. I'm an early riser."

"That right?" A startled laugh tumbled out of me. "Eh, I'll get used to it." Truth was, I was an early riser too. Just another reason this female was meant for me.

My stomach churned. After what happened last night, I needed to tell her. She deserved to know what part fate was playing in bringing us together. But every time I tried to work up the nerve, I'd remember how much she hated the concept of fated mates. Would she even accept that it was happening?

Ren ducked into the forest while I scrounged up some breakfast. As I set out haldi bread and sliced some fruit and vegetables, a blast of heat washed over me.

Harlx's beard... I'd been worried this would happen. I'd heard that once a bonded pair surrendered to the physical pull between them, the heat became stronger until they completed the bond. If I was feeling it now, Ren must be too.

I popped one of Asani's tablets into my mouth and washed it down with a gulp of water just as Ren returned to the cave. "Here." I handed her a tablet. "Don't forget to take your medicine."

Ren's nose wrinkled. "How long will I need to keep taking these? Did Asani say?"

Sweat beaded on my lower back. Turning aside, I said, "I think it depends on a number of factors. Mind if I head out for a moment? I could use a break." It was a lame excuse, I know, but I couldn't seem to work up the courage to come clean.

"Okay." She settled on the floor beside the food.

I scarfed down some haldi bread on the way out, and by the time I returned, Ren had finished eating too. After packing up, we locked the cave and walked toward the rider.

This was it. If I wanted to tell her before we climbed on the rider and I couldn't even look her in the eyes, then I had to do it now. "Ren... I—"

Ren gasped, her hand flying to cover her mouth. "Oh fuck! This is bad." She rushed forward, her gaze glued to a puddle of black gunk under the vehicle. "It's leaking coolant. And I don't have any replacement fluids."

Well, there goes that plan. I couldn't exactly tell her when she was upset already, right? "No worries. We'll get there just as easily walking."

That statement did nothing to wipe away her pout. She just stood there, looking dejected. Perhaps a joke would help... what was that Terran word she taught me yesterday? Ah! "I was looking forward to being your bitch rider again today. But I can still be your bitch walker." I waggled my brows, and she giggled.

"Jalen, I promise you can be my bitch whenever you want." She patted my shoulder and headed for the footpath.

"I don't mind. Great view back here." I'd happily trail behind her anywhere as long as she let me admire her toned ass once in a while.

She smirked over her shoulder when she caught me staring. "I thought guides were supposed to lead the way?"

Chuckling, I replied, "And I—" Rustling in the trees halted me midsentence. "Hold on." I pressed a finger to my lips, listening.

Ren inched backward and whispered, "What is it?"

"I heard something." It happened again just as I finished whispering back—the crunch of footsteps in the underbrush. And since we were a day's walk from any villages, I doubted we'd stumbled across a Dionion. "We have company."

Her eyes widened. "Dradhowlers?"

I shook my head. "Not in the day. More likely it's poachers."

Ren shifted from one foot to another. "What do we do?"

We could return to the cave, but from the sound of those steps, we'd never make it in time. That didn't leave us many options.

I stepped into the forest. "Let's hide off the path. If we're lucky, they'll walk right past us."

"What if they don't?" Ren hurried to a nearby tree.

"I'll take care of them." I stopped behind her, shielding her back while the tree trunk hid her body from the path. "You run for the cave. You remember how to open it, right?"

Ren peeked at me, her face pale and her lower lip trembling. "No. I won't leave you—"

"Yes, you will," I ordered gruffly. She stiffened. "I'm the guide. It's my job to keep you safe."

Her eyes burned, her glare so hot it nearly seared a hole through me. But as she opened her mouth again, a branch snapped. She clamped her lips closed and twisted around, tilting her head to peek out from our hiding spot. I gently tugged her back, not wanting to give away our position just as a male stumbled into sight.

It was immediately clear he wasn't native, though he wore Dionion garb. My heart raced as I dragged my gaze over the Terran's black hair and dimpled chin. What was he doing out here, dressed like one of us? Had we truly crossed paths with a poacher?

He certainly didn't look the part. The single pack he carried was stuffed but seemed far too small for a smuggler. And he wasn't skulking about in the trees but confidently striding down the path in full daylight, though I noticed something wrong with his gait. He was definitely favoring one leg.

Ren tried again to lean out for a peek, and I lifted a hand, halting her. She let out the tiniest puff of air, making a barely discernible huff.

"Hello?" The male squinted, staring right at our hiding place. "Is someone there? I can hear you."

Harlx's bane! No way he heard that... He must've spotted me when I moved. I drew a deep breath through my nose, preparing to fight.

But then Ren darted out, slipping around the trunk so quickly I couldn't stop her.

"My god, what are the odds—" she began.

What is she thinking? I burst out and snagged her sleeve. "Ren," I barked, and with my free hand, I pointed frantically behind me. "My bitch!"

Ren whipped to face me, horrified.

And from across the path, the mystery male roared, "Like hell she is!"

24

Dumb Joke

Ren

It was just supposed to be a dumb joke.

Yeah, when I first told Jalen riding bitch meant being in the back, I snickered a little. And when he told me he'd be my bitch walker, I had a good laugh. But I never imagined he'd dub me his bitch while staring down my brother like he wanted to do unholy things to his corpse.

Yep, color me surprised when the suspected poacher turned out to be none other than my foster brother, Demetri. Only now the joy that had overcome me when I first heard his voice had melted away, replaced with enough embarrassment I wanted to stuff my head in the jungle dirt and hide for, oh, about a century.

Alas, that was not in the cards for me. Instead, I was cursed to watch the awful scene I'd unwittingly orchestrated unfold in slow-mo.

The righteous anger slipped from Jalen's face as he clocked my horrified expression. His brows squished together, and he glanced around as if looking for answers, completely baffled by what was happening.

At the same time, Demi marched across the path, his fist pulled back, clearly seeing red.

I lifted a hand and took a step, my mouth falling open. But before I could hop in between them or spit out, *No*, the crack of flesh hitting flesh reached my ears.

The men collided in a mad tumble, punching, kicking, and rolling around like a pair of wolves fighting to see who was the alpha.

"Stop!" I shouted, my heart in my throat. "Jalen, stop! He's my brother."

Jalen stilled, but Demi didn't. He landed a blow to Jalen's gut, making him grunt and double over.

"Demi, you too! He's with me. Jalen's my guide. Stop hurting him. Please!"

Demi blinked, pausing with his fist in the air. "Your guide? Then why'd he call you his bitch?"

I cringed. "I'll explain, I promise. Just let him go."

Demi released his grip on Jalen's vest. "Fine." He stood, brushing the dirt off his long shorts. "What are you doing out here, Ren?" He tentatively reached down, and Jalen clasped his hand, letting Demi help him to his feet.

"It's a long story." I winced as Jalen turned to me. The skin around his eye had already begun to bruise, and I suspected he'd end up with an awful shiner. "Are you okay?"

He forced a smile. "I think so. I'll be better once I understand what just happened. I don't recall learning that Terrans start family introductions with a brawl..."

Demi laughed humorlessly. "No. That wasn't normal at all." His eyes narrowed at me. "Spill, Sis. What was that?"

I twisted my hands. "I may have told Jalen the other day that riding bitch meant you were the one in back."

As understanding dawned on Demi, his brows lifted, and then his lips pressed together into a thin line. "Why would you say that?"

Jalen cocked his head. "Wait, what *does* it mean?"

Demi, always the linguist, couldn't resist jumping in to explain. "It's a Terran word that has several meanings. It's sometimes used to refer to a female dog. It can also be spoken as an insult, usually to a woman. But I believe our dear Ren used it in that context to imply that you were subservient to her. You know, like a servant, or a minion."

By the time he finished, my face burned. "It was just a dumb joke. I'm sorry, okay?" My voice rose, sounding far shriller than I'd intended it to.

Jalen split a glance between Demi and me, his expression unreadable. My stomach clenched.

He scrubbed a hand down his face, and for half a heartbeat, I worried that this was the end. The universe had given me the sexiest, most easy-going man that existed, and I'd pushed him too far with my stupidity.

Jalen would tell me—nicely, of course—to get lost. He'd go home and find some sweet little thing who'd never trick him into getting sucker punched. Some perfect Dionion woman who'd smile at his jokes and let him use his hands when they fucked.

Ugh... *Please say something, Jalen!*

Then Jalen's hand fell to his side, and a huge belly laugh exploded from him.

I couldn't help it. I scowled. "I'm glad you find this funny."

He met my gaze, his green eyes shining with glee. "Don't you?"

"Well..." I poked his side. "Now that you guys aren't trying to murder each other, I guess it is kind of funny."

Jalen's laughter subsided, and he turned to Demi, raising a fist. I tensed until I realized he was only offering a Dionion greeting.

Demi caught on instantly, pressing the side of his fist to Jalen's. "Sorry, I know Ren said it, but I seem to have forgotten your name."

"It's Jalen. And you're..."

"Demi."

They retracted their fists and stared at each other warily.

"You're Ren's brother?" Jalen gave Demi a cool once-over. "I don't see the resemblance."

"He's my foster brother."

Jalen glanced at me, his eyes widening. "You're an orphan?"

I nodded, my gaze downcast.

Demi cut in. "Ren and I met at an orphanage when we were teens. We've been best friends ever since."

Jalen grunted, and I got the feeling he wasn't too happy with that answer.

Time to change the subject. "Demi, you still haven't explained why you're out here."

Demi sighed. "Okay, fine. But then you better tell me what you're doing here. After what you said when Cassidy invited us, you were the last person I expected to meet in a Dionion jungle."

"I'll tell you everything. Promise. You first."

Demi started, "I've been out here for a few months, traveling from village to village so I can incorporate any regional phrases into the Dionion translator upgrades." He frowned, scratching his chin. "Remind me to add some Terran slang in there too. Maybe we can avoid more miscommunications like—"

"You're getting off track, Demi," I said.

"Oh, sorry. I left my last village yesterday, but just after sunset, I ran into a problem. Smugglers."

Jalen's nostrils flared. "How did you know they were smugglers?"

He shrugged. "I caught them red-handed digging up these pretty flowers. What are they called again..."

"Ellbright?" I guessed.

"That's it! I knew they were trouble, so I hid until they took off. But by then it was nearly full dark. So I hunkered down for the night, and now I'm back on the road. I should make it to my destination tomorrow morning, barring more complications."

"Where are you headed?" Jalen asked.

"Onatel Village."

I spied recognition on Jalen's face. "Is that where we're going, too?" I couldn't contain the hint of hope in my voice.

Jalen shook his head. "It's not."

"Oh." My shoulders slumped. It'd been years since I'd hung out with Demi in person. But it looked like we'd have to go our separate ways after this chat.

Jalen's brows dipped. He opened his mouth, but before he got in a word, Demi said, "All right, I've told you my story. What about you, Ren?"

I faced Demi and quickly filled him in, explaining enough about Arda's genetic mystery to have him intrigued, and a brief recounting of where we'd traveled so far. I left out my weird collapse, since I didn't want to worry him. And of course, he didn't need to know how I'd been sleepwalking in just my panties, or that I'd rubbed myself to completion on Jalen's vibrating cocks last night.

"Huh, you've been through a lot. Sounds like you need a hug." He threw out his arms, and I leaned in without hesitation.

"Thanks, Demi." I sighed, taking comfort in his embrace like I could with hardly anyone else. But then my gaze slid to Jalen, and I spotted a scowl flash where his smile was usually plastered. I pulled away. "I guess this is goodbye. Since we're headed in different—"

Jalen cut me off. "We should go with him."

My jaw fell open. "Really? Why?"

"If there are poachers about, it's not safe to travel alone. We'll drop Demi at Onatel and continue our hike from there. Since we made it so far on the rider yesterday, we're ahead of schedule, anyway."

I clapped my hands together. "This is great! I'll feel so much better knowing my bro won't be all alone."

Demi grinned. "I'm glad too." He glanced at Jalen. "Should give us a chance to get to know each other a lot better." He slung an arm over my shoulder. "Come on. It's this way."

I sent Jalen a smile and mouthed, *Thank you*. He smiled back, but I couldn't help worrying that his expression was a little off.

25

Campfire Confessions

Jalen

Two crescent moons hung in the sky, lighting the clearing we'd camped in well enough that we had no need for a campfire. Ren had perked up at the mention of one, though, so I'd obliged. Logs crackled and hissed, and the flames sent flickering shadows across her beautiful face as she laughed at another one of her *brother's* jokes.

It had taken me a while to warm up to Demetri. When I learned he wasn't Ren's family by blood, a spark of suspicion flared to life in my gut.

Was he truly just her best friend? Or did he crave more from their relationship? Did she? It was clear Ren was excited to run into him, so I'd held my tongue while keeping a close watch of their interactions.

Now, I was beginning to realize my suspicions were unfounded. Yes, Demi wasn't shy about touching Ren, and she was comfortable enough with him to allow it, but there were no lingering glances. No flirting. Just lots of laughter and the easy companionship you'd expect from siblings.

Frankly, I was relieved. Normally, I was the guy who thought the best of everyone—unless they proved otherwise. But I couldn't seem to help myself from being overprotective—and yes, a tad jealous—where Ren was concerned. It was the pair bond's influence, no doubt. Some lingering evolutionary urge to tear any male to pieces who looked at my mate sideways.

"So, how about you, Jalen?" Demi asked, his head tilted.

I blinked, forcing myself back into the moment. "Sorry. What's the question?"

"You don't have to answer that." Ren scowled and jabbed Demi with her elbow. "He's being nosy, like usual."

Demi rubbed his side. "It's not an inquisition. I was just wondering where you grew up, Jalen."

I chuckled. "Well, that's no secret. We're headed there, actually."

Ren's eyes widened. "You grew up in Onatel Village?"

"I did. My aunt's still there. We can stop by and say hello, if you don't mind the detour."

She twisted her lips. "You want me to meet your aunt?"

"Certainly. I bet she'll like you."

Ren glanced at Demi, who sent her a knowing look. Then their expressions changed rapidly, and it was almost like I was watching them have a silent conversation—one I wasn't privy to.

"What else do you want to know?" I dug into my vest pocket, pulling out a burner. "I'm an open book."

Demi's face lit up. "Is that what I think it is?"

I grinned and tossed him the burner and a light. "Here. I have plenty."

Demi lifted the burner to his nose and sniffed. "The weed on this planet is insane. Can you imagine if we had this stuff when we were younger?"

Ren giggled. "Probably good that we didn't. Remember when you snuck a bong into Oraxis Station? We had a hell of a time keeping the smell out of the ventilation system."

I'd thought from the expert way Ren had handled my burner the other night she'd smoked before. Only how? "I didn't realize we had the same plants growing on our home worlds." I used to assume other planets would be completely alien from mine, but it appeared we had more in common than I'd realized.

Ren explained, "We do, but back home, it's hard to find marijuana you can smoke. Too many people were worried about their lungs, I guess. Not like we had any plants that needed to be tamed with smoke, either."

"How do you use it if you don't smoke it?" I asked.

Demi sparked the burner. "They cook it into edibles. Gummies, brownies, that kind of thing."

My nose wrinkled. "And it tastes good?"

"Not really." Demi chuckled, blowing smoke at the fire before passing the burner to me. "There's only so much sugar can disguise."

Ren smirked. "That didn't stop you from scarfing down three brownies at Mika's graduation party."

Demi groaned. "Don't remind me." He clasped his stomach like the memory pained him. "I was already half-drunk when I ate them. I just thought he couldn't cook..."

I sat by the fire for a long time, listening to Demi and Ren reminisce. I shared a few stories of my own when prompted, but mostly I just listened. Ren had been stingy with details of her life so far, and I greedily absorbed Demi's stories, eager for a glimpse at her past.

Shortly before the first moon set, Ren rose from her seat. "This has been great, but I need to sl—" She wobbled, and my heart dropped.

I lurched up, catching her before she tumbled into the fire. "I got you." As I stared into her face, a powerful urge to kiss her rosy lips washed over me.

Not now, Jalen. She almost fainted.

"Thanks." Her lashes fluttered up and down, and she gripped my vest, still a tad unsteady on her feet. "Got really hot all of a sudden. Do you think I'm getting sick again?"

Demi appeared at her elbow. "Sick? What are you talking about, Ren?"

"It's nothing." Ren pushed out of my arms and waved a hand. "I bet it was the weed."

"Like hell. You said sick *again*. What happened the first time?"

She rolled her eyes. "I got a little overheated is all. Jalen brought me to a healer who gave me these tablets." Her face brightened. "The tablets! That's what the problem is. I forgot to take one earlier." She thrust her hand out to me.

I pulled the bottle out of my vest pocket. Demi's eyes widened as she shook out a pill and snagged my thermos off the ground. "There, all better," she announced after she swallowed it. "Now, I'd like to get some rest. Are you guys coming?"

Demi cleared his throat. "I'm not tired yet. You want to hang by the fire a little longer, Jalen?" I sensed from his hard tone that the invitation wasn't one I should ignore.

I smiled breezily. "Let me get Ren settled first." I stopped at a lionettle plant—we didn't have a cave nearby that night, so we were back to roughing it—and lit a burner. "You're certain you're okay?"

"Yeah, I'm good." Ren plucked the burner from my fingers and took a big puff. "This ought to help me sleep, right?" With a grin, she blew enough smoke at the plant to climb inside, then passed me the burner. "Goodnight."

"Night, Ren." I strode back to the campfire, my stomach sinking.

Demi's jaw clenched as he spotted me returning. "She doesn't know yet, does she?"

I didn't even bother to play dumb. It was clear from his reaction that Demi knew exactly what those tablets were for. "No." I sighed and sank next to him.

He snagged the burner out of my fingers. "She's not gonna take it well."

"That's what has me worried."

Demi blew out a huge puff of smoke. "Ren and I might laugh about the good times growing up, but she had it harder than most. You want my advice?"

I turned, staring at him full on in the dim night. "Please."

"When you tell her, give her time to process. Ren's always been... guarded. After what happened when we were younger, I can't say I blame her."

My heart twinged. "What happened?"

Demi chuckled. "Nope. Not my story to tell, man." He passed me the burner. "She'll share when she's ready."

"Guess secrets run in the family." I raised a brow, then let my gaze trail down to Demi's shorts. I'd noticed something *off* when we'd tussled earlier. And from the way his head cocked at every sound in the forest—even a few that were so quiet a Terran shouldn't be able to hear them—I suspected he wasn't being entirely truthful either. "What are you hiding?"

"Ask me again after you talk to Ren, and maybe I'll tell you." He grabbed the burner again and stood. "Come on. You can have this back after I find a bush to sleep in."

I followed Demi to a different lionettle, then stomped out the campfire. My thoughts swam as I approached the plant where Ren slept soundly with no clue that her future was about to change forever.

Perhaps Demi had thought his advice was helpful, but honestly, it just made me even more worried. Would she ever accept that we were fated to be together?

How was I going to tell her?

I needed to figure it out fast. If her symptoms were returning, then we didn't have much time before they hit us with full force. From what I'd heard, the mating instinct eventually grew so intense that it would make up her mind for her. And as much as I craved her, I hated the thought of rushing her into intimacy before she was mentally prepared for it.

As I climbed in beside her, I made myself a silent promise. *Tomorrow. No matter what happens, I need to tell her tomorrow.*

26

Onatel

Ren

"Onatel is close. I'll run ahead, open the gates." Jalen turned, gracing me with a blinding grin. He'd led the way all morning, in proper guide fashion, while Demi and I chatted.

My cheeks warmed as his eyes locked with mine, reminding me of earlier this morning. Those gorgeous greens had been the first thing I'd seen when I woke with him beside me. If I hadn't remembered that Demi was sleeping within earshot, I might've tried for a repeat hump session.

"Go ahead," Demi said. "We'll catch up."

As Jalen jogged away, Demi lifted a brow. "Well, well. Never thought I'd live to see the day. You're smitten with our guide... aren't you?"

My cheeks burned. "Not sure if I'd go that far."

Was I smitten? With his vibrating cocks... definitely. As for the rest of him... maybe. *Ugh. How did this happen?*

I'd never been the girl who swooned over guys. I'd always been content alone. I had my friends and my work. Some might even say I was a little obsessed with the latter, but it never bothered me. Getting my hands dirty fixing things made me happy. My lack of a relationship never factored into my overall contentment. Not to mention that the few interactions I'd had with men were either so traumatic I did my best never to think of them, or entirely forgettable.

But something told me that when I left Dionus, I wouldn't forget Jalen so easily.

"What's the matter?" Demi tilted his head. "It's okay for you to like him, you know. I'm pretty positive he likes you back."

I worried my lower lip with my teeth. "Yeah... if you say so."

"Don't think I missed you two sleeping in the same lionettle last night."

"It's not a big deal. Not like anything is gonna come of it after this trip is through."

He scoffed. "You didn't see the way he was looking at you when he saved you from falling into the fire last night."

The guy was a recluse. It was no surprise he'd be attracted to the first chick who'd come along. "I don't know about all that..."

Demi leaned in. "I have a feeling he'd follow you to the end of the universe if you asked him to."

I spat caustically, "Well, I'm not asking."

"What are we asking?" Jalen's voice boomed from ahead. We turned a corner, and the trees blocking the way thinned, revealing Jalen standing at the end of the path beside an open gate similar to the one at Asani's village.

I shot Demi a dirty look before flashing Jalen a sheepish grin. "Nothing. Demi's just messing with me."

Jalen's eyes narrowed. "Is he? Say the word and I'll teach him to watch his mouth."

"Me? Who's the one calling people bitches around here?" Demi crossed his arms, staring Jalen down.

God, I don't need to deal with this pissing match right now. "If anyone needs to watch their mouth around here, it's me, you fucks." I brushed past them both, ducking inside the village gate. "Now come on. Let's go."

My eyes widened as I emerged onto a busy street and strode into a town far larger than the last one we'd stopped in. Wood cabins lined the winding roads, built in the same fashion as the homes in the capital. Dozens of Dionions wandered about, and all those close enough to spot us eyed us curiously.

"Hey, Jalen!" a squeaky voice called. It belonged to a boy a head shorter than me, who wore clothes a touch too small, like he'd just finished shooting up a few inches.

Jalen answered cheerfully, "Tun. Good to see you." More children gathered around, the older ones clearly excited, though some of the younger ones stared at him curiously with no sign of recognition.

As they broke into a conversation full of names of people I didn't recognize, I hung back with Demi. "Is someone here expecting you?"

Demi nodded and pulled a folded paper out of his pack. "The official from the last village sent me with a letter of introduction. Seems that's the way of things in these parts."

"How... quaint." It certainly wasn't how we were used to doing things. I could contact Arda with a single touch as long as she stayed on the planet.

"Hey, if it works." He shrugged. "Now I just need to find the village official."

"Official?" I asked.

"They're the ones in charge. Always at least one in a settlement this big," he explained.

As if the words had summoned him, an older Dionion wearing a vest so long it was more of a robe appeared in the doorway of the large cabin that sat closest to the gate. "Greetings, visitors," he began, speaking formally as he tossed his long blue hair over one shoulder.

Jalen spun around. As soon as the official spotted him, he lost the pomp and grinned widely.

"Jalen! What a pleasure to see you. Karln will be thrilled." He stopped at Jalen's side, forgoing the formal greeting and pulling him into a tight hug.

"It's good to be back, Official Minra." Jalen hugged him back—and was that a tear gathering in the corner of his eye?

"Who are your companions?" Official Minra asked.

Demi cleared his throat. "I'm actually here on a separate matter, Official." He thrust out the letter, following it up with the formal fist press. "You may have heard about me already. I'm Demetri, the linguist working on the translator upgrades that were commissioned out of Harlxston."

Minra glanced over the letter with pursed lips. "I see. You're right. We've heard about your travels." He snapped his fingers three times, and the teen who'd first spoken to Jalen appeared at his elbow. "Please, run ahead and inform the hostel Demetri will need a room. I hope you enjoy your stay with us." He turned to me. "Are you his... assistant?"

"I'm with him." I jabbed my thumb at Jalen.

"We're passing through on our way to the old ruins," Jalen said smoothly. "We ran into Demetri in the jungle and thought it wise to travel together, after we encountered some trouble."

Minra lifted a hand, palm out. "Say no more." His gaze darted around the children gathered within earshot. "We should discuss this in private, I think." Then his brow furrowed. "After you've settled in, of course. I'll have someone take you to get cleaned up. We'll put out fresh clothes and a bite to eat for each of you."

I could sense from the way his gaze lingered on the worst of the stains I'd acquired, the mention of clothing was meant for me. "Thank you, Official Minra. I lost my pack early on—"

"It's no trouble at all." He grinned widely, and the expression completely changed his face, making his resemblance to Jalen stand out starkly. "Some say we have the most skilled weavers in all of Dionus living within Onatel." Minra shot a sharp glance behind me into the crowd of teens, and two broke free from the pack as if summoned. "Take them to the bathhouses, please." With that, he spun on his heel and headed back to the house he'd emerged from.

A young woman with wide violet eyes, her long blue locks styled in a dozen braids woven into an intricate series of loops, approached me. I smiled tentatively, but before I said hello, a young man beckoned Demi and Jalen to follow him, and my heart dropped. "Are we splitting up?"

She nodded. "Females and males have separate bathhouses in Onatel. Is it not the same where you live?"

Jalen must've sensed my distress. He sidestepped the boy and stopped beside me. "Hey, Ren. Are you okay with this? I can come with you and wait outside if you'd feel more comfortable."

"No, it's fine." I could handle a bathhouse full of women. "We'll meet after?"

He nodded and turned to the girl. "Kiki, can you walk her to Karln's cabin when she's finished?"

"Certainly," she replied.

With a final smile, Jalen returned to his guide.

"Kiki, is that your name?"

The girl smoothed a hand down her thigh-length skirt before holding out her fist in Dioinon style. "It is. And you are?"

"Ren." I pressed the side of my fist to hers. After we dropped our arms, she strolled in the opposite direction from Jalen and Demi.

"It's nice to meet you, Ren. We don't get a lot of off-worlders here." Even though she wasn't shy about examining me, her innocent curiosity didn't make me squirm the way other people's gazes normally did. But when her gaze trailed to my hair, her face fell, and she said, "I'm sorry for your loss."

What is she talking about? "What loss?"

She waved a hand at my short blonde curls. "When did you lose him? It must've been pretty recent. I'm so sorry you had to endure losing your mate at such a young age."

A startled chuckle escaped me. "I'm not sure why you think that, but I've never had a mate—much less lost one."

"You didn't cut your hair short when your mate died?" she asked in such a shocked tone, I knew she wasn't messing with me.

"No. I promise you, that's not a thing where I come from."

Kiki tilted her head. "Huh. So you just cut your hair because you like it short?"

A pang of discomfort lodged in my chest. *Not exactly... but we're not gonna get into that.* "Pretty much."

"Off-worlders are so bizarre." She giggled. Then her eyes widened, and she quickly added, "No offense."

"None taken."

I had about a dozen follow-up questions. Did they really cut their hair as a sign of grief? Was it only for mates—what about children or parents? But at that moment, Kiki strode up the porch steps of a log cabin, one of the few buildings without open windows and big airy rooms visible from the street.

I slotted my questions away for later and followed Kiki into the dim interior. Lamps set to low provided a peaceful ambiance, and light fruity perfume smacked me in the nose.

An old Dionion woman, far plumper than most I'd met so far, rose from behind a desk. "Kiki. Who have you brought me today?" She frowned as her gaze raked over my clothes. "Oh dear. You've come not a moment too soon, I see."

A wave of heat stung my cheeks. "Lost my pack a few days back. Been down to one skinsuit since then."

"Don't worry." She rushed forward, hands outstretched. I backed away before she made contact with my shoulder, but the woman's smile didn't slip in the slightest. She let her hands fall to her sides and cocked her head at a wooden door behind the desk. "We'll get you cleaned up. Come along."

I followed warily, but as I wandered into a fresh-scented room with soft music playing, my shoulders relaxed. A curtain covered the back half of the room, and two young Dionions stood in the front, their posture stiff and attention focused on the plump proprietor.

"This is Tirra." She waved forward a pretty girl slightly older than Kiki, her long blue hair styled in loose waves, and a second girl, whose long lashes fluttered as she looked me up and down. "And Novri. They'll be your attendants today."

"Attendants?" I shook my head. "I don't need help bathing."

"I see. Well, they'll be just outside, should you need anything." With that, the boss pulled back a curtain, revealing a tub similar to the ones I'd used in the caves with one major difference. More than a dozen jars, bottles, and brushes littered the tub's edge.

Talk about overkill. No wonder they need assistants. "Thanks. I'll manage."

Kiki hurried forward as I ducked inside. "Ren, would you mind handing me your clothing once you step out of it? We'll have it cleaned for you while you're bathing."

"Oh... Um, sure."

The boss winked at me before slipping out. I slid the curtain closed and pulled down my zipper. The outer door had barely swung closed before voices rose from the other side of the curtain.

"Are the rumors true, Kiki?" one attendant asked.

The second, her voice slightly higher pitched, chimed in. "I heard Jalen's returned."

Kiki said, "It's true. He said he was just passing through."

"How did he look? I bet the years have been kind to him," the first said.

The second didn't give Kiki a chance to reply before she asked breathlessly, "I wonder if he'll stay for the festival tonight? I'd love a dance with him."

I rolled my eyes, wondering if the girl was out there swooning. "Here's my stuff, Kiki." I thrust my clothes outside the curtain, interrupting their conversation.

"Thank you." Maybe it was just me, but Kiki sounded relieved. "I better take these to the cleaners."

The barely there hum of whispers rose from beyond the curtain after the door shut, but I tried to put the attendants out of my mind.

So there was a village full of cute, young things itching for a chance to get their hands on my guide. I shouldn't be surprised. Jalen was gorgeous. And that smile of his... Any girl would be lucky to have him as her mate.

I sank into the warm water and willed the jealous thoughts away. I had to face the facts. Jalen wasn't meant to be mine. I mean, how often did Dionions end up with someone outside of their race, anyway?

Of course, it was possible. If it wasn't, then Cass wouldn't be with Rhelt.

Cassidy... Her name filled my thoughts at the same moment I slathered sweet-smelling gunk on my hair. Clarity hit me full blast, making my eyes widen. *That's why Jalen was so upset when we first met.* He must've assumed I was Cassidy, and that the short hair meant Rhelt was dead.

Odd... He didn't talk about Rhelt much. The few times his name came up in conversation, Jalen's brows pinched in and his shoulders slumped, leading me to believe their relationship was strained. But then why would he be so distraught over Rhelt's loss?

Noise in the outer chamber drew my attention. "Kiki, you're back quick," one of the girls said.

"I have new clothes for Ren." Footsteps slapped the tile, and then Kiki called from behind the curtain. "Can I come in and place some clean clothes on a chair for you?"

I could duck under the water. Or better yet... "Just a second." I snagged a towel off a hook on the wall and wrapped it around me, thankful I'd already finished washing. "Come in."

Kiki smiled politely as she slipped inside. "It will take several hours to launder your clothes. You're welcome to wear these while you wait."

"Thank you." I crossed the room, my stomach sinking. The thigh-high skirt and tight-fitted tank top would show off a lot more skin than I was used to. "I'm guessing you don't have any pants instead, do you?"

Kiki shook her head. "I can ask around, if you'd like."

"No. I'll be fine. It's just for a few hours." I fingered the shirt, sighing as the buttery fabric slipped across my skin. At least I'd be clean. Then I'd change back into my stuff when it was time to leave.

Kiki ducked behind the curtain, and I dressed quickly. But when I searched for my boots, my brow furrowed. "Have you seen my boots?"

The girl with the higher voice replied, "We have them out here. We're almost done shining them for you."

The curtain whooshed as I pushed it aside. Both the attendants looked up, their hands busy scrubbing the mud and gunk off my hiking boots.

"You didn't need to clean those. They're just gonna get filthy again."

Novri replied, allowing me to put a name to the high-pitched voice. "It's no trouble at all."

I shifted from foot to foot in my borrowed socks. "Okay. Thanks, then, I guess." I glanced around, wondering what to talk about while I waited for them to surrender my footwear. Maybe I could ask Kiki some of those questions from earlier. But as I spotted her standing beside the doorway, my stomach clenched.

Kiki's bronze skin was flush, and her lashes fluttered at the same time she wobbled on her feet.

I gasped, rushing to her side as she fainted. "Get the healer!" I shouted. "Kiki needs help." I lowered her gently to the floor, resting her head in my lap.

"Don't worry." Tirra calmly rose and handed her boot to Novri. "I'll find who she needs."

As the door swung shut, Kiki slowly came to. "So... hot," she muttered, tugging at the neck of her shirt.

My heart raced. Was this the same sickness that'd struck me? From what I could tell, the symptoms certainly lined up.

"Here she is," Tirra announced lightly as she led a lanky teen inside.

What the hell? "I thought you were getting the healer?"

"It's all right. He'll help Kiki," Novri said. "Watch."

The teen bent and lifted Kiki gently from my arms. Then, before I could do more than gasp, he planted a kiss on her lips.

"Hey!" I stood, intending to smack the filthy pervert off her. "She's not in any condition to—" My words died in my throat as Kiki's loose limbs locked around the guy's neck, dragging him closer. I averted my eyes as they pulled apart.

"Ebam. You didn't have to come," Kiki said breathlessly.

Ebam caressed her face, which had returned to her normal bronze hue. "Of course I did. Let me guess. You forgot your tablets again this morning." He reached into his vest pocket, and I had a sinking feeling I knew exactly what he was about to pull out. He turned before I could confirm my suspicions, leading Kiki to the door. "Come on. Let's get you some water."

As the door swung behind them, I spun to the girls. "What was *that*?"

Novri sighed. "She's so lucky, isn't she? I wish I'd found my harmonic when I was Kiki's age."

"Harmonic..." Where had I heard that before? "What's that?"

"Her mate," Tirra replied matter-of-factly.

I blinked repeatedly. "Her... mate? What does that have to do with her collapsing?"

Novri scrubbed the sole of my boot. "It's the heat. Since they're waiting to complete the bond, they take blockers to stop it."

Blood zinged through my veins like it'd been turbocharged.

"I'm planning to wait when I first meet my mate, too." Tirra sat beside Novri and picked up the other boot and cloth. "Back when my gran was young, there was no choice. That was before the healers discovered how to block the heat symptoms."

I wasn't entirely sure how I made my voice work, but somehow I asked, "How do they... complete the bond?"

Novri and Tirra shared a knowing look. Then Novri leaned in, her brows raised. "You truly don't know?"

I shook my head, not caring that I probably looked like an idiot.

Tirra stated baldly, "They complete the bond by *mating*." Her lips thinned. "You do know what that is, don't you?"

I nodded blankly as a thousand scattered pieces clicked together. Then the answer to my earlier question struck me in a flash. Asani had called Jalen my harmonic before she'd tried to sear off my taste buds. It couldn't be true... could it?

Is Jalen my mate?

27

Serious Wooing

Jalen

I held my breath as I slipped inside the cabin I'd grown up in. "Auntie Karln?" No answer. But with Ren busy bathing, I resigned myself to wait inside for them both.

My footsteps echoed on the wooden floors. Dozens of plants greeted me, their meticulously trimmed leaves dangling in every window. Even more hung from the ceiling, making the living area feel like I was back in the jungle.

My aunt had always had a love for plants. Once I'd gotten the travel bug, I'd fed her obsession by bringing her the rarest blossoms to tend. And when I was locked away in my personal purgatory, she'd sent me clippings, giving me something to focus on.

I ought to thank Karln for that. Without my garden, I'd have ended up like all the other outcasts—whiling away the lonely days and nights mired in misery. Those plants had kept me from going crazy, wondering why everything went wrong...

I sighed as I wandered further inside. Reaching out, I plucked a framed picture off the side table next to Karln's favorite rocking chair. Rhelt and I stared out, big smiles on our faces and our arms slung around each other's shoulders. A pang hit me in the ribs.

"Such a shame. You two used to be so close."

I whipped around, nearly dropping the photo. "Aunt Karln. I didn't hear you come in." She strolled out of the kitchen, a sad look in her violet eyes.

"Have you spoken to Rhelt lately?" she asked softly as she plucked the frame from my fingers.

My stomach churned. "No. He sent me a letter, though."

She shook her head, making the loose bun she'd piled her blue curls up in wobble. "I'm sorry to hear that. I assumed that since you were here, the two of you had mended your issues."

"Not quite. I doubt he'll ever forgive me."

Karln set the photo down gently. "Don't give up. He'll come around." She lifted her gaze to mine. "It might help if you find your mate."

I rubbed the back of my neck. "About that..."

Karln's face lit up. "You found her? But who..." Her eyes narrowed. "Is it the human you arrived with?"

Aunt Karln had always been too quick-witted to sneak anything past. It seemed a few years hadn't changed that. "Yes. But... it's complicated."

Karln sank into her rocker and waved a hand at the old couch across from it. "Sit. Tell me what's troubling you."

"I don't even know where to begin." I plopped on the couch.

"Finding one's mate should be a joyous time. Why do you look so disturbed? Were you hoping she'd be Dionion?"

"No, I don't mind that she's Terran. It's just... Ren told me when we first met that she hates the idea of fated mates. I'm afraid when I tell her, she's going to..."

"Reject you?"

My chest tightened. "Exactly."

"You can't let that stop you, Jalen. If you two are experiencing the heat"—she glanced at me as if to confirm, and at my nod, she continued—"then you have to explore your connection."

"I know that." I rubbed my temples. "She's just so different from me, Auntie. And I don't mean that she's an off-worlder. I think something happened in her past that made her give up on relationships. Half the time, she glares at me like she wants to murder me."

Aunt Karln chuckled. "I like her already. You need a female who won't spend her life swooning at that smile of yours." She leaned back on the rocker. "What about the other half?"

"Hm?"

"You said *half* the time she wants to murder you. What about the other half?"

A flash of Ren writhing on my lap, her eyes half-lidded and her mouth agape with pleasure, flooded my memory.

Aunt Karln laughed again. "I'm guessing the other half you don't want to talk about with your old aunt."

"Perhaps." The tips of my ears burned. "But I'm worried when she finds out, she'll think we're only drawn to each other because of the bond."

"Then you must show her that's not so." Karln leaned forward on her rocker and patted my knee. "Get to know her. Prove that you enjoy spending time with her and you aren't just interested in mating her."

I twisted my lips. "You think that will work?"

Karln reached over and plucked a different frame off her side table. She flashed the picture at me before placing it on her lap and staring at it.

My parents. I'd been so young when they passed I had no memories of them, but I knew them well enough from staring at that picture and listening to countless tales my aunt shared.

Karln looked up. "It's funny, I remember my brother sitting right where you are and sharing something very similar the day he met your mother."

"But I thought they were deeply in love." At least, that was what Karln had always led me to believe.

"They were. Only... not at first." Karln smiled nostalgically. "Your mother was a tribe runner. While most females would be too frightened to brave the jungles on their own, your mother loved it. You get your love of travel from her."

"I thought father was a runner too?"

"Not until after they met. Your father knew she wouldn't settle for a life led in one place. So he went with her. And when he showed he valued her—exactly the way she was—that was when she knew fate had chosen correctly."

Perhaps Karln was right... I had to prove to Ren that we made sense together. Then, when I came clean about the bond, she'd realize we were meant to be.

Karln placed the frame back on the side table with a clunk. "Treasure her, Jalen." Her lip wobbled. "You never know how long your time together will last." She rubbed her thumb across her brother's likeness. "I'm just thankful they had each other in the end."

My parents had died in a freak accident. It couldn't have been easy on Karln, though normally she was good at hiding it. Times like these when she let her sadness show, I realized the enormous hole my parents' deaths had opened in her life. It could be why she never sought a new relationship after my uncle passed.

"I'm glad too," I admitted softly. "Thank you for the advice, Auntie."

"Happy to help." Her face brightened. "Now, when do I get to meet her?"

I chuckled. "Soon, I hope. I asked Kiki to walk her here when they were done in the bathhouse."

Karln hopped out of her chair. "She's coming now? I need to tidy this mess."

Shaking my head, I rose. "Let me help you." As we rushed around, clearing the few piles of junk Karln had lying around, her words rang in my mind.

My aunt was right. If I wanted any chance of making Ren mine, then I had some serious wooing to do.

28

Delayed

Ren

"Here you are." Tirra led me into a small room that I suspected they used for breaks. A few tables and chairs sat empty, except for one table where a small plate of fruit and cheese waited for me. "I'll see if Kiki is feeling better yet. I hear she promised to take you to Karln's after this."

I sank into the hard wooden chair and stared at the food. It smelled inviting, but I couldn't bring myself to eat any of it.

"You're certain you don't want any company? I can ask Novri to sit with you."

"No, I'm fine." I grabbed a cube of cheese and popped it into my mouth, hoping that would convince her to leave. Not that I didn't want her around, but I was dying to call Arda. I needed some advice about all this mate crap.

Tirra disappeared through the doorway, and I barely waited for the door to swing closed before I slapped my neck.

Time ticked slowly as I chewed the tasteless hunk of cheese, waiting... "Hello? That you, Arda?" Apparently, I was so desperate to talk I couldn't even wait for her to squeeze out a word of greeting when the call connected.

Chuckles echoed in my head. "Yep, I'm here. I swear, you must be psychic, Ren. Your call came in just after we heard the good news."

"Good news?"

"After we didn't find Smudge yesterday, I called your sister for advice. I was hoping she'd have a more detailed map, but she flew over with a whole ass search party! We just got word that someone spotted Smudge. Won't be long now until Lux has his baby back."

"That's great. I'm glad she's okay."

Arda cleared her throat. "Something wrong?"

It had to be bad if she could glean that just from the sound of my voice. "Yeah... you could say that." I drew a deep breath and spilled everything. The attraction for Jalen I couldn't seem to shake. How I'd nearly collapsed again into the fire last night. And even what happened in the cave tub the other day. Then I wrapped up with what I'd learned about Dionion mates in the bathhouse. "So, what do you think? Am I crazy, or is he my... my..."

"Your mate." Arda whistled. "I'm no Dionus expert, but it sure as shit sounds like it."

I groaned. "Fuck. What am I going to do?"

"Hm... I might know fuck all about how mating works on this planet, but we both know someone who does. Why don't you call Cassidy?"

I shook my head. "I can't. I've never been able to talk to her about stuff like this."

"But you *are* sisters. I'm sure she'd help."

"Maybe."

After a weighted pause, Arda carefully asked, "What happened between you two?"

"I don't want to get into it."

Arda sighed. "Ren, I know you're worried about what you're experiencing with Jalen. About your future. But have you ever considered that you might need to come to terms with your past first?"

I propped my elbows on the table and cradled my head in my hands. Would I be better equipped to handle everything if I dealt with my unresolved issues with Cass? She could provide some insight into the mating stuff. She was the only person I knew who'd mated a Dionion.

But that meant I had to talk to her—*really* talk, about more than just surface-level things. And with me and Cass, that was easier said than done.

Footsteps pounded in the hall. "I need to go, Arda. I'll call you later, 'kay?" I slapped my neck, ending the transmission.

Kiki poked her head in the door a second later. "You ready to go?" She frowned as she spotted my practically untouched plate.

"I don't have much of an appetite." I stood, then joined her in the hall.

"Don't worry. I bet Karln will set something out for you before the festival. She makes amazing salads. You'll see why once we arrive."

My heart sped as we left the bathhouse and emerged into the afternoon sunshine. An air of excitement filled the village, and I suspected it wasn't merely news of our arrival that had caused it. Everywhere I looked, someone was hurrying past, many carrying baskets or hauling overloaded packs on their backs. "What's with everyone rushing?"

"They're preparing for the festival tonight. We hold one every year on this day. It's a celebration of the end of forice."

"What's forice?"

"It's our name for the season that just passed, which is marked with infrequent rain and long, bright nights. The next season brings ample rain, darker nights, and extended daylight—which is a boon for hunters and planters alike."

"I see..." My belly twinged. I could understand why they'd want to celebrate, but those conditions didn't sound ideal for tramping around the jungle. Maybe that was another reason Jalen hadn't wanted to put off leaving when we'd first met. "What's the celebration like?"

"Everyone gathers by the bonfire at dusk, and we dance until full dark."

"Sounds like... fun." Maybe for some. Honestly, it wasn't my kind of scene. I'd much rather spend a quiet night in with friends than party out in public, where I'd need to worry about making a fool of myself.

Kiki marched down a side street. "I hope you can stay the night and attend."

"I don't know about that. We're just passing through."

"Too bad. Seems a shame to miss it when you're already here." She stopped in front of a small garden, the varied plants and flowers lined up in neat rows that made it clear they'd been planted, and so densely packed they hid much of the cabin behind them. "This is it."

She turned down a cramped walkway and led me to the porch. I tucked my elbows close to my torso, not wanting the foreign plants to brush against my skin. But after carefully examining a few, I spotted a pattern. "So, this explains the amazing salads?"

Kiki grinned. "Karln grows the best vegetables and herbs in all of Onatel." Her dainty boots pounded the porch stairs.

My fingers tangled in the hem of my borrowed top as she knocked. I cocked my head at the front windows, but unlike virtually every other house on the planet, I couldn't sneak a peek inside. Potted plants sat on every inch of space, blocking my view.

Guess I know where Jalen got his green thumb...

The door swung open, and a beautiful older Dionion wearing a silver sundress, her hair piled up in a bun, popped out. "Kiki, so nice to see you." She grinned warmly at her before her gaze darted to me. "And you must be Ren. Come in. I've been expecting you."

I gulped and forced a smile. "Thanks." I slipped past Karln while she said a quick goodbye to Kiki. My eyes widened as I scanned the inside. More plants. Some worn seating. But there was one thing suspiciously absent. "Is Jalen here?"

Karln eased the door closed before facing me. "Not at the moment. Official Minra sent a runner for him. But he won't be long. I told him to hurry. I'm almost finished preparing our midday meal."

I shifted from one foot to the other. "Can I help?"

"No need. Sit and relax." Karln waved to the sofa as she glided across the cabin to the small kitchenette. With the open floor plan, I had no problem seeing her, even once I took a seat on the couch.

As she began chopping vegetables, I examined the room. "You have a lovely home. Did you grow all these plants yourself?"

"Most. Though I wouldn't have half of them without Jalen." Karln lifted the knife, using it to point out a spindly green fern in the front window that reminded me of a spider plant. "He brought that one back from the Yeranium Mountains." She pointed to another with bright-yellow blossoms hanging in the kitchen window. "This one's from the Tipolis Valley. Both are places most Dionions wouldn't dream of traveling to—but not Jalen."

Huh... weird. "He doesn't seem to travel much these days."

"Yes. Such a shame. To be honest, I expected him to leave this world long ago. Take his adventures to the stars." She went back to chopping, the rhythmic slicing oddly soothing. "At one time, he was even scheduled to go on a peacekeeping mission to your system."

"He was?" That was news to me. Though it made sense, seeing how knowledgeable Jalen was about humans... Well, except for their slang.

"About five years ago, he was selected to be the Dionion representative at a meeting regarding intersystem boundaries and trade. But just before he left, he had to be replaced." Karln sighed. "I know he regrets missing that journey."

My stomach clenched as an odd sense of déjà vu washed over me. "Wait... where have I heard about that before?"

"I imagine from your sister. That's where she and Rhelt first met."

Eyes widening, I slumped back on the sofa. If Jalen was meant to go, then he would've met Cassidy instead of Rhelt meeting her.

Wasn't that just... lovely? My stomach sank. Would Jalen have wanted her instead?

Of course he would've, Ren. Who are you kidding? Everyone loves Cassidy more than you. Hell, even Arda's half-obsessed with Little Miss Perfect after her rescue mission went off without a hitch.

Karln interrupted my pity party with a cough. "I suspect fate kept Jalen home because it had other plans for him." She grinned and set down the knife. "What do you think, Ren?"

God... does she know? "I don't put much stock into what fate wants." I swallowed, hoping she hadn't somehow figured out that Jalen and I were... ugh, mates. "So what kept Jalen home if he was so eager to leave?"

"It's a sad tale." She rounded the countertop and settled into the rocker across from me. "We received word of a series of cave-ins in the Yeranium Mountains shortly before the shuttle was set to depart. Jalen was one of the few guides familiar with traveling there. He volunteered to head up the search party."

"Oh. That's terrible."

"A handful were lost in the rubble, but the party saved several males and one female." A tiny smile crossed her face. "I doubt they'd have survived if not for Jalen's expertise. He has much to be proud of."

Warmth spread through my insides. "Yeah... I guess he does." *How am I supposed to tell him to take a hike now? My* mate *is a goddamn hero.*

Was that even what I wanted? If you'd asked me last week, I'd have sworn up and down I wanted nothing to do with the entire male half of the universe. But now...

A knock pounded on the door just before it swung open. "Auntie Karln?" Jalen strolled in, a radiant smile spreading as he spotted me sitting across from his aunt in the living area. And damn, he sure did clean up nice. He'd traded his dusty shorts and vest for a fresh set that clung to his muscles, and he'd brushed his long blue hair until it gleamed.

"Ren. You look..."—his gaze trailed down my frame, making me hyperaware of how my short skirt had ridden up my thighs—"comfortable."

I was tempted to leave it as-is and revel in his heated gaze, but when Official Minra wandered in the house after him, I tugged the hem lower. "Um, thanks. I'm good to head out as soon as Kiki delivers my skinsuit. She promised to drop it off after the cleaners finish with it."

Minra cleared his throat. "I'm sorry to be the bearer of bad news, but I don't think that would be wise. You two ought to stay the night. After what Jalen and Demetri have shared, I don't want you leaving so close to nightfall."

"Seriously? Why not?" I asked.

Minra sank onto the sofa beside me. "We've been keeping it quiet within the village, but this isn't the first encounter we've had with poachers in recent days. One of our males was attacked twelve nights past. I think it's prudent you get a fresh start in the morning. Then, when you make camp, you're more likely to have traveled out of their search radius."

"You don't want to tangle with these off-worlders." Karln leaned in and lowered her voice. "The healer sent for some of my strongest pain-relieving herbs after that attack. I can only imagine why."

Jalen frowned. "Do we know what they're after?"

"Ellbright," Minra explained. "The villager caught them in the midst of harvesting it."

"What do they want it for?" My brow furrowed.

Minra shrugged. "No one knows. But since tonight is mostly full dark, there's bound to be plenty of blooms. Chances are good they'll be out scouring the jungle for more of it."

I couldn't exactly insist we leave when it would be putting us in danger. "Well, I guess staying the night won't set us back too much."

"Great." Jalen turned to me. "In that case, would you like to accompany me to the bonfire tonight, Ren?"

As their expectant gazes landed on me, my heart thrashed like haywire. I couldn't tell him I'd rather stay in and hide when everyone had been so friendly since we'd arrived. Looked like I'd be dancing the night away after all. "Umm... sure. Why not?"

"Wonderful!" Karln clapped her hands. "There's plenty of room for you two to stay here. I'll air out your room, Jalen. And Ren can stay in Rhelt's room."

"Thank you." I forced a smile.

Karln rose from her rocker. "Would you like to stay and eat with us, Official?"

He shook his head. "Can't. I'm expected elsewhere, though I appreciate the invitation."

"Of course." Karln strode across the floor. "I'll walk you out."

As they disappeared onto the porch, Jalen sat beside me. "I'm sorry our plans were delayed. Thank you for being so understanding."

My belly fluttered as our gazes clashed. "It's fine. I get it."

He inched closer, but stopped well before we touched—yet somehow, I still felt the heat of him on my skin. "I promise, I'll make it a night to remember," he said softly.

Yeah... that's what I'm afraid of.

Ren

Drums thumped hypnotically. A trio of curved woodwinds and a curious stringed instrument reminiscent of a cello played along, their dueling harmonies adding to the festive atmosphere. Twinkle lights strung between trees and cabins circled an enormous fire cracking in the center of the village square. And all around it, Dionions danced, the women's skirts swishing as the men twirled them about.

"You ready to dance?" Jalen asked, raising his voice to be heard over the din.

"Not yet." *Maybe never.*

We'd been at the celebration for at least an hour. So far, we'd sampled some delicious baked goods that could rival the best Terran cakes and sipped some tangy juice that was unfortunately nonalcoholic. *I sure could use a little liquid courage right about now...*

I'd insisted on hanging on the sidelines instead of joining the dancers gaily spinning around the fire. Jalen had been nice enough not to insist, but I didn't miss his toe tapping in time with the beat. Or the dozens of pretty village girls sending longing glances in his direction.

I lifted on my toes, bringing my mouth closer to his ear. "Why don't you ask one of them to dance?"

Jalen shifted, bringing our faces so close his warm breath washed over my neck. "Are you trying to pawn me off on someone else, Ren?"

"No." My breath caught. "You just look like you'd be having more fun out there." I waved at the revelers, but he didn't reply until I returned my focus to him.

"I'll wait until you're ready." His eyes met mine as his words wrapped around me without a hint of wavering in his tone.

"You might be waiting a long time."

He smiled slyly, his gaze sliding slowly down my body. "Did you forget I'm a planter? We know the most delicious things are worth the wait."

Holy mother of innuendos. My panties just flooded.

I backed away a pace, putting more space between myself and the fire. When Jalen cocked a brow, I said, "What?" I stared pointedly at the flames before fanning my face. "It's hot out here."

A crooked grin spread across his face. "Want another drink?"

I nodded, grateful for the reprieve.

"Be right back." Jalen sauntered off, and I had to drag my gaze away from his fine backside.

Get ahold of yourself, Ren.

I needed to talk to him about the mate stuff. I knew that. But every time I tried to broach the topic, I got flustered and fell back on my go-to coping mechanism—bottling everything up inside.

It didn't help that we'd been surrounded by people since I'd learned the truth. The last thing I wanted was to cause a huge scene.

What if he didn't know? Hell, what if he knew and was keeping it from me? Or what if I was completely off base, and this attraction was one-sided?

No. He wouldn't have just looked at me like *that* if he didn't want me. But wanting to fuck and wanting to be together forever—the way we would be if we were mated—were two entirely different things.

I should've peppered Kiki with questions earlier. There was still so much I didn't know about Dionus.

My gaze flicked sideways as movement caught my attention. A woman with her hair cropped shorter than mine nodded politely as she passed. She crossed the clearing and sank into a chair beside the fire, her forlorn gaze locked on the dancing flames.

Kiki's assumption earlier rose to the forefront of my mind. *She must be a widow...*

Jalen returned and handed me a full cup.

I took a sip. "Hey, why didn't you ever explain what short hair means to your people?"

"Sounds like someone filled you in."

"Yeah." I frowned. "Is that why you freaked out when you first saw me and thought I was Cassidy?"

"It was. I thought Rhelt was..."

"Dead," I finished.

"Yes."

"Well, sorry for that, I guess."

"You have nothing to apologize for." He sighed. "I made a quick judgement back then, but it didn't take me long to realize my mistake."

"Why didn't you tell me? I know there wasn't much time for it with Arda getting loopy, but you could've afterward, when we were on the trail."

"You mean when you were giving me the silent treatment?"

I scowled, and my cheeks heated.

He shrugged. "By then, I'd remembered that Terran customs were different. I didn't see a point in lecturing you about our cultural differences when you barely wanted to talk to me."

My gaze sank to the ground. *Is that a nice way to say I was being a bitch?* "I guess—"

"Ren!" a familiar voice called.

I whipped around. "Demi. You look like you're having fun." He'd changed, his dirty traveling gear replaced with long shorts and a vest. His cheeks were rosy, his breath coming hard and fast, like he'd run a marathon—or more likely, danced with a dozen villagers.

He pursed his lips, his eyes narrowing. "And you don't." With a single smooth motion, he plucked the cup from my hands and thrust it toward Jalen. "Come on. Let's show 'em how we do it out in space."

"Oh, no. I don't think—"

With a wink, he snagged my waist with one hand and my wrist with the other. Then he swung me out into the crowd before I could finish my rant.

"Demi, are you insane?" I followed his erratic steps as best I could, certain I looked like a complete idiot. "I can't keep up with them." I jerked my head at the revelers, but Demi just laughed.

"Relax, Ren. They don't care what you look like. Just dance."

I clenched my jaw. "You didn't give me much of a goddamn choice."

Demi rolled his eyes, then twirled me into a spin. I let him lead, cursing inwardly until he stumbled.

"Hey." I caught his elbow. "You all right?"

He recovered quickly, righting his balance and widening his grin. "Yep. Damn knee's acting up again."

My heart twinged. Demi had an old injury that liked to bother him from time to time, mainly affecting his balance. He refused to talk about whatever in his past had caused it—even to me. I'd always been fine with his silence. I understood more than most that sometimes people needed to keep their secrets to themselves.

"Sorry. You need anything?" I asked, concern wrinkling my brow.

He pulled me into another spin. "Just for you to shut up and dance."

I spotted Jalen across the clearing, and for a moment our gazes locked. Heat sizzled in my belly.

Demi twirled me sideways, breaking the connection. He peered closely at me. "You okay, Sis?"

Blinking, I shook off the strange sensation. "I... I don't know." I grabbed his vest and dragged him closer, making sure no one nearby heard. "Jalen and I... I think we're mates. Is that crazy? Please tell me I'm crazy."

I pulled back, examining my brother's face. Firelight danced over his features, his expression so flat he might as well be wearing a mask. He opened his mouth.

The music cut off and clanging echoed through the clearing. Everyone spun forward, focusing on Official Minra, who stood beside the drummer, beating on a cymbal.

"I'd like to take a moment to welcome everyone to the annual forice celebration."

Cheers exploded, and I sighed, resigning myself to wait for Demi's answer.

Minra let the clamor die before continuing. "We gather here to give thanks for the abundant bounty of our land and to praise Harlx for..."

I toed at the dirt, only half listening to Minra as he droned on. At least the speech gave me an excuse not to dance. Now, if only I could sneak away while he was talking. But then I wouldn't get to finish asking Demi for his opinion.

It might be worth it. Especially if I could remember the way to Karln's place.

"...Demetri, Jalen, and Ren." Minra's voice sliced through the air, and I froze, my heart beating frantically.

Holy crap... What did he say?

The gaze of every Dionion present bored into me. I smiled wanly, completely lost. *Am I supposed to say something?* I cut a glance at Demi, who appeared just as lost as I was. Panic tore at my chest, but before I hyperventilated, Jalen appeared at my elbow.

"Thank you, Official. We're so pleased fate brought us here at this auspicious time. We thank you for bestowing us with your most cherished honor." He bowed his head, and Demi and I followed suit. As our heads lifted, the crowd burst into more cheers, and my speeding pulse finally slowed.

"Wonderfully said," Mirna shouted. "Let's dance!"

The music struck up again, and my shoulders slumped. I turned back to Demi, but before I could open my mouth, Jalen snagged my hand in his and wrapped the other around my waist.

"Now that you're ready, I'll take that dance." A mischievous grin lit his face, and I couldn't slow my answering smile that mirrored it.

"I guess one dance won't hurt," I breathed, tingles shooting across my skin everywhere he touched me.

Demi peered over Jalen's shoulder and met my gaze. Then, with another wink, he took off, quickly disappearing into the sea of dancers.

Don't leave me, I wanted to shout. But another part of me was quick to choke the words back before they flew off my tongue. Because the truth was, nothing had ever felt so right as being in Jalen's arms, his sure steps twirling us across the clearing like we were floating. And for once, I just wanted to shut my brain off for a while and enjoy the moment.

"You having fun?" he asked.

"Yeah. Surprisingly, I am."

29

Breathtaking

Jalen

I spotted Karln's scowl as I twirled Ren to the beat. To my people, cutting in on a dance was an insult worthy of a duel. Yet that knowledge hadn't been enough to still my feet after our eyes had met a few moments ago.

Until then, I'd been locked in a trance, watching her. Every roll of her hips. Each spin that sent her skirt inching higher up her lithe thighs. The light flush that spread across her chest I was desperate to trace with my tongue.

Then our gazes clashed. In that instant, my fingers burned from the pain of holding back. My lungs ached, needing to be close enough to breathe in her scent. And I'd had about all I could stand of the sight of my mate in another male's arms. Luckily for me, Demi hadn't put up a fight when I claimed her.

Neither had Ren. I'd half expected her to slap my hand away when I slipped my fingers into hers. Instead, they'd wrapped around mine like they were made to fit. She'd even admitted she was having fun—albeit grudgingly.

Tingles shot up my wrists as I pulled her into a spin. She followed my lead effortlessly, though her gaze constantly darted to the side, as if tracking the dancers around us. As the move ended, I tugged her closer than was decent.

I didn't need to look up to know Karln was scowling again. I couldn't help it. I was greedy for Ren's attention. Now that I held her so close, I couldn't contain the want burning within me. And if I couldn't have her hands on me the way I craved, the least I would settle for was her eyes.

She complied, her gaze shooting to mine. "Are you sure these are the right moves?" she whispered hastily.

I fought the urge to drag her even closer. "I am. Why do you ask?"

She glanced around nervously. "Because everyone's staring at us." Her face paled, and my smile fell.

"Do you need a break?"

"Please," she said gratefully.

I led her to the crowd's edge, my stomach sinking. *Great job, idiot. You're supposed to be wooing her, not ruining her fun.*

As we slipped past the last dancers, Ren stumbled. I grabbed her upper arms before she took a tumble. Her hands landed on my chest. I ignored the thrill of her warm touch and asked, "You all right?"

Gulping, she nodded. "I think so. Just... got a little dizzy."

"Did you take your tablet already?"

She nodded again. "Before we left. Maybe I need a drink."

It was a bad sign if the medicine was losing its effectiveness already. I snagged a couple cups of juice from a nearby stand. We drank in silence, and after a moment, a bit of color returned to her cheeks. "Feeling better?"

She tugged at the neck of her tunic. "Somewhat. Still kinda hot. Can we back away from the fire?"

That was the second time tonight she'd complained about the heat. I had a sinking feeling it wasn't the bonfire causing it. My heart twinged. I had to tell her. But what about proving we fit together first? No way I'd done enough to show that yet.

A torch flared to light in my mind's eye. "I can do better than that. Follow me."

"Where are we going?" Ren lifted a brow as we wandered away from the village square. Cobblestone gave way to a dirt path heading to the town's outskirts. Two partially full moons hung high in the sky, lighting the overgrown footpath.

"You'll see." I flashed a grin at her. "You're not too hot walking?"

"I'm okay."

"If you get dizzy again, I can carry you."

She scoffed. "You'd like that, wouldn't you?"

Yes, please. Having her body pressed against mine sounded like bliss. "More like hate it. You'd poke me with your knobby Terran elbows."

Her eyes narrowed. "You really want to complain about being poked? I bet my ass still has a bruise on it after that day on the rider."

Laughter burst out of my chest. "I can check if you want to be certain." My gaze slid to her skirt. In her Dionion garb, it would be a simple enough task to complete. One I would be thrilled to undertake.

"No thanks." She tugged the hem lower.

"Offer stands, if you change your mind," I said playfully, but Ren didn't take the bait. If anything, the teasing suggestion made her more distant. Her pace slowed slightly, widening the gap between us.

Harlx's bane. Why don't you keep your dumb mouth shut for a change? Every time I thought I was getting her to loosen up, I couldn't help ruining the progress a heartbeat later. I sighed, hoping my surprise would help.

After a short hike, I slowed to a halt.

Ren crossed her arms and frowned. "I don't see anything."

"That's because we're not there yet." I bent, lifting several low-hanging branches to reveal a barely discernible path leading up a steep, densely forested hillside. "Come on. It's this way."

She cautiously stepped forward. "It's dark in here."

"Don't worry." I dug into a vest pocket and sparked my lighter. "Path opens up again just ahead."

Ren grunted as she ascended, her breath labored. "How did you find this place? Looks like no one's been here for ages."

I kept a close watch of her movements, ready to catch her if she lost her balance. "I've always loved to explore, even when I was a puny tike. Found this trail when my hair barely swept my shoulders."

"I can't imagine you ever being *puny*." She glanced back. "And you kept it a secret?"

I nodded. "Used it as my escape. This is where I came when I needed a moment alone. I've never showed it to anyone until now."

Ren scrambled up the last rise. "Is that supposed to make me feel special?"

Shadows danced on her face as I caught up to her. I snapped the lighter closed, washing us in near darkness. "Special? Perhaps. Now you know where to find me if I run away." I stepped into her personal space but held back from touching her. Still, it was close enough to greedily breathe in her scent.

She whispered, "What makes you think I'd come looking?"

Dipping my head by her ear, I said, "Because if you were the one missing, I would want to find you."

Her breath hitched. I closed my eyes, sampling her sweetness in a deep, slow inhale.

Then I stepped back and lit the lighter again. "Sorry. This was getting hot. Had to let it cool off."

Ren swallowed. "Sure... Hot. I get that." She tilted her head. "Hey, is that water?"

I'd barely noticed with her occupying my thoughts. "Good ear. Come on." I waved the lighter ahead. "We won't need this much longer."

The elevation leveled out, and soon the path opened, revealing a moonlit cliffside topped with a waterfall. I'd crossed more impressive falls in my travels, but this secluded spot brought back so many memories from my youth.

Ren strode to the edge, eyes wide. "Wow. It's beautiful. I'm surprised you kept this place a secret."

"I didn't, exactly." I stopped beside her and pointed to a larger, higher vantage point on the far side of the falls. "The falls aren't a secret. Just the trail. No need to tromp through the woods when there's an easier hike over there."

"Hey! Why'd you take me the hard way?" She shoved my shoulder.

"I don't mind putting in extra effort when the reward's breathtaking." I dropped my gaze to her mouth, certain she'd be worth every bit of my effort, too.

Ren licked her lips, and for a tense moment, I wondered if she might lean in and put me out of my misery. But then she shook her head, blinking rapidly. "Breathtaking? That little thing? Remind me to take you to Niagara Falls one day."

"It's a date." I winked, enjoying how her cheeks reddened in the moonlight. "Only I wasn't talking about the falls." I stretched out a hand. "Ready to cool off?"

"Wait... You want to jump in?" She backed away, eyeing my hand like I might toss her over the edge. "No way."

"I've done it a thousand times. Even when I was just a puny tike." This was the reason I loved this spot so much. Yes, the higher vantage made for a better view. Perhaps we'd even visit there one day, have a picnic with the falls trickling in front of us. But my secret trail let out at the perfect spot for cliff diving.

"You swear it's safe?" She inched forward again, peering over the edge cautiously.

"Promise." I wiggled my fingers. "Come on. Or are you afraid your breath will be taken, and you'll be forced to admit you were so very wrong?"

"You're lucky I really want to swim, or I would've shoved you in for that remark."

Her fingers slipped into mine, and I smiled.

"You ready?"

She nodded. I tugged her gently forward, and my pulse raced as she joined me at the edge.

This has to mean something, right? A few days ago, she would barely speak to me and backed away every time it looked like I might touch her. Here she was, holding my hand. Trusting me to lead her into the unknown. To keep her safe in an unfamiliar world. It might not be much, but to me, it meant everything.

"On the count of three, we jump."

"Okay." She sucked in a deep breath.

"One. Two. Three."

We leaped in tandem. A startled yelp escaped her lips before the cool water enveloped us. We sank fast before lightly slapping the bottom. I pushed off, using the momentum to lift us to the water's surface.

She emerged with a gasp. I laughed, flinging long blue strands out of my eyes. "That was fun, wasn't it?"

"Sure." Ren twisted in the water, facing me. "I'm still breathing just fine, though." As the last word slipped off her tongue, her jaw dropped. Brilliant glowing specks in varied shades of pink, orange, and yellow floated around us, blooming from below and spreading out to coat the surface of the lake. "What is that?"

"Tiny creatures that live in the mud. When we kicked off the bottom, we disturbed them. Beautiful, aren't they?"

She smiled as she treaded water, staring openly at the dancing lights. "They are."

"Did I hear a snag in your throat?" I smirked.

"No." Her lips pursed, and her gaze shot to mine. "I'm just not used to treading water like this."

I swam closer. "Come here. I'll tread for both of us." No part of me expected her to take me up on the offer. But barely a moment passed before she glided closer, then wrapped her arms around my neck and her legs around my waist.

"Is this okay?" she asked softly.

Is she kidding? We were alone, out in this breathtaking pool, flickering lights reflecting off her lovely face. "It's perfect." Well, it would've been better if we'd lost the clothes before jumping in. Still, feeling her curves pressed against me had me so hard I ached.

My arms and legs lazily flicked, keeping us afloat. Ren inched closer, bringing her face so close I could've leaned forward and captured her lips if I wanted to. And yes, I wanted to.

But something held me back. Perhaps it was the realization that—once again—she'd only felt comfortable enough getting close when my hands weren't part of the equation. Or it could be I just wanted to know how far she would go without me spurring her on.

So, I bit my tongue and kept treading. One by one, the neon embers winked out around us. My body quivered, my gaze locked on her perfect lips as they drifted closer... and closer.

Yeeesss. Shivers rushed down my spine at the first tentative press of her lips against mine. I sighed, kissing her back softly.

That one perfect taste left me eager for so much *more*. I wanted to drag her to the bank, strip her naked, then lick, suck, and stroke every delectable inch. To spread her thighs and sink one cock after the other into her heat.

No. I shoved the lustful desires aside. This was enough—for now. I'd cherish every delicious scrap she fed me until she was ready to let me feast.

Ren's mouth opened, and her tongue flicked out. The sensation was surprising—Dionion teeth were far sharper than Terrans, so we typically kissed closed-mouthed—but not unwelcome. She teased my lips with the wet point of her tongue, clearly wanting me to do the same.

I leaned my forehead against hers. "I don't want to hurt you. My teeth—"

She tugged my neck, dragging my lips back down to hers. "You won't hurt me." Her mouth skimmed mine again. Then her tongue was back, flicking insistently.

I opened the tiniest fraction, groaning as she sucked my lower lip into her mouth. Tingles shot out, spreading through my chest and igniting a fire in my loins. Then her tongue slipped into my mouth, tangling with mine so exquisitely I nearly forgot to keep treading.

A deep moan vibrated my chest. I was on the verge of swimming us both to the edge and giving in to the need burning within me, when she suddenly slipped away. "What? Where—" I blinked, feeling like she'd fed me a dose of drosse along with her tongue.

"How's that for breathtaking?" She grinned cheekily as she swam away.

I chuckled, catching up to her as she reached the shallows. "You win. I can admit when I've been bested."

She wrapped her arms around her middle as she emerged from the water. "Glad to hear it." The grin she flashed barely could be called a smile.

"Hey. What's wrong?" My heart pounded as she whipped around, crossing her arms.

"I don't know. Why don't you tell me?"

"Tell you what?" I thought we were having a nice time. Especially after that kiss.

She stomped out of the shallows and plopped on a boulder by the lake's edge. "I still barely know you, and you barely know me." She unlaced her boot before upending it, dumping the water out. "This might come as a surprise, considering how... forward I've been on this trip, but I don't usually go around kissing men I've just met."

"I won't lie. I'm happy to hear that." I grinned as I sat beside her.

She shot me a glare before turning her attention to her other boot. "Well, I'm not happy." My heart sank as the murky lake water splashed out of her boot onto the ground. "What aren't you telling me, Jalen? I don't want to go to sleep tonight feeling like I just made out with a stranger."

Harlx's bones. I'd been so hopeful that by bringing Ren here, she'd realize we were meant to be.

No. She wanted the truth... and it was beyond time I started opening up to her. Only how could I tell her we were fated now, when she was already on edge? Perhaps a different confession would appease her... I'd work my way up to the one that might send her running.

Then again... this one might be just as bad.

"I wasn't in that cabin by choice."

Ren shoved her boot back on. "Yeah, I figured. So why were you there?"

I bent over, unlacing my first boot. It'd be easier to admit to the humiliating past if I wasn't watching her reaction. "On Dionus, when you have a personal conflict with someone, you can challenge them to a duel. If you lose, the winner selects your punishment."

"Wait, seriously? That's—"

"Barbaric?" I tugged off the boot with a shrug. "It may not be how the rest of the universe does it, but it's always been our way."

"So that's why you didn't want to tell me. You were embarrassed." She nudged me with her shoulder. "You can relax. I don't care if you lost some dumb fight, Jalen."

My heart hammered painfully. *Will she still feel the same when she learns the rest?* I dumped out my other boot, buying myself some time.

"Don't leave me hanging." She stood, pinning me with a serious stare. "What was the duel about?"

After pulling the wet shoe back on, I busied myself with the laces and drew a steadying breath. "It's—"

"Jalen. Ren. There you are!" My aunt's voice rang out from the path connecting the lake to the village, and I'd never been so thrilled to be interrupted in my entire life. "I've been looking all over for you. It's nearly full dark. You two need to get some rest if you're still planning to head out at first light."

I shot Ren an apologetic look. "Mind if I fill you in tomorrow?"

Her eyes narrowed. "You better." Then she turned to Karln with a wave and a warm smile. "Sorry we ducked out on you. How was the rest of the party?"

As my aunt took over the conversation, I heaved out a sigh. I hadn't earned much of a reprieve, but it was something.

Tomorrow, I'll tell her everything... Now to spend the night worrying if that kiss would be our first—or our last.

30

Lies of Omission

Ren

Daylight awakened me, streaming through the leaves of some monstrous fern that'd claimed my temporary bedroom window as its home. I stretched, blinking lazily before the memory of what house I was in—and whose bed I'd borrowed—returned to plague me.

I jolted up with a shudder. It had been easy to shove the facts out of my head last night, when I was exhausted enough to sink into a dreamless sleep. But in the cold light of day, a shiver chased up my spine. I tore the covers off my legs and clambered out, trying to wash the image of my brother-in-law's face from my brain.

I'd kill for a damn coffee right about now. No such luck on Dionus. They'd never imported the beans, though I wagered they'd have no trouble growing plenty, if anyone had the desire. *Could be a nice gift for Karln. Bet she'd have it growing in no time, if she could scrounge up some space in that crowded garden.*

What was I thinking? I'd probably never see Karln after today. For some reason, the thought didn't sit well.

As I finger combed my hair and straightened my sleep-rumbled clothes, my lips tingled. That kiss... Why had I thought kissing Jalen was a good idea?

It wasn't that it was bad—truth be told, it was the best damn kiss I'd ever experienced. And yeah, he'd looked like every woman's wet dream bathed in moonlight, his muscles flexing as he kept us both afloat. But I should've resisted. Now it would be impossible not to recall how fucking incredible he tasted when I ought to be mad at him.

I'd broken the kiss as soon as my lust-drunk mind remembered that he wasn't being entirely honest with me. I mean, how could I have figured out we were mates first? As a native, he had to know what those tablets were for. It seemed pretty damn likely he was keeping me in the dark.

But when I'd called him out for it, he'd fed me that dumb half-assed confession instead. I couldn't care less if he lost some stupid duel. I needed to know if we were mates. As soon as he woke, I'd ask him point-blank. It was time for answers.

I slipped into the hall on silent feet. Wouldn't be very kind of me to tromp around waking everyone while they were still sleeping. Only the hum of voices quickly alerted me they were already up. I was on the verge of clearing my throat and calling good morning when I froze in my tracks.

"Don't be a stranger once you're mated. I swear Rhelt never comes home anymore now that he has Cassidy," Karln said, sounding a bit peeved.

My eyes widened and my heartbeat thrashed in my ears.

"Don't get ahead of yourself, Auntie," Jalen answered. "The future's not written in granite yet."

Karln's scoff set my nerves on edge. "They say *fated* for a reason. If you're both feeling the heat, then—"

"I know. Just... save me the lecture, please. I have a lot on my mind already."

Why does he sound so frustrated? I cursed myself for the thought. I should be livid right now. Raging. There was no question anymore if he knew. Jalen was fully aware that we were mates—and he was choosing to keep me in the dark.

I should've stormed in there and demanded answers. But that wasn't what happened. I tiptoed backward, worrying my lip between my teeth. Then I slammed my bedroom door shut before shuffling down the hall.

"Good morning," I bellowed as I stepped into the living room.

"Good morning." Jalen greeted me with that same stupid, sunshiny grin he always wore. And when my belly fluttered in response, I cursed myself for the second time that morning.

"I'm ready to head out when you are," I announced curtly. His smile lost a little luster but didn't fall before I tore my gaze off him and strode into the kitchen.

"Did you sleep all right?" Karln asked. "I hope Rhelt's mattress wasn't too lumpy. I've been meaning to replace the filling."

"It was fine. Thank you." I forced a grin for her sake and snagged a piece of haldi bread off the platter she held.

She smiled back warmly. "You're welcome, Ren. It was such a pleasure having visitors. I'd love it if you came back again soon."

"Um... Thanks." I bit into the bread, hoping that if I stuffed my mouth, she'd give the doting-mother routine a rest.

It felt wrong in a visceral way. She was offering me something that I'd always craved but had never been given—a parent's love. Getting such a tiny taste, here in the wild of what was supposed to be a barbaric world, made tears of longing well in my eyes.

I turned aside, blinking furiously.

And because luck was clearly not playing nice, Jalen noticed, his brow etched with concern. "You all right?"

I nodded and faked a cough. "Swallowed wrong." I rubbed my eyes before shoving the last bite of bread into my mouth.

"Perhaps you shouldn't take such big bites." Karln chuckled, seeming to miss the tension simmering in the air. "Here you go, Ren. Freshly filled from the village well."

She handed me a thermos, and I smiled gratefully before I swallowed. "Thanks again."

"It's my pleasure." Karln shooed me with a deft flick of the wrist. "Go on, then. You ought to head out if you want to make it a good distance on the trails before nightfall."

Jalen pulled her into a hug. "We'll talk soon."

I strode out the front door, fighting back tears once again. And this time, I wasn't sure it was only from that sweet woman's kindness.

Why hasn't he told me? His words to his aunt kept ringing in my ears. It wasn't what he'd said so much as his tone. The frustration had been easy to spot, but was there more behind it? Fear... Disappointment.

Was he keeping the truth from me because he didn't want me? *No one's ever wanted you before. Why should it be any different now?*

Jalen joined me on the porch, his gaze sliding down my limbs slowly enough it made liquid pool in my belly. "Thought you'd be wearing your skinsuit today."

Shit. I'd planned to change out of the short Dionion skirt and tank before we left, but that idea flew out the window when Karln got all motherly with me. I couldn't fathom going back in there now. "Doesn't matter. I'll change later."

"If you're certain." He offered me a pack. "Karln insisted you take this to replace the one you lost. Your clothes are inside, along with some snacks and necessities."

I swallowed thickly. "That was nice of her." Too nice. I snagged the bag, feeling more uncomfortable than I should've.

Jalen's eyes narrowed. "You're acting strange. What's going on in that pretty head of yours?"

Scowling, I set off down the cramped path. "I'm not used to having someone dote on me. I'm an orphan, remember? And unlike you, I didn't have some kindly relative to take me in. Just a flawed system that stuck me in a tin can out in space, where I grew up alone and forgotten."

I winced, hardly believing what had spewed out of me. I never shared anything about my past. Not with Arda, or Zen. Not with anyone.

"Ren!" Jalen's footsteps pounded behind me. "Wait."

No thanks. I planted one foot in front of the other, wishing I could outrun the pain of my past just like I was running from him. *But everything catches up in the end, doesn't it?*

Jalen caught me before I made it out of his aunt's garden and onto the street. His fingers closed around my forearm tightly enough to make me gasp.

"Let go of me," I hissed, glaring daggers at his hand. Horrible, sickening memories fought to surface, making me quiver in place.

He dropped my arm instantly. "I'm sorry." The depth of emotion in the simple phrase made me certain he wasn't just apologizing for grabbing me. It was for my confession. For my sad excuse of a childhood that no one should have to suffer through.

I drew a deep breath, willing the maddening wash of shame and rage roiling within me to subside. "It's fine. Let's go." I turned on my heel and sped through the village streets, not caring if Jalen followed.

Fuck. No wonder Jalen didn't want me. I couldn't even stand feeling his hand wrapped around my arm for two seconds without freaking out.

Thankfully, the streets were far less crowded than they'd been the day before. Everyone probably slept in after dancing half the night away. But one familiar face appeared just before we reached the gates.

"Ren." Demi ducked out of the shadows of a nearby porch and jogged toward us. "Can't let my sis leave without a hug goodbye."

I summoned my first genuine smile of the day. "Demi. I'm gonna miss you." A sigh spilled out of me as his arms wrapped around me tightly. I closed my eyes, but not before I spotted Jalen stiffening, his jaw clenched.

Whatever. His little show of jealousy wouldn't stop me from enjoying a hug from one of the few men in the universe I could actually trust. I'd thought I could add Jalen's name to that list, but not any longer. Not while he was actively lying to me through omission.

I squeezed Demi tightly. "How much longer are you planning to slum it on Dionus?"

"Not too much longer." He pulled back, smiling. "My work here is close to complete. This is my last stop before I head back to deliver one more translator upgrade to Harlxston and start looking for a new gig."

"If you need a ride out of the system, I bet Arda would be happy to lend you a guest room on the *Verne*. We could catch up more during the flight."

"Hm... You know what? That sounds great. Guess I'll see you soon, then." He squeezed my forearm—in the same spot that still burned with the ghostly remnants of Jalen's touch—and released me.

Jalen's voice rang out, far deeper and gruffer than normal. "Demetri." With a curt nod, he brushed past him and marched to the gate.

"See you around, Jay." Demi wiggled his brows and lowered his voice to a hushed murmur. "Someone woke up on the wrong side of the mat today."

I stifled a giggle. "Or with a stick up his ass."

Demi's lips thinned. "I know it's useless to try to convince you to stay, but promise me you'll be careful out there. Those poachers are no joke."

"I will." With a wave, I strode into the jungle.

31

Pouty

Jalen

We spent the entire morning hiking in silence. It was like we'd been sucked into a time portal, brought back to our first tense interaction. Ren walked by my side, silent and stiff, keeping her distance both mentally and physically.

Especially physically.

It was like she'd never kissed me so deliciously under the stars. Like she'd never climbed onto my lap in that cave and rubbed her hot cunt all over my cocks.

She was back to treating me like I was her own personal villain. And for once, I couldn't summon the desire to warm her cold demeanor. Not while ire burned through my veins. Each time I thought I'd calmed enough to talk, the memory of Demetri's *hug* returned, driving me mad with envy.

What did he have that I didn't? She'd let him touch her. Hold her. He'd wrapped her in his arms, and she'd sighed like it was the only place she'd ever feel safe in the whole damned universe.

I wanted her sighs. I craved her warmth. Couldn't bear the thought of another day spent without dragging her into my arms. But as the day wore on, it grew more likely that it wouldn't be happening. Not now. Perhaps never.

Suddenly, Ren stopped, planting her feet firmly and facing me with her arms crossed. "All right, enough!"

I halted directly in front of her, leaving a barely there gap between us. "Enough what?"

"This... this"—she circled a hand in front of my face—"pouty bullshit. I don't know what wiped the stupid smile off your face, but I'm done with the moping. The frown looks like shit on you, anyway."

The corners of my lips ticked up just a hair. "That was likely the rudest 'what's wrong' I'll ever hear in my life, but if you must know, it's *you*."

"Me?" She jabbed a thumb at her chest, incredulous. "You're fucking insane! That's what's goddamn wrong—not me."

I cocked a brow. "Then why won't you let me touch you?"

Her face fell like a wilted blossom. "I don't let anyone touch me."

"You let him. Demetri." I fought to keep my tone even, but a sliver of anguish colored it. "Why?"

"Because he saved me!" she shouted. Then her eyes widened, and she slapped her hands over her mouth.

"What did he save you from?" Hadn't I saved her too? Didn't that earn me a modicum of trust? Her eyes pinched closed, and I worried she'd never explain. I needed this. I needed to know what secrets she buried that still affected her so deeply. "Please. Tell me."

She opened her eyes at the same time her hands fell to her sides. "Okay." She nodded at a downed log nearby. "Can we sit?"

"Certainly." I followed her and sat beside her, leaving a small gap between us.

"I never had an easy time making friends as a kid. I was the weird girl obsessed with machines. Cass always stuck up for me, though. Until she couldn't." She twisted her fingers in her lap. "She got adopted when we were eight. The couple who took her swore they'd come back for me. At first, I believed them, but after a few months, I realized they didn't want me. I wasn't bubbly and sweet like Cassidy. I was just... me."

"Ren—"

She cut me off with a lift of her hand. "After that, I was truly alone. I kept to myself, finding enough joy tinkering with engines to keep sane. It was a lonely childhood, but at least I was warm and fed. And for a long time, that was enough." A visible shudder worked its way through her, starting at her head and rolling to the tips of her toes.

"What changed?" I prompted softly, my heart already breaking. Whatever it was, it had to be bad. I sensed it deep down in my bones.

"Puberty, I suppose. There were a few guys around my age at the space station, and one of them started treating me differently. He was a few years older than me, the son of the station's mayor. He would save me a spot in the mess. Then he'd smile and flirt. At first, I even liked it. It was nice to be noticed, after so long with no one paying attention to me. I started to trust him. I even told him the truth about how lonely I was feeling. And when he asked me on a date, I said yes."

I tried to picture her, young and all alone. Craving a relationship and being forced to settle for the company of machines. She'd be an easy target for an entitled male looking for a body to warm his sheets. "I'm guessing the date didn't go well."

"That's the understatement of the millennia." Her hand clenched into a fist. "He led me to a secluded part of the ship that was under construction."

Rage burned in my veins. I could guess what happened next.

"He grabbed me." She rubbed her arm in the same spot I'd touched that morning. "I begged him to stop, but he wouldn't listen. He forced me to my knees and wrapped his hand around my hair."

I didn't want to hear the rest. But she'd *lived* it.

"That's what Demi saved me from." Her voice hardened. "If he hadn't been walking by and heard me struggling..."

Thank ellios for Demetri's uncanny hearing.

"Demi had barely known me, but he burst in, demanding to know why the asshole wasn't listening to my pleas to stop. The fucker had the gall to claim he couldn't hear me. Can you believe that?" She shook her head in disgust.

"I hope Demetri ripped his heart out and fed it to him piece by piece."

A startled chuckle escaped her. "Not quite. But he clocked the fucker hard enough that I got away. And he held me when I cried my eyes out later. He even tried to stop me from chopping off my hair... but I wouldn't listen." She dragged a hand through her short locks. "I guess, in a twisted way, I have to thank the prick for that. Demi's been my honorary brother ever since."

"And what about the male? Was he punished?" A sneer curled my lips. "What did you say his name was?"

She heaved a big sigh. "Travis. And nothing much happened to him, besides the shiner Demi gave him."

"That's not acceptable. If a male committed such heinous acts on Dionus, he'd suffer far more than a single blow." I filed the name away. If I ever crossed paths with Travis, he'd learn a hard truth at my hands.

"He was practically royalty there, and I was just a lowly orphan." She smirked. "But I got him back good a few weeks ago. Laid him flat on his ass last time I visited Oraxis Station."

"Good." Seemed my mate had taken her own vengeance. And yet, the memory of that day still haunted her. It was clear enough in her words and actions. I shifted on the log, turning so we were eye to eye. "Ren, I vow no male will ever put his hands on you again—or I'll tear them off his wrists."

Her lips quirked sideways. "I appreciate the vow and all, but I've learned how to cope on my own."

"Cope..."

"Do you think he was the only one?" A tired smile flitted across her lips. "I hate to break it to you, Jalen, but the universe is full of creeps. Luckily, most of them stay far away from oil-stained mechanics who have ample access to tools that can rearrange their insides."

My gut clenched. This explained so much. It must be why she wore her hair short and lived in those rumpled skinsuits. She was hiding her beauty so the so-called *creeps* wouldn't target her.

I tensed as a terrible thought filtered through my head. Each of our interactions flashed in front of me, a whirlwind of flirting and fun and lust. I'd been a willing participant in all of them. Harlx help me, I'd be lying if I didn't admit to wanting to go further.

But was it different for her? What if she was *trapped* by the mate bond? What if she wanted nothing to do with me at all?

My voice broke as I asked, "Am I one of the creeps? Do you want me to stay far away from you, too?"

32

Complete Panic

Ren

I stared at Jalen with dawning horror as the gravity of his question sank in. *Fuck. I know my resting bitch face is on point, but he doesn't actually believe that, does he?*

Then again, it wasn't so long ago that a similar thought had crossed my mind. I'd dismissed it back then, and that was before he showed me—yet again—that he could be trusted. When he'd grabbed my arm that morning, he hadn't hesitated to let go when I'd asked. But I'd been doing a shit job of showing how much I appreciated his inherent decency.

I grabbed his hand, my heart pounding furiously. "No, you're about as far from a creep as it gets." I flashed a tentative smile.

Jalen's answering grin nearly blinded me. "That's a relief." His fingers tightened around mine, and his touch was so comforting it made most of the anger simmering in my belly dissipate.

But there was still one matter keeping me from relaxing completely. I slipped my fingers out of his and cleared my throat. "I know you well enough by now that I trust you'll never hurt me. But tell me, Jalen." I lifted my gaze to his. "Why are you lying to me?"

He blinked, his green eyes swimming with wariness. "What are you—"

"Don't play innocent. I heard you talking to Karln this morning. And I know what those tablets do too. No thanks to you." I crossed my arms. "Were you ever planning to tell me we're... we're..."

"Mates," he finished lamely.

"Yes," I hissed, holding tight to the last sliver of my frustration as I forced out the rest. "Why am I the last to know? Is it because you don't want me, because if that's the case, then—" My voice broke, cutting off my rant before I could finish.

"Then what?" Jalen asked softly.

My eyes welled with tears, all the potential foster parents I'd met over the years flashing through my mind. "You wouldn't be the first."

Soft words spilled out of him, too quiet for me to make out, though I thought I heard Harlx's name in the mix. Was he cursing me? Maybe saying a prayer for the strength to let me down easy...

My eyes pinched shut, a last-ditch effort to stave off the tears that were about to fall.

Then Jalen's arms closed around me, and for once in my life, I didn't feel the urge to push back or flinch. I sank into his warmth, allowing myself that single fleeting moment of connection.

"Ren, don't cry."

"I'm not." But my choked-up voice belied my words.

Jalen rubbed soothing circles on my back. "I'm sorry. I know I should've told you earlier. But after I learned how much you hated fated mates, I was worried you'd want nothing to do with me. And that's the last thing I want, Ren. I swear I was planning to tell you. I just hadn't worked up the courage."

The weirdest, most surreal feeling washed over me. For a second, it was almost like I was living a stranger's life. I *never* poured my heart out about my past. Not since I'd been burned by Travis. Even in the aftermath of his attack, when Demi had comforted me, I'd kept my mouth shut about my deeper feelings of loneliness.

But now, here I was, laying my soul bare to a man I wanted more than my next breath… and he wanted me back.

"You really mean that?" I peeked at him, disbelief threatening to swallow me whole.

He nodded solemnly. "Why do you think I got so jealous over a hug? I want you so badly it hurts, Ren."

He meant it. I spied the truth in his eyes.

Panic swamped me. Visceral, boiling panic.

I jumped to my feet, scrubbing my eyes violently. "I-I need to think. Can I… Can we…"

Jalen rose much more slowly. "There's a cave just ahead. I'll drop you off while I do some foraging for an evening meal. Sound good?"

I nodded blankly, feeling like utter shit. I was sure he was hoping I'd throw myself at him when he confessed his feelings. Or at the least, that I'd admit how much I wanted him too.

But I couldn't. Not now. I needed time to wrap my head around this.

I followed him silently for a few minutes, until the cave appeared right where he'd said it'd be. He bent and opened the lock, then tossed me his lighter. "I'll be back soon."

"Okay." I flashed him a weak smile.

When he turned away without grinning back, pain stabbed my gut.

I lit a lantern, then barely waited for the cave door to close before slapping my neck to activate my comms implant.

"Ren. I've been dying for an update." Arda's voice rang through my mind. "Did you talk to your sis—"

Cassidy was the least of my worries right now. "No. I need some advice." In fact, I could use all the help I could get. "Can you loop Kar in too? Is she busy?"

"No, she's here. Just give me a sec…"

"Hey, Ren." Karsen's peppy greeting echoed a moment later. "Before you say anything, I'm sorry about our last conversation. Arda filled me in on how your illness progressed. I should've taken your symptoms more seriously. That was very unprofessional of me."

I waited impatiently for Karsen to get that off her chest. "No biggie. You can make it up to me by telling me what the fuck to do next."

Kar asked, "What's wrong? Are you feeling sick again?"

"No. Nothing like that." I sighed. "It's Jalen. We got into a fight this morning and he came clean about all the mate stuff. And he… wants me."

Arda chuckled. "No shit."

I rolled my eyes. "Come on, this is serious! I don't know what to do."

"What did you say when he told you?" Karsen asked.

"I told him I needed to think. Fuck my life! How is this happening to *me*? You know me, guys. When we landed on this planet, did you ever imagine I'd have some big alien begging to *mate* me?"

"You are considering it, aren't you?" Arda replied shrewdly. "I mean, why else would you be freaking out if you weren't at least a little interested?"

Sure, Jalen might be my complete opposite. The sunshine to my stormy day. But he was strong, funny, achingly sweet, and so damn sexy it made my head spin. Fate had sent me the most patient, caring man who hadn't run from the ugly truth of my past.

"He is kind of... amazing." For the second time that day, tears welled in my eyes. I dashed them away with the back of my fist. "I-I think I want him too. Is that crazy?"

"No. It's not crazy at all," Arda said. "Talk to him. I know you don't like talking about your feelings, Ren, but you have to if you want this to work out."

Karsen started, "Better yet, you should follow through with the advice I gave you last time."

I scoffed. "Really, Kar?"

"What did you advise?" Arda's voice was thick with curiosity.

"What do you think that maneater said? She told me to fuck him. But I can't. Not until we figure this out. Mating is what locks the bond. I asked around at our last stop."

"Actually," Karsen began, "after Arda told me about your situation, I did some digging. It's truly a fascinating medical—"

I rubbed my temples. "Kar, you're rambling."

"I'll cut to the chase. Dionion pair-bonds alleviate heat symptoms only after a *complete* connection has been made. Anything less than that is fair game."

"So that means what, exactly?" Arda asked.

"She can take him for a test drive as long as she doesn't activate both engines at once."

Arda groaned. "The fuck, Kar? What kind of metaphor is that?"

"What?" Karsen giggled. "I thought our mechanic would appreciate it."

"It's fine. I get it." A shiver raced through me. There was a lot we could do together before doubling down...

"There's one other thing I discovered that you need to know," Karsen said. "There is a way out, if you want it."

My stomach clenched. "There is?"

"Yes. Before the healers invented heat blockers, there were only two options for mated pairs. Either you fuck or you flee. A couple hundred miles of distance was enough to negate the effects."

Arda added, "This is good. If you keep taking the blockers, then once we head off-world, you'll be back to normal."

My heart thudded painfully in my chest. Would I ever be back to *normal* after everything I'd experienced on this trip?

"Sorry if I made your decision a million times harder. I just thought you should have all the facts," Karsen said.

"No. I appreciate it." Guess my fate wasn't so set in stone after all… But just because I discovered this out didn't mean I had to take it.

Karsen cleared her throat. "I still think you ought to test the goods. Can't make an informed decision without seeking all the facts."

"Thanks for the advice, Kar, but I think Arda's right. Jalen and I need to talk."

Arda sighed. "Good. I'm glad you're ready to face your feelings. Trust me, you'll feel a lot better once you know for sure where you both stand."

"Good luck," Karsen added.

"Thanks. I'm gonna need it."

Ren

When the cave door swung open a few minutes later, I'd worked myself into a panic again. I was sure Jalen would be back to moping, wearing that stupid frown that fit his face so badly I wanted to rip it off. Knowing me, I'd end up picking a fight and making everything worse.

Luckily, he strolled in smiling brightly and humming softly. "Hey, Ren." He swung his pack off and made a beeline for the closest table. "I hope you're hungry. There was some great foraging nearby." He halted with his back facing me and dumped out the contents of his pack.

What the hell is this? Is he just going to go about his day acting like he didn't tell me he wants me? Blood boiling, I opened my mouth, ready to tell him where to shove those plants, but before I got a word out, he sucked in a huge breath and faced me.

"Listen, before you say anything, I need you to know that what I said earlier... I won't let it become a problem."

"What?" My brows pinched together.

He flipped back around and busied himself sorting the vegetables. "When I told you how much I want you. If you're not there yet, that's perfectly all right. I'm willing to wait as long as it takes."

My heart sped, blood pumping through my veins like a fuel injection. "Is that right? And what if I'm never ready? What if I want to leave this world after we finish our hike and never come back?"

He spun back to face me, fire burning in his eyes. "Then that's your right. But don't be surprised when I come looking for you."

I sucked in a startled breath, my body heating from more than just anger. "So your plan is to stalk me until I give in?"

"No. My plan is to show you I want to be with you for more than just physical reasons. Don't get me wrong, I'm dying to see your face filled with pleasure again." He took a slow step closer, and my breath quickened. "To hear you scream my name when you come."

He stopped with just a few inches separating us. "But I want *you* too, Ren. Your kind heart, your strange jokes, and even your scowls."

My skin warmed, and I wasn't sure if it was from the heat or his confession. I glanced down and spotted his fingers twitching.

"I love making you smile, Ren. Do you know why?"

His question made my gaze lift. "Why?"

"Some people give their smiles freely—but not you. Each time you smile, I know it's been earned. I would gladly spend the rest of my life earning more, if you let me. But only if that's what you want."

"What I want..." After ending the call with my crewmates, I'd been certain talking was the way to go, but now I could only think of one thing I wanted. *And don't they say the doctor's always right?* "Touch me, Jalen."

He lifted a hand instantly but stopped with it hovering next to my cheek. "Are you certain?"

"Yes. Just... take it slow."

A breathtaking smile crossed his lips. "I wouldn't want it any other way." His palm met my flesh, the heat of his skin searing me where I stood. "I want to savor you." The tips of his fingers trailed down my neck to my collarbone. "Would you like that?"

I gulped. Nodded.

"Then say it," he demanded, stepping closer and bringing our bodies flush. My nipples turned into stone as they grazed his chest. My belly tingled as his hard lengths pressed against me, washing away every lingering doubt I had. *Can't fake that.* "I need to hear it, Ren."

I choked out, "I want you too," my words breathy and stilted.

He tipped up my chin with a finger and met my gaze. "If you need to stop, just say so. I promise I'll always listen. No matter what."

Tears pricked the corners of my eyes. Hearing that meant more than I could ever express. But I refused to let the tears fall this time. Not when I was dying to feel Jalen's hands on me. "I will. I promise."

His fingers finally moved, tracing from my collarbone to my shoulder and bringing the strap of my tank top with it. My stomach fluttered as he dragged my shirt down my arms. My bare skin prickled with goosebumps as it met the warm air.

Jalen stared hungrily at my breasts as his fingers lightly trailed down my arms to my wrists and back up again. "Where do you want me to touch you, Ren?" He pulled back, shrugging his vest off and leaving us both topless.

I gulped again, so turned on with his eyes on me I answered readily, "Everywhere."

A sexy smirk painted his lips. "Do you just want my hands?" He leaned in, and his hot breath warmed my neck. "What about my mouth?"

"Yes, please," I breathed, skin tingling. I tipped my head to the side, giving him better access.

He rewarded me with a lick that made me shiver. Then his hands closed around mine, and he tugged, directing me to a pallet, keeping eye contact the entire time. He sat first and gently pulled me toward him.

For a split second, that awful memory fought to surface. I was alone again with a man who could easily overpower me...

I shoved the thought aside. This was not the same. Jalen would *never* hurt me.

Jalen's brows dipped. "Do you need a—"

"No," I cut him off sharply as I slipped my fingers out of his, and his face fell. But then I planted my palms on his shoulders and straddled his hips. My pussy landed in the perfect spot to make us both groan. "I don't need anything except for this. Touch me, Jalen. Please."

The smile he unleashed would've been enough to bring me to my knees—if I hadn't already been kneeling. My body thrummed as his fingers grazed my bare back before coasting across my stomach.

I leaned down and kissed him, threading my hands through his hair and swallowing his moans as my hips started rocking. It was like they had a mind of their own, driven mad for so long by the heat ignited between us I'd stubbornly ignored.

But the moment Jalen reached up, closing his fingers around one pebbled nipple, I stilled. Pulling away from his lips, I stared between us and watched him slowly tug, rub, and deliciously torture one breast. Then the next.

Jalen's attention was just as rapt. He licked his lips and said in a voice coated with honey, "Look how beautiful you are in my hands, Ren. These breasts were made for me." His praise sank into my soul and lit a fuse I hadn't known existed. "They were made for my hands," he cooed as he captured one peak in his big palm. "And my mouth."

Then he bent his head, and I whimpered as his tongue flicked out to tease me. My hips jerked, refusing to stay still for a second longer. But the next thing Jalen whispered against my heaving breast made me freeze in place. "I can't wait to make you mine, Ren."

I bit my lip. "I-I don't know when I'll be ready for that. Definitely not now." My stomach clenched, and he must've felt me tense.

Jalen lifted his head, his lust-drunk eyes connecting with mine. "Don't worry. I'm a planter, remember?" His hand left my breast as his mouth dipped to my ear. "I'm quite familiar with tending to beauty and waiting for it to bloom." I shivered as he glided lower, slipping into the top of my skirt and beneath my panties. "Always remembering to keep it good and *wet*." As the word rolled off his tongue, his finger sank between my soaked lips and circled my clit.

I quivered in his arms as euphoria pulsed through me. Sure, I'd never had a partner I trusted to go this far, but I was no stranger to being touched. I'd played with my fingers or toys countless times in the past. But nothing compared to this.

Jalen caressed me with the perfect amount of pressure and speed to keep me on edge without falling over. My breathing shallowed and my hips jerked, chasing the teasing touches he doled out so expertly.

For a moment, I wondered how he was doing it. How could he be so in tune with me that he had me panting and moaning with just the flick of his fingers?

But when I focused on his face, it all clicked. His rapt attention had never wavered, not for a second. He studied my reactions, that gorgeous smile of his filled with what I could only describe as pure bliss.

"Do you like watching me while you play with my pussy?" I asked bluntly.

A low growl rumbled in Jalen's chest. "I think I've found a new obsession."

"Jalen, fuck!" I choked out as he finally sank two thick fingers inside of me. Tingling waves of pleasure shot through me, though it still wasn't enough to make me come. But as Jalen curved his fingers, making me writhe and gasp on his lap, I'd had enough. I grabbed his wrist and wrenched his hand out of my panties.

His smile fell. "Are you—"

"I'm more than okay." I hooked my fingers in my skirt and shucked it off as fast as I could. "I need you naked. Now."

Jalen grinned. "As you wish." His shorts quickly joined my skirt, discarded on the floor.

I gasped as I got my first look at him in all his glory. Yeah, I'd seen him before in the tub, but now I was getting the full picture with no water to block my greedy gaze. I licked my dry lips as a sliver of fear creeped up my spine.

How the hell am I supposed to take on two of those? Jalen was slightly longer and thicker than the biggest toy I owned. One I could definitely manage. But two?

Some sign of apprehension must've shown on my face. "Ren, we can stop now if you want to."

"No. I don't want to stop." I stretched out beside him so we lay side by side, not quite touching, my gaze glued to his twitching cocks as they jutted against his belly. "I hear the bond doesn't lock until we…"

"Until both my cocks are inside you at the same time."

His words made a delicious fission of lust flash through my veins. I couldn't deny the thought of it had me practically panting. I wasn't sure how much of it was the heat drawing us together, and how much was my own suppressed desire raising its hand and shouting, *Yes, please!*

But I hadn't been lying before. No matter how turned on I was right now, I wasn't ready to be bonded forever. Still… "I was thinking… could we start off with one?"

Jalen smirked. "I was hoping you'd ask that." His voice dropped an octave. "Where do you want me?"

I huffed out a shaky breath, thanking the stars once again that it was *this* man I'd been fated to. A lot of women might find the constant reassurances grating. They might hate being given a choice instead of being tossed around like a ragdoll. I could certainly see the appeal in that, but right now, I desperately needed that sense of control to feel comfortable. And Jalen wasn't shy about giving me exactly what I needed.

Now it's my turn to make him thank the universe he got me.

A smirk of my own painted my lips. "On your back."

Jalen rolled over, and I wasted no time making my move. But instead of straddling his hips, I climbed in between them. My pulse quickened as my mouth lowered dangerously close to his beautiful cocks.

Once again, a tiny thread of fear spooled around my heart. The last time I'd been this close to a man's dick, he'd been trying to shove it down my throat.

He lifted his head. "You don't have to—" His words garbled as I sucked the head of his lower dick into my mouth. Then when I swirled my tongue around the tip, he hissed, "I take it back. Don't stop. Your mouth feels like paradise, Ren."

Heat spread through my core. With each moan I coaxed out of him, I could feel my desire swelling. By the time I'd gotten his first dick completely wet and moved on to the next, I was clenching my thighs together tightly.

Jalen's muscles strained, his gaze glued on every move I made between his legs. "Ren, if you keep that up, I'll come in your mouth."

My pussy throbbed. I'd like that—one day. Not today.

I released his top cock, giving the underside one last long lick. Jalen groaned, and his hands shot out to grab my hips as I climbed up his body. He settled me hastily over his hips, but he didn't bear down, just left me hovering above the straining length of his lower cock.

"Need to be inside you," he muttered, jaw clenched.

"Yeess." I used his chest for balance and sank onto him slowly. Jalen breathed out harshly, holding steady as my inner walls adjusted to his girth. I whimpered, fighting to accept being filled. "You're so... big. Fuck."

"Here." He reached between us and grabbed his upper cock. He lightly slapped it against my pussy lips, making me mewl. "This should help." As his top dick slipped inside and brushed my clit, he closed his eyes, brows pinching together.

"Oh god. Oh my fucking god, Jalen!" Both of his cocks began to vibrate, and I nearly came on the spot. "Jalen, you feel so fucking *good*." Within a few euphoric thrusts, he was seated to the hilt inside me.

Then my hips took on a rhythm of their own, mindlessly rocking, driving our bodies together and apart relentlessly. And through it all, I was a writhing, moaning mess, chasing an orgasm that I sensed would completely wreck me.

As my thighs started to quiver, Jalen sat up and drove his fingers through my hair. The move pressed us even closer, setting off fireworks on my clit and hitting an angle within me that had my toes curling. "That's it, Ren. Come with me," he ordered.

I shattered instantly. Electric sparks of ecstasy flooded me in waves that seemed to last forever. I vaguely registered Jalen grunting and a hot gush of fluid spilling across my stomach at the same time warmth flashed inside of me.

I collapsed on his chest, all the energy leaving my body as little aftershocks of pleasure came and went. In the back of my mind, I knew I ought to say something. At the very least, get off and thank him for getting *me* off, but all I summoned was a sleepy, "Mmm," before Jalen shifted.

With a chuckle, he laid me down, cleaned me up, and draped a blanket over me. "I'll let you rest while I get our meal ready. How's that sound?"

My eyes fluttered closed, a crooked grin etched on my lips. "Hm. Wonderful." I sighed contentedly as I listened to him putter around, floating on the wave of bliss he'd unleashed within me.

But when I heard the cave door scratching over the floor, my eyes popped open. "Hey. Where are you going?"

Jalen waved at the table where the ingredients for our salad sat neatly lined up in a row. "I just realized I forgot to grab a haldi fruit for the dressing. But I spotted a tree a short hike from here. I'll be right back."

"Okay." My head sank into the pillow. "See you soon."

33

Breaking Her In

I sprawled there, boneless, with a smile that refused to wipe away.

Wow... That was a hell of a test drive.

But it wasn't long before the doubts Jalen had so easily demolished creeped back in his absence.

Was it good for him, too? Sure, he'd been all smiles when he'd left, but that didn't change the fact that he *had* left. Blew right out of the cave as soon as he could find an excuse.

Fuck. Arda was right. We needed to talk. I wouldn't feel comfortable until we hashed it out. With that thought in mind, I forced my sated limbs to move. Shoving my discarded skirt and top back on, I shuffled to the entrance. He said he wouldn't be long. Maybe I could catch him walking in and we could clear everything up before I lost my nerve.

I flung open the door and grinned when I spotted a figure hunched over just ahead of me. "Jalen, we need to—" I gasped, eyes widening as the man stood. "Who the fuck are you?"

It sure as shit wasn't Jalen. As soon as he straightened, that was blatantly clear. Before he turned, I realized he wasn't even Dionion. The hair was all wrong, short and dirty blonde, and though he was stacked with muscle, he was shorter than the average Dionion. The clothes were a dead giveaway, too. Mystery guy wore a skinsuit, much like the one I was currently cursing myself for not slipping back on.

Then he turned, and I took a step back. Human. Why was another Terran here, alone in the jungle?

"Yuri, you about ready to head back?" a man called from somewhere in the trees.

My skin prickled. Not alone, then.

I forgot about waiting for an answer and bolted for the cave. My heart pounded wildly as I grabbed the door and pulled, only to have it wrenched out of my fingers. Then I went airborne, shoved into the cave so violently I smashed into the stone floor. My chin slammed into the rock, rattling my skull.

Thankfully, my arms absorbed the brunt of the hit, but the attack was so unexpected I couldn't protect my face completely. A trickle of warm liquid gushed down my neck, and when I lifted my hand to my aching jaw, red painted my fingers. My stomach revolted, forcing me to close my eyes to avoid retching.

"What do we have here?" Yuri called over his shoulder, "Roland, get in here. I found something you're gonna want to see."

As I flipped over, my rattled brain picked up on a clue that I hadn't noticed when the last guy—Roland, maybe—spoke from the woods. These guys weren't Terrans. Anyone else might have missed the slight difference in their accent, but I had an advantage. Namely, my linguist brother who had spent the better part of his college career studying the mysterious colony that had broken contact with the Terran system nearly a century ago.

"If you know what's good for you, you'll leave me alone, Thrin scum." A sneer curled my lips, and I forced as much venom into my tone as I could muster. I had to do something. Maybe if I kept him talking, it would give Jalen time to return and find me. "My mate is out foraging. When he sees what you did—"

"Shut up, Terran." Yuri pulled back his booted foot, aiming it at my stomach.

"Stop!" The voice I recognized from earlier stopped Yuri's boot in its tracks.

It belonged to a man who stood in the doorway, scowling. He wore an identical black skinsuit and boots, but that was where the similarities ended. This guy was far darker, with black hair that fell over his forehead and partially hid his piercing brown eyes. "What the hell do you think you're doing?" he barked, crossing his beefy arms across his barrel chest. "You know what our orders were."

"But look at her." Yuri's lecherous gaze raked over me, making my skin crawl. "We can have a lot of fun with this one on the way back to—" A hard crack rang out, Roland's hand moving lightning fast to slap Yuri. I winced but couldn't bring myself to feel sorry for the prick.

"Idiot. Don't tell her where we're from!"

"She already knows." Yuri rubbed his reddening jaw. "The bitch called me Thrin scum."

Oh no. My stomach sank.

"Fucking hell." Roland paced back and forth twice, his long stride eating up the cave floor. Then he halted and waved a hand. "Bring her."

"What? No!" I scrambled back, desperate. There had to be a way out of this. If not Jalen, then Arda. I slapped my neck. "Verne, come in!" I shouted. "Help! I need your help!"

"You're wasting your breath." Roland lifted his sleeve, flashing a watch I vaguely recognized from the pages of *Visionary Tech Magazine*. "This is the best comm-blocker on the market. No one is coming to save you."

"That's where you're wrong." I yelped as Yuri grabbed my arm and yanked me to my feet. "My mate is out foraging. He'll come for me! He'll kill you on the spot."

Roland's shoulders stiffened. "Guess we better move fast, then." He turned to Yuri. "Gag her and bind her wrists." Roland snatched my pack and riffled through it as Yuri released me, a violent gleam in his eyes.

No. This isn't happening.

I froze as the brute grabbed a sheet off the nearest pallet and shredded it. But no matter how many times I blinked, I couldn't make the nightmare disappear.

I had two choices. I could stand there and accept my fate, or I could fight back.

Not much of a choice, is it?

Still, I had to be smart. There was no way I could overpower them. They were both far too big. But maybe I could outsmart them.

I cast my gaze around, looking for anything that I could use. If I was about to be bound and gagged, I wouldn't be able to scream for Jalen. I needed some other way to show him where they were taking me. My lips twitched as I spotted something that might work.

First things first. I couldn't leave the cave like this. With how unpredictable I'd been, Jalen might think I'd run away. The small patch of blood on the cave floor would help, but that was easy to overlook. I had to make it clear I'd been taken.

So as Yuri lifted the first strip of cloth to my mouth and demanded, "Open," I lurched for the table.

With a wild sweep of my arms, I scattered the plants Jalen had foraged and stacked so neatly for our meal. "No! You won't take me! Leave me a—" My rant cut off as pain blasted through my stomach.

Yuri hauled me against his chest, clenching my belly so tightly I wanted to weep. "Feisty, are you? Good. I can't stand a dead fish in my bed."

Nausea bit the back of my throat, but I was careful to hide the small treasure I'd scooped up into my fist.

"Hold her still," Roland ordered. "I'll clean up your mess—again. You owe me, Yuri."

Yuri's arms banded even tighter around me, and I could hear the smile in his voice. "Don't worry. I'll let you have the first go breaking her in. How's that for payback?"

We'll see about that, Thrin asshole.

34

Taken

Jalen

I strolled back to the cave, tossing a ripe haldi fruit between my hands. It'd taken longer than I'd expected to hike back to the tree I'd spotted, but Ren would thank me when she tasted her salad.

That's not all she ought to be thankful for. The smug grin I'd been wearing since I left her half-passed out on the pallet still hadn't budged. *Relax,* I told myself as I spotted the door ahead. *She still hasn't agreed to—Wait. Why is the door open?*

My heart instantly climbed into my throat. "Ren!" I raced forward, ducking inside.

The haldi splattered on the floor with a wet plop. Instead of the blissed-out female I was expecting, I found chaos.

Vegetables were splattered everywhere, as if someone had tried to use them to paint the walls. Ren's bag had been upended, the once neatly folded clothing and supplies strewn on the sheets.

And worse, she was gone.

No, not gone. Taken.

There was no question in my mind that Ren wouldn't leave like this. She was serious about helping her friend, and she had no clue where to go next. Besides, she wouldn't leave after what we just shared. Would she?

I shook off the lingering doubt as a splotch of red caught my eye. I bent, dipping my fingers into the small pool of blood I'd nearly missed. Still wet. "She can't be far."

With a determined stride, I marched out of the cave. I had to find her. And when I did, whoever had taken my mate would pay with their life.

Ice coursed through my veins as I stopped in the clearing. "Ren... Where are you?" There were countless paths she could've taken through the jungle. If I chose the wrong one, I might never find her.

Horrid, nauseating images rose to plague me. The blood... was that hers? What if her captors were hurting her while I stood there hesitating? What if I was too late? I might find her body on the trail, broken and lifeless.

I dragged my hands through my hair, pacing. No. I *would* find her. I just had to start moving.

Wait... if she was still bleeding, then there might be a trail.

Hope bloomed in my heart as I combed the trees, starting in the opposite direction from where I'd come. It made sense that they'd have taken a different path. I'd have heard footsteps otherwise.

But after long moments of searching, the hope withered to dust. Nothing. No blood drops, at least. My heart lifted as I realized the stain in the cave must not belong to a serious wound as I'd first feared. Even so, it didn't help me find her.

I sucked in a shaky breath, resolved to expand my search grid, when I spotted something that made my eyes widen. A bright dash of orange decorated a tree trunk just ahead. I strolled toward it, smiling as I recognized the biteroot stain.

Scanning further, my smile deepened as I spotted another stain. And another.

"Clever." Ren remembered my lessons. Somehow, she'd gotten hold of some biteroot leaves and left me a trail.

I wasn't about to waste it. Keeping my steps light, I marched into the forest, following as fast as I could while staying silent.

There was no way of knowing how many villains had taken her. I could be rushing into a battle I had no chance of winning. Still, I wouldn't let that stop me. The thought of her hurt and scared drew me forward incessantly.

She didn't deserve that. After everything she'd been through, all the men who'd treated her like a piece of meat, the last thing she deserved was being taken prisoner.

What did they even want her for? The horrific possibilities bloomed in my mind and made my chest ache. They could be slavers intent on selling her to whoever paid the highest price, or butchers ready to cut her to pieces and sell her organs on the black market. Or worse, they could want her for the same reason as the others—her body.

No! *I'll find her and make those bastards pay, even if it kills me.*

35

Sitting on a Gold Mine

Ren

I stumbled again, catching myself against the nearest tree. By now, after what I guessed to be nearly a half hour of traipsing through the jungle, my upper arms were scraped so badly from hitting rough bark that I bit back a yelp. But it would be worth it, since each time I crashed into a tree, I left a mark with the dwindling handful of leaves clasped in my fists.

"Hurry up." Yuri tugged mercilessly on the rope Roland had stolen out of my pack and ordered Yuri to wrap around my neck. Gasping, I lurched forward, gulping in air.

"Easy," Roland said, though his voice held no hint of compassion. "We won't fetch a good price for her if she suffocates."

Yuri sneered. "If I knew Terrans were this clumsy, I would've slit her throat in that cave."

Shivers rushed through me. I hadn't missed the blade at Yuri's waist. Or the blaster tucked into Roland's ankle holster.

Stay calm, Ren. They want you alive. I mean, they were planning to sell me. But that was better than wanting me dead. As long as I stayed alive, I could keep leaving a trail. Jalen would find me. He had to.

Yuri's eyes narrowed. "Wait... what do you mean fetch a price?"

I'd realized pretty quickly the brute wasn't the brains of their operation, but that reaction was slow, even for him.

"You don't think Zan will let you keep a pet once we make it home, do you?" Roland dug into his ear before flicking a speck into the trees.

"Fuck. You're right." Yuri tugged on the rope again, making me lurch forward and gag. "Guess I'll have to get my fill quick before we dump her." The lecherous look he sent my way made my skin crawl.

Jalen... where are you?

He'd come. I had to keep trying. Keep leaving breadcrumbs for him to follow.

As Yuri faced forward, jerking the rope viciously, I used the momentum to propel myself into another tree. I slipped open my bound hands, dragging a leaf across the bark. "I said move, whore."

Fuck you, you fucking fuck! At least, that was what I would've said if not for the damn gag. With the torn sheet stuffed in my mouth, every curse I leveled at them came out garbled. All I could do was stare daggers with my eyes, but that only made the fiend chuckle darkly.

Yuri's vile hand reached out, gripping my chin tightly. "Do what you're told, and I might even fuck your pussy after I'm done with your ass."

For once, I was thankful for the gag. I definitely would've puked in my mouth if it weren't there.

"Stop playing around with her, you idiot. We need to get out of here." Roland's gaze flitted around the jungle, and his voice rumbled with urgency.

"What are you worried about? We're almost back to the ship, aren't we?"

My stomach bottomed out. If they loaded me on a spaceship, then I was done for. Given enough time, Jalen would find me in the jungle, but there was nothing he could do if they took me off the planet.

"Yeah, we're close," Roland admitted, though his gaze still flicked about nervously. "But I got a bad feeling all of a sudden."

"You're just being paranoid." All the same, Yuri tugged me forward with renewed haste. "Anyway, we're coming. Right, pretty? The sooner we make it to the ship, the sooner we can get you out of that ugly skirt." He flashed an oily grin at me, which did nothing except increase my worries.

If we were close, then I had to stall them. I couldn't let them drag me into their ship. As Yuri tugged again, I dropped to the ground, howling as best I could behind the gag and staring at my ankle.

"What is it now?" Roland barked.

"Looks like the bitch sprained her ankle." Yuri turned, a murderous gleam in his eyes. "I'll grab her."

He advanced on me, and my heart pounded like an engine with a faulty crankshaft. I continued whining, putting on the act of a lifetime. Then the idiot did exactly what I'd been hoping he'd do. As he bent to lift me off the jungle floor, he dropped the rope.

I leaped to my feet and tore off, running faster than I'd ever run in my entire life.

Not fast enough.

I crashed into the ground, landing on my battered bound wrists, gagging as the rope tightened around my neck. My vision blurred, agony bursting to life in a thousand places. My lungs screamed for air.

Fuck, he's gonna kill me this time. Black seeped around the edges of my vision.

"Bitch! I told you to—" Yuri's voice cut off with a startled yelp.

As the pressure around my neck lifted, my vision slowly cleared. Coughing, I rolled over, blinking furiously.

Jalen! He found me. *And he's pissed.*

My pulse hammered with every blow he landed. Blood splattered the trees, and the scent of copper permeated the air so strongly my stomach wobbled. Yuri reached for his knife, but Jalen gripped the brute's hand and viciously tossed the blade aside. Again and again, he pounded Yuri into the ground with his bare hands.

I sat there wide-eyed, awed by his power. His savagery. All to protect me.

Yep... I can see the barbarian now. Forcing the thought aside, I crawled to Yuri's blade. The wet smack of flesh hitting flesh echoed in my ears as I sliced through my bindings.

Free! Relief pulsed through me, but I couldn't rejoice yet. Roland was still out there.

Where *was* Roland?

My stomach sank with an awful premonition of danger as I turned back to the fight. I ripped the gag out of my mouth. "Jalen! Look out!"

Roland stood half-hidden behind a tree with his blaster aimed at Jalen's face.

"No!" I screamed at the same moment a shot rang out.

Jalen dodged, narrowly missing being blown to smithereens. Then quicker than I could track, he bolted up, abandoning Yuri's bloody corpse. He raced for Roland, a battle cry on his lips that would make even the stoutest warrior piss in his boots.

Roland never stood a chance. Jalen was on him before he aimed the blaster again. Blow after blow landed, and Roland's screams soon took on the gurgling, wet sound of a man close to death.

"Wait!" I yelled. "Jalen, stop."

At the sound of my voice, he halted. After kicking the blaster out of reach, he spun, chest heaving.

He was covered in blood and guts and worse. I should've been sickened by the sight. But fuck, I'd never been so happy to see someone in my entire life. "You found me," I choked out, my voice breaking.

"I'll always come for you, Ren. I swear it."

We collided, and for once in my life, I couldn't care less about the disgusting mess squashed between us. Not as long as his arms were there, holding me softly yet strongly, like I was the most precious gift he'd ever been given.

After a long hug, he pulled back, just far enough to meet my eyes. "Now, can you tell me why I shouldn't finish sending that sorry excuse for a male to ellios where he belongs?"

I drew a shuddering breath and lowered my voice. "We should question him. We need to find out what they were doing here." I nodded to Yuri, who lay so still on the forest floor it was clear he was no longer breathing. I couldn't say I was sorry about it. The fucker deserved worse. "I got a peek in his pack. It was full of ellbright blooms. They're the smugglers terrorizing Onatel."

"Hm... Very well. I suppose we can... talk." The way he drew out the last word, like the taste of it sickened him, made it clear Jalen had no intention of having a calm chat.

"Let me do the talking, 'kay? Then you can send him to whatever hell will take him."

"As you wish."

We slowly approached, and when I got my first clear view of Roland's face, I almost felt sorry for him. Teeth and bone protruded from places they had no right being. Blood gushed from dozens of places, making it hard for me to look at him without heaving, but I forced my revulsion aside. He wheezed, sounding even worse than I had when his good buddy Yuri had been choking me a little while ago.

Yeah... I'm so not sorry. Resisting the urge to kick him in the balls, I bent over Roland, making sure he could see me with the only eye he had not swollen shut. "Tell us what you're doing here, and we'll let you live."

Beside me, Jalen grunted but let no other sign of his displeasure show.

Roland coughed, a stream of blood spilling down his chin. "I-I don't believe y-you."

Yep. He was the brains. Couldn't fault him for being suspicious. I honestly had no plans to nurse my captor back to health. But he didn't need to know that.

"What? You don't think Terrans like making a quick buck off the slave market too?" I leaned closer, letting him see a calculated expression flash across my face. "I can let my mate finish killing you, or I can clean you up and let you be someone else's problem. Granted, it's not ideal, but at least you won't be dead."

Roland's pained gaze rolled from me to Jalen and back again. "I don't trust h-him."

"Don't worry." I turned to Jalen with a soft smile and patted his arm. "Jalen is much fiercer than you thought, but he isn't beyond reason. He listened to me when I asked him to stop, and he'll listen to me now, too."

Jalen's eyes narrowed, but he wisely kept his mouth shut.

"Tell us what you're doing here. Why are you smuggling ellbright off Dionus?" I demanded.

Roland's body slumped against the ground, and all the fight faded from him. "Ellbright is the f-future."

"What?" Maybe Jalen had pummeled him too hard. He wasn't making any sense. "I don't understand. They're just flowers."

"N-no. They're not. T-they'll change the universe." Roland gulped. "I-if I tell you how, d-do you swear on your life you'll save me?"

I forced my tone to stay level. "I do. Tell us."

Roland struggled to prop himself against a tree, but only managed to get his head at a slightly better angle before he gave up. "P-prince Zan sent us. One of his sci-sci—researchers discovered a b-byproduct of ellbright c-can boost sub-light engine performance by s-seventy percent."

Jalen's brow furrowed.

I rocked back on my heels, stunned. "You're kidding."

"N-no. I've seen it w-work."

"What's he talking about?" Jalen asked.

Adrenaline coursed through my veins so swiftly my insides vibrated. "Sub-light engines have been stuck at the same speed for centuries. This could revolutionize space travel. If what he's saying is true, then Dionus is sitting on a gold mine."

"I thought everyone uses jump tech now?"

"That's true, but it's not always safe to jump. Like when you're close to an asteroid belt or flying through a planetary system. But if ellbright can increase the sub-light that much, it would save a crazy amount of time. You could cut a month-long journey down to a week, giving anyone who possesses it a serious tactical advantage."

Jalen glared at Roland. "Something tells me we don't want them having it."

"No. No, we don't." I turned to Roland with a hardened stare.

"W-wait, you p-promised," he wheezed.

"You must've misheard. I'm probably not talking straight since your friend tried to strangle me."

"N-no!" He lurched forward, only to cough out another nauseating mouthful of blood. "Y-you can't leave me here."

Jalen's hands shook before he clenched them into fists. I reached over, squeezing his forearm.

I sighed. "Look, you're not thinking clearly, Roland. Even if I wanted to save you, how could I? There are no med-bots around. And from the looks of what you just coughed up, it's too late for you, even if I had one." I straightened and waved for Jalen to follow. "You should've listened when I told you my mate was coming for me. You sealed your fate when you abducted me."

Roland trembled, his face blanching. "I-I don't want to d-die here all alone."

Jalen rose beside me. "That's one wish I can grant." With a measured stride, he marched to Roland's blaster and retrieved it.

"Wait!" Roland coughed again, his words barely distinguishable among the crimson flood. "I take it back! P-please—"

A shot pierced the jungle, and Roland breathed his last breath.

I spun around, swallowing thickly as Jalen tossed the blaster aside. "Come on. Let's get out of here," he said.

"Gladly."

36

As You Wish

Jalen

Ren fell asleep exhausted that night after letting me tend to her wounds. With each scrape I bandaged, I wished I could kill those bastards all over again. Luckily, she hadn't been through worse.

I'd snuck up on her captors shortly before I'd struck. I'd heard the way they'd spoken to her. The vile things they'd planned to do.

Fear nearly paralyzed me then. A worry so strong that the trust I'd cultivated with Ren would wither in the face of my error.

I should've never left her alone.

What kind of guide lets their charge be captured by slavers?

What kind of male lets his mate be taken by rapists?

Ren deserved better. My heart clenched as the realization spread through my soul. *Perhaps she'd be better off without me...*

As her eyes fluttered open and connected with mine in the morning, I tried to bury my worries. "Hey." I smiled softly. "How are you feeling?"

She levered herself up on the pallet and winced. "Sore." Her head slanted as she performed a cool once-over on me. "You look like hell. Did you sleep at all?"

"Couldn't. But don't worry." I forced my smile to brighten. "I won't let it slow us down. We ought to reach the old ruins today. Unless you don't feel up to it? We can rest here—"

"No. I'm okay." She swung her legs off the pallet and grabbed her boots. "I'm sure my muscles will feel better once I start walking." She paused before sliding them on. "Is it just me, or is it darker than it should be in here?"

"You're not wrong. It's raining today. Less sun shining outside and seeping in." Her nose wrinkled, and she looked so annoyed—and downright cute—laughter burst out of my throat. "Don't worry. It shouldn't slow us down. It's only a light rainfall."

"If you say so." She set down her boot and grabbed her pack. "Think I better put my skinsuit on today."

"As you wish," I drawled, watching with interest.

Her cheeks pinked adorably, and she circled her hand. "Turn around, you perv."

I chuckled but did as requested. "Pretty positive you confirmed I wasn't one of those, right before you showed me everything you're hiding now."

She scoffed, and the rustle of fabric made my pulse race. "Yeah, well, I reserve the right to take that back if you stop acting like a gentleman."

"You won't ever have to." The words settled between us, filling the silence with the weight of their promise.

Shortly after she announced, "I'm ready," we set off. I tore a piece of haldi bread in two, which we chewed as we walked, the rain coating our skin with the lightest mist.

"It's actually kind of nice." Ren lifted one shoulder in a lopsided shrug. "I'm not as hot as usual with the rain falling."

I grinned. "True. Just be thankful it's not a heavy rainfall."

"What happens then?"

"The paths turn into mud quickly. You spend the whole hike soaked to the bone and sucking each boot out of the muck after every footstep."

"Yikes." She gazed at the sky. "Think we'll get hit with a storm like that?"

"Undoubtedly. This is the rainy season on Dionus. Light rain like this is typically a precursor to bigger storms. But if we're lucky, it won't start until nightfall."

"Great. More fun to look forward to." Ren grimaced and hastened her steps.

I chuckled, following with a spring in my step that likely had her internally cursing me for frolicking again. "What's the rush?"

She glanced at me with a grin. "There's only one thing I want sucking on me today, and it isn't the damn mud."

Harlx's bane. That mouth of hers was bound to drive me to insanity if I wasn't careful. "Let's get a move on, then, and we'll see if we can't make that happen later." I winked, leading the way while planning exactly what I wanted to do with my feisty mate.

Jalen

"This is it." I halted at a break in the tree cover, waving Ren forward.

She squinted. "Where? I don't see any ruins."

I pointed to a small mound that looked like a typical hillside to the untrained eye. "It's hard to see from here, but once we duck behind those trees, we'll find the entrance to the old ruins. The jungle sprang up around it, but the construction was sound. It was built around the same time as the caves—we think."

A fat raindrop splattered my nose. I scanned the darkening sky with a frown. "Seems we arrived just in time." I held out a hand, catching another drop in my open palm before Ren clasped my palm with hers. "It's about to start pouring. We need to hurry."

"Race you there?" She wiggled her brows, and I couldn't help smiling in response.

"All right." I dropped her hand and counted. "On the count of three. One. Two. Hey!"

She bolted on two with a devious cackle that made my skin tingle with joy. I sprinted after her, laughing. Just before we reached the entrance, the sky opened, spilling rain in a sheet that drenched us both within seconds.

"Ren!" I shouted, my vision blurring as water poured into my eyes.

Her fingers slipped into mine, clenching tightly. "I'm here. Fuck, you weren't kidding. It's like a damn monsoon!"

"Come on!" I tugged her with me the last few steps to the ruins' entrance. We sheltered under a small overhang as I worked the lock, and it was almost like we'd found a hidden cove to hide in behind a waterfall.

I cursed under my breath when I spotted Ren shivering. Why wasn't the stupid lock—there! "Inside. Quick, before we let the wet in."

She didn't need to be told twice. Ren hurried inside as I dug my lighter out of my vest pocket. Within moments, I'd slammed the door behind us and lit a lantern, washing the chamber in soft light and shadows.

"Wow. Big step up from the caves." Ren scanned the building, awed. "This looks so... modern."

Banks of cabinets lined the walls. Tables held rusting boxes filled with what might be ancient tools or medical equipment. And in the far corner, a strange blank monitor overlooked a huge seat surrounded with crystals, each of the multicolored gems shimmering dimly in the lantern light.

Who built this place? What was it for?

Yet, as Ren shivered again, I forced the questions aside. "Let's get you out of those soaked clothes and into something warm."

She arched a brow. "Why do I get the feeling the only thing you intend to warm me with is body heat?"

I chuckled softly. "While that is certainly an option, there are some blankets around here somewhere..." I grinned as I spotted the hall that was half-hidden behind a table piled high with boxes. "This way."

Ren trailed me through the hall toward the far end. "Seems like you know this place pretty well."

"I've been here a few times. It always fascinated me."

"Really? Why's that?"

I shrugged. "I suppose I enjoyed wondering about who built it and why."

"Your people never figured it out?"

"No. Just like with the caves, the knowledge is lost to the ages."

She twisted her lips. "There's stuff like that on Earth, too. Big monuments built out of enormous rocks that should've been impossible to move with ancient technology."

"Guess we aren't so different." I eased open the door to a small bedchamber, dusty but otherwise tidy, with a proper bed instead of the simple pallets we were used to finding in the caves.

"No. We aren't," Ren said, her voice lowering to practically a whisper.

I hung the lantern on a ceiling hook. Then I lifted the blanket off the bed and shook off the dust. "Wrap yourself in this. I'll wait in the hall."

But when Ren reached out, it wasn't to take the blanket. Her small fingers wrapped around my forearm and pulled me closer. "And if I don't want you out in the hall?"

My pulse turned molten as her sultry voice reached my ears. I'd been so worried she'd want nothing to do with me. Thank ellios I was wrong. "Then you can have me wherever you want me."

Her fingers slipped to the nape of my neck and pulled my head down. Her lips crashed into mine, and I was gone. Lost in the bliss of her hands tracing my skin and the sweetness of her tongue in my mouth.

She shuddered again, and I couldn't be certain if it was from my kiss or the wet cloth clinging to her curves.

I can fix that. I snagged the zipper at her throat and slowly dragged it down, moving slowly enough she had time to stop me if she wanted to. When she tugged at her sleeves, helping me shuck off the offending cloth, I sighed into her mouth. But as I reached her waist, I was forced to leave her tempting tongue behind.

Leaving a trail of kisses down her neck and between her breasts, I dropped to my knees, working the zipper down until I could finish stripping her. She toed off her boots, her stomach hollowing and chest heaving as she stood before me, her hands in my hair, and her back pressed against the wall for balance.

Then it was just that puny triangle staring at me again. Hiding the treasure I craved with every fiber of my being. My fingers traced up her inner thighs. "Is that all that's wet?"

She moaned, spreading her legs wider. Her head fell back against the wall, her eyes closing in anticipation.

"Is it?" I asked again, feathering the lightest touch on the edge of her panties.

Ren's gaze shot to mine. The hunger in her eyes made my cocks throb. "My panties are wet too. Take them off." She groaned as my fingertip slid under the elastic. "Please, Jalen."

It was my turn to groan as her nectar coated my fingers. "You're right. They're soaked."

Ren mewled, her hips jerking as I circled her clit with my thumb. Then she gasped as I pulled my hand free, and her expression turned murderous.

"Just doing as ordered," I said as I hooked the band in my fingers and tugged her panties down.

I stared, entranced with the perfection before me. At this angle, I had a phenomenal view of the slick paradise between my mate's thighs. A fluffy mound of hair, the same shade of blonde as on her head, topped the juiciest lips I'd ever seen. My mouth watered, and I couldn't resist dipping in for a taste.

"Jalen!" She bucked against the wall, grinding her pussy on my tongue.

Ellios, yes! A wicked thrill shot through me. With canines as sharp as my species possessed, few females let their partner taste them, too frightened that their tender parts would be accidentally sliced in the heat of passion.

But Ren wasn't scared at all. She rode my mouth fearlessly, and I *loved* it. All the same, I was careful to keep my teeth tucked back, resolved to never hurt her. My heart swelled even more than my cocks. Ren trusted me to keep her safe. To bring her pleasure. And I wanted to give her everything she deserved.

Through it all, I watched her. I studied every move she made and memorized every gasp and moan. Soon, my exploratory strokes became more precise as I discovered what drove her crazy.

As soon as her thighs started to quiver, I slipped a finger inside her. She gasped. "Jalen, yesss!" But there was one last thing I was dying to try. Now would be a good time, while she was on the verge of coming.

I slicked a second finger inside her, coating it with her nectar. Then I slipped it down, wondering if the move would set her off or make her recoil. Either way, I had to know. My cocks ached painfully as I ringed the wet finger around her asshole.

Ren's eyes shot wide, but she didn't tense up. As a small smile lifted her lips, I took that as a sign and sank in to the knuckle.

With my mouth on her clit, one finger in her cunt, and another in her ass, Ren screamed and came—hard. Her hands clenched in my hair as her legs clamped down on my face. I stayed with her through it all, loving the way her walls clenched around my fingers and she chanted my name like a litany.

"God, Jalen. That was incredible." Ren beamed at me as I pulled back, licking my lips. She traced my tongue with her gaze until I sat back on my heels. Her breath caught as she spotted the bulge in my shorts straining to be set free. "There's one problem, though."

My brow furrowed. "What problem? Did you not like it when I—"

She squeezed my shoulders. "Jalen, I loved every second of what you just did. The problem is that we've been ignoring that bed." She patted my cheek once, then stepped around me, hopping up on the mattress.

I grinned as I stood, following her to the edge. She stopped me with a naked foot pressed to my chest, her finger wagging. "Uh-uh. You can't come to bed all wet. Strip."

If she insists... "As you wish."

37

Unearthing Secrets

Ren

A few hours later, with the blanket wrapped securely around my shoulders, I sat on the weird stone chair and stared at the black monitor. The smooth expanse stared back at me, mocking me with its hidden secrets.

We'd spent ages opening dozens of cabinets—all empty—and scouring practically every nook and cranny in the small building for clues. Well, after we put that bed to use, of course.

A blush warmed my cheeks as my mind wandered to earlier. I'd never come as hard as I had with Jalen's tongue on my clit and my back pressed against the wall. Until he fucked me on all fours on the bed, with one cock in my pussy and the other rubbing against my ass.

The wicked thrill of what might happen next—of what *would* happen once I gave in to the mating heat—had keyed me up like nothing else ever had. And with Jalen's dirty words in my ears, and his hands roaming over every inch of me, I'd detonated, screaming so loud it probably scared off every wild critter in a one-mile radius.

But now was not the time to get caught up in reminiscing. I had a job to do, and a hunch that everything I needed was hiding in the one spot we couldn't access.

"Are you sure we've searched everywhere?" I asked finally.

Jalen sighed. "Yes. We've been through every room. Twice."

My lips thinned into a flat line. I knew the answer was on that strange computer. But no matter what I tried, I couldn't figure out how to boot it up. And for someone who prided herself on fixing broken machines, that knowledge didn't sit right. No. It really fucking sucked.

How could I go back and tell Arda I had left with nothing? That it was an ancient machine that stopped me from discovering what secrets this old facility held?

"Wait..." Jalen perked up, flashing a grin that made me feel all melty. "What is it?"

"There is one spot I could never explore, but you might be able to."

I brightened, bouncing on my toes as I stood. "Really? Where is it?"

"Right here." He strode across the room and bent beside one of the cabinets set closest to the floor. One we'd already checked and found empty.

The hope brewing within me faded. "There's nothing there. Remember?"

"Yes, the cabinet is empty. But I nearly forgot about this." He threw open the door and reached inside, his big body blocking my view of what he was doing. "Grab a lantern, would you? The smallest you can find."

"Okay." I spun on my heel, searching. There. With the lantern in hand, I bent beside him just as a loud creak echoed in the room. "What was that?"

Jalen shifted, allowing me to finally see what lay inside. "A crawl space." I inched the lantern closer, my heart lifting. "This could be it! It looks like this leads behind that crystal monstrosity. If I go in, I might figure out how to fix it."

"I hope so. Just... be careful. You're small enough to fit back there, but I'm not. If it comes down to it, I'd tear down the wall to get you out, but I'd hate to destroy this place."

Adrenaline pumped through my veins. "Don't worry. I was born for this. I lost count of how many crawl spaces I'd squeezed into before I turned ten."

"I believe that," he said with a chuckle. But as I made my first move into the cabinet, the humor drained out of him. "Don't take any chances back there. We don't know what that ancient tech can do."

It was cute how worried he was about me. "Relax. I've never let a machine kill me before, and I'm not about to start now." Sure, I'd been maimed a time or two—or a few dozen, as Zen and Karsen could attest—but now probably wasn't the best time to be bringing up that fact.

With a parting grin, I slipped into the cabinet. "Fuck. Whatever species made this must've been super slim," I grumbled, forced to hold my breath to squeeze through.

"Are you inside yet?" Jalen asked nervously.

"Yep." I waved the lantern ahead of me, spotting a bunch of wiring and components I recognized. "It opens up a bit once you're through the door." A little, but not much. If I stuck out my arms, I could touch both walls of the narrow corridor without fully unbending my elbows.

I wouldn't have a ton of room to work with, but hopefully it'd be enough to start the screen.

I turned back and thrust a hand into the cabinet. "Can you pass me my tools, please?"

"Certainly." I heard rustling as Jalen dug into his pack, and then he handed me my portable tool kit. "So, do you think you can fix it?"

"I hope so." With the kit in hand, I shimmied down the hall. "I've gotta say, the stuff back here looks a lot more familiar than that crystal interface."

Jalen's voice became more muffled the further I explored, but I didn't have any trouble hearing him. "What strikes me as odd is why the seat out here is so large, while the space in there was clearly built for a smaller creature to service."

"Huh. You're right." I shrugged. "Maybe whoever built it had a slave race they forced to do their repairs."

Jalen grunted. "If they were slavers, then I'm glad all they left behind was ruins."

I frowned, wondering if he was thinking about the Thrin who'd almost sold me. I hadn't hesitated to tell him how grateful I was he'd saved me. How I didn't blame him for what happened or regret how he'd chosen to end things. Yet, as I listened to the pounding beat of his pacing footsteps, I almost brought up the topic again to soothe his misdirected guilt. But if I wanted to get any work done, I couldn't keep up the chatter.

"You mind heading outside to check the weather?" We'd thought we heard the storm tapering off from inside, but the ruins' thick stone walls made it hard to know for sure.

"You want me to leave you alone in there?"

"Do you mind? I need to concentrate."

"I'll be back to check on you soon."

As Jalen's footsteps faded, I studied the wiring. Dozens of potential fixes flared to life in my head. I mentally catalogued them all, sorting out which were most likely to work, and a few that I'd save for a last-ditch effort if all else failed.

Then I set down the lantern, opened my tool kit, and got to work. I wasn't sure how much time had passed, but I kept tinkering until a loud gasp interrupted my flow.

"Ren, get out here!" Jalen shouted.

I hurriedly shuffled out. "What is it? Did the weather take a turn?"

"No. The monitor." His gaze was glued to the formally black monitor, which now featured a full screen of static. "Look! You got it started."

"Hm..." I strode back to the cabinet. "I think I can fix that." Sucking in a breath, I crammed myself through the door. Then I returned to work, detaching wires and swapping their positions.

"Wait, Ren!" Jalen yelled. "Whatever you just did shut it off."

"I knew that would happen. Hold on." I chewed on my lip, standing on tiptoe to make a final attachment. "There. How about now?"

"Nothing."

Shit. Now that I'd had it started once, determination poured through me. This machine wouldn't best me. I'd stay here for days if that was what it took to figure out how to fix it.

I backed away, studying the components from afar. There! "What about now?"

"Still noth—Wait." A few seconds passed before Jalen announced, "It's working!"

I crawled out, and I was willing to bet that for once, the smile on my face was a match for Jalen's. "What did I tell you? I was born for this."

Jalen slung an arm over my shoulder. "So you were. Come on. Let's see what's on this thing."

"Sure, one sec." I grabbed my tool kit and aimed a recorder at the screen. "In case I can't figure out how to download what pops up, I better get a record of this."

Jalen tilted his head at the crystals. "Any clue how these work?"

"I think so." I touched the blue crystal, and it moved easily beneath my fingers.

"Whoa. Those have always been stuck in place before."

"Booting up the computer unlocked them."

"Is that what you think this is? A computer?"

I nodded. "I just hope we can find what Arda needs on it."

After a few experimental moves, I'd figured out how to get the crystals to cycle through screens of text. With the static gone, countless words and the occasional sketch flashed across the monitor.

"Can you read this?" I couldn't make heads or tails of any of it.

Jalen squinted. "No. It's not Dionion writing."

"Damn."

"Wait..." He clasped my shoulder. "Go back."

I scrolled the text slowly. "There are a few excerpts written in Dionion here. An old dialect, but I recognize it... mostly."

"What's it say?"

He shook his head. "I'm not certain. Try going further."

I obeyed, and within moments, Jalen pointed again. "Here's another. I'm not positive, but it looks like... medical research."

A gasp spilled out of me. "This is it! That's exactly what we're looking for!"

His brow wrinkled. "That's good, though most of it doesn't make sense—to me, at least. There's so much medical jargon mixed in with the old dialect that it might as well not be Dionion."

"That's okay. We can dig into all that once we're back on the *Verne*."

"Hold on..."

I stopped scrolling. "What is it?"

Jalen strolled forward and pointed to the lower portion of the screen. "Here's something that I can understand for a change." He cleared his throat. "Significant findings to note. Use caution when introducing monozygotic twins to the Dionion project. Preliminary results have been destructive to the host species' mating rituals."

My hand fell off the crystal as my eyes widened.

"Monozygotic... I wonder what that means?" Jalen mused.

"I know. It's what Cass and I are. Identical." A strange tingle shot between my shoulder blades. Why would there be a warning about twins? I blinked, trying to make sense of it all. But then I turned to Jalen and spotted his normal bronze skin looking a lot grayer. "Hey... What is it?"

Jalen gulped. "I need to tell you something. It's about your sister."

38

Spit it Out

Jalen

Heart pumping, I stared into the beautiful face of my mate. I couldn't keep silent any longer. Not after what we'd just read. It might explain why I'd made such a terrible mistake so long ago.

I ought to be elated. Once I'd read that warning and connected it with everything that had happened, the truth bloomed to life in my mind. This was the *why* I'd spent years pondering over. I knew it deep down in my bones.

Yet, I couldn't help worrying that once I confessed my past, Ren would be... less than pleased.

"Spit it out already, Jalen. What do you need to tell me about my sister?"

I grabbed Ren's hand. "Remember that duel I lost?"

Her eyes narrowed. "Yes..."

"I lost to Rhelt." My stomach turned, everything within it souring. "When Cassidy first arrived on Dionus, I thought she was meant to be my mate."

Ren backed away, snatching her hand out of my reach. "What the fuck?"

"The healers explained after that I'd been experiencing a false heat. They could never figure out why it had started. Don't you see?" I gestured to the text still visible on the screen. "This must be it!"

Ren blinked repeatedly, a palm pressed to her chest.

"The moment I met you, I started feeling it again, but so much stronger. I worried it was happening again. But it wasn't. This time, it was real. Everything I felt before barely compares to what I feel with you."

She met my gaze directly. "Did you and Cass ever...? Did you two...?"

"Nothing more than a handshake. Rhelt saw to that." I sighed. "It all happened so fast. I met them in town, shook her hand, and in the next heartbeat, I was challenging my cousin to a duel. In some ways, it feels like a dream."

Well, more like a nightmare. I'd spent years wondering what went wrong that day. I still wasn't certain exactly what made identical twins different for Dionions, but now that I'd learned Ren was my mate, the way I was instantly drawn to Cassidy made sense in a way it never had before. Perhaps once we translated the rest of the research, the full truth would become clear.

"Oh god. I-I believe it. All of it."

"You do?"

She waved at the screen. "Something happened to me, too, the first time I met Rhelt." She shuddered, wrapping her arms around her middle. "I just thought he was a creep. But now..."

Fire blazed in my gut. "What did he do?"

Ren closed her eyes. "It started when Cassidy brought Rhelt to meet me and Demi, after they'd mated. It was little things, really. If it had only been once, I could've excused it as an honest mistake. Cassidy and I look so much alike... But it kept happening. He'd pull me into a too-close hug or slap my ass when I had my back turned."

The thought of Rhelt's hands on my mate was enough to make me want to murder him. *Is this how Rhelt felt when I'd tried to take Cassidy from him?*

"When he realized it was me, he always looked so *shocked*. He'd apologize. Promise it wouldn't happen again. Only it kept happening." She shook her head. "Cassidy had already bragged about how Dionions mated for life. They'd never stray. It wasn't in their nature. I didn't have the heart to tell her that her precious mate had wandering hands."

"Ren... I'm so sorry." That couldn't have been easy for her. At every turn, the males in her life had taken what she'd been unwilling to give. "I'll make him regret ever touching you."

She spun to me, eyes narrowing. "No, you won't. Don't you see? You've both made mistakes because of this... quirk of nature. We should use this knowledge to fix things, not ruin them more." A tentative touch landed on my forearm. "Your aunt told me you two used to be close. Don't you want to be close with Rhelt again?"

"You're right." I hung my head. "We were like brothers, once. I miss him."

"Then let's get your brother back. And my sister too."

As I lifted my gaze and spotted the resolve shining in Ren's eyes, a wash of emotion rushed over me.

Back when I'd thought Rhelt had stolen my mate, I'd cursed fate. And after, when I'd realized my mistake, I'd tried to put it all behind me. To live my life as happily as I could—to be useful, even as an imprisoned castaway.

But now, I could see that fate had always had my best interests in mind. When fate stopped me from getting on that spaceship so long ago, it kept me from making the worst mistake of my life. If I had been the first to meet Cassidy instead of Rhelt, that would've been a tragedy I couldn't bear. Not now that I'd had a taste of the utter joy of Ren being mine. She could've stormed out after she heard my confession. Instead, here she was, with a fix for the mistakes I'd made.

"I'm so glad I found you." I tucked an errant curl behind her ear, unable to stop myself from touching her. "You're incredible. Have I ever told you that?"

Her cheeks reddened adorably, and then she smirked. "Yep. Pretty sure you said so the last time I had your dick in my mouth."

Harlx's bones. I had... hadn't I? The memory flared to life, making my cocks swell, but before I could pull her in for a kiss, she darted away, wagging a finger.

"Hold that thought. We need to record the rest of this info in case the computer loses power."

With a sigh, I followed her to the monitor. "How can I help?"

39

Heavy

Ren

The sun burned bright and hot as we exited the ruins the next day with the recording tucked safely in my pack. Luckily, the mud wasn't too bad, and by midmorning we were back to walking on mostly dry topsoil. The jungle was as beautiful and loud as ever, buzzing with countless insects and animal calls. Now that our mission was nearly through, with only the long hike back to complete, I almost wished I could stay a little longer.

But I couldn't help missing my friends. "I'm gonna call the *Verne* with an update," I said once the hiking was easy.

"I'll trek ahead. Give you some privacy."

"Thanks." As Jalen hurried out of earshot, I tapped my neck. "Verne, come in. It's Ren."

Arda's voice rang through my ears a moment later. "Ren, it's good to hear from you. How did your search go?"

For some reason, I hadn't been able to use my comm implant within the old research facility, so this was the first report I'd made since we'd ventured inside. "It's a good thing I went instead of you. There was an ancient computer that needed fixing."

"And you made it your bitch, I bet?"

"Basically..." I chuckled. "We're headed back now with a lot of info that'll need to be translated."

"That's fantastic! I knew you could do it. There have been some interesting developments here, but nothing you need to worry about. In fact, I think it'll be a fun surprise when you get back."

"Come on, you know I hate surprises."

Arda clicked her tongue teasingly, and I knew I'd never get it out of her. Then she cleared her throat. "Now... how about you tell me what's going on with that man of yours? Did you make him your bitch yet, too?"

"Not quite, but I'm coming around to the idea." Might help that the man in question hadn't stopped making me come. It was getting kind of ridiculous, but we couldn't keep our hands off each other. We'd fucked two more times before leaving the ruins, and I was already itching for another go.

"Aww. I'm so happy for you, Ren." Arda fell quiet for a moment before she asked, "So you guys talked, right?"

"We did." I'd shared things with Jalen I was still keeping secret from my best friends. Neither of us were perfect, but I couldn't deny that we fit. It was like all our experiences had shaped us into two imperfect beings who were just right for each other. "I honestly never thought I'd say this, but I think he's perfect for me."

"If that's the case, what's stopping you from pulling the trigger? It can't be comfortable dealing with those heat symptoms."

"It's not so bad with the tablets." Still, the meds weren't meant to work forever. And now that Jalen and I were getting freaky regularly, they weren't working as well as they had a few days ago. "I guess I just want to be *really* sure."

"I can understand that. If I were in your shoes, I'd want the same." She chuckled. "In a way, I *was* in your place when I met Lux. Pherians mate for life, too, you know."

"It's just so different from how we do things. When divorce isn't an option, it feels so *heavy*. What helped you decide what to do?"

"Lux being there for me no matter what. Plus, when I looked ahead at the future, I couldn't imagine my life without him in it." Arda giggled, and with her next words, I could picture her on the *Verne's* bridge, waggling her brows. "The incredible sex was hard to pass up, too."

"True, that would be hard to give up."

"Ooo, now look who's holding back secrets from me? When are you planning to dish on all your test drives?"

My cheeks burned. I was glad Arda couldn't see how badly I must be blushing. "How did you know there was more than one?"

"Puh-lease, I was there when you met him, remember? I don't think there's a woman alive who'd be able to resist hopping on that ride more than once. Unless she was already happily settled, of course."

"Yeah... right. I think there're some secrets better left unsaid."

Arda scoffed. "Fine. Keep the dirty details to yourself. It *is* good, though, right?"

I smirked. "Let's just say you might want to invest in a pair of noise-canceling headphones, too."

Her delighted laughter spilled through my ears. "Oh, before I forget, have you given any thought to my proposal? Or should I say, has Jalen?"

I adjusted my pack's straps with a sigh. "Actually, I haven't brought it up." Once Arda realized I was seriously considering becoming Jalen's mate, she'd offered him a spot on board the *Verne* as a resident botanist. He certainly had the knack for it... "It seemed a little premature to mention it when I haven't decided if I'm ready to mate for life yet."

"Once you do, *if* you do, don't forget to ask him! And remember, whatever you decide, I'm happy for you. But... let's hope he says yes."

"Thanks, Capt."

As I ended the call, the weight of the life-changing decision I needed to make hung over me. I just hoped that the long hike through the jungle would give me the clarity I needed to make it.

Ren

We arrived at Onatel at midmorning a couple days later. I halted outside the gate. "Do you mind if I hang here while you head in? I need to hop on my comms." My heart pounded, but I ignored it, forcing a smile.

"Certainly. I won't be long." With a parting grin, Jalen entered the village.

A quick stop was all we had time for if we wanted to arrive at the river at an optimal time to cross. Jalen could handle filling the official in on what he'd learned about the smugglers. I had something else I'd been putting off that might be just as important.

My pulse revved higher as I activated my comms. As I waited for the call to connect, my mind warred with conflicting thoughts.

Don't pick up.

No, you need this.

Fuck... Don't pick up.

Can't start your future with the past hanging over you...

"Hello? Cassidy speaking."

Silence fell between us before I finally spat out, "It's me. Ren."

"Hey, it's about time. I thought with you here, we'd have a chance to catch up. I didn't realize the mere mention of a conversation with me would make you run into the jungle." Cassidy kept her tone light, but I couldn't mistake the tinge of hurt hiding within her words.

"I'm sorry, Cass. I guess I still wasn't ready when I got here. But I think I am now."

"I'm glad to hear that. So, what changed your mind?"

I sighed. "A lot of things, actually. The truth is, there's been something that I've been keeping from you that I should've told you. I realize now that when you came back into my life, I wasn't in a place to give you any trust. But now, I'd like to change that."

"I'd like that too. I want us to be close again, like when we were kids. I've said it before and I'll say it again. I should've fought harder for you when my parents didn't go back to adopt you."

One of the first things Cass had done when we were reunited as teens was apologize—profusely—for how our adoption played out. "I get it. You were just a kid."

Honestly, I truly didn't blame her. I knew it was her parents who had chosen not to come back for me. They were the ones who had insisted on sealing Cassidy's records while she was a minor, keeping her from finding me until after she turned eighteen. But that knowledge hadn't helped me trust her. Not after everything I'd been through.

"I mean it, Ren. I wish I'd never met them. Then we'd have grown up together like we were meant to."

I'd had the same thought countless times. But this time, the words felt wrong.

"No. Both of us need to stop living with regrets. If our lives had turned out any differently, we wouldn't be here right now. How would you feel if you'd never met Rhelt, Cassidy?"

"You're right. That would be a tragedy." She paused before adding, "Funny. I got the feeling you didn't like Rhelt."

There was a reason for that. But I didn't want to get into the why behind it until we talked in person. "Maybe I'm starting to see things differently now that I've met someone, too."

"You have!" Cassidy squealed. "Oh my god, is it Jalen?"

"It is."

"Oh, yay! I don't know why—I don't even know him that well, really only from stories Rhelt has told me—but for some weird reason, I *knew* Jalen would be perfect for you."

I chuckled. "I guess some of those freaky twin skills are still intact." I added another thing to the list of topics to cover once we were face-to-face. Now didn't seem the right time to spill about the warning we'd dug up at that facility, or what it had caused our mates to do. Not while Cass could barely contain her excitement.

"Are you two mated yet?" she asked.

"Not yet."

"You won't regret it. Trust me." She sighed contentedly. "Rhelt made our first time so... incredible. I'm sure Jalen will too—"

"Thanks, Cass." I cut her off before she got too detailed. "Listen, I need to go, but I'd like to talk more once I get back to the *Verne*. In person this time."

"I'd like that. Love you, Sis."

My heart squeezed and my voice wobbled a little as I replied, "Love you, too."

As the call cut off, tension seeped out of my muscles, and a strange lightness overcame me. We might not be thick as thieves like when we were kids just yet, but taking the first step toward reconciling with my sister gave me a sense of relief I hadn't realized I'd been missing.

That wasn't so hard after all.

Maybe it was time I stopped delaying another important conversation...

40

Focus

Ren

"We're almost there," Jalen said, a tired smile shining on his lips in the moons' light. "Hope you're ready for a well-deserved break."

We'd pushed hard for the last few days, both of us eager to make the crossing during the brief window nature had allotted us. I had no doubt if it came to it that Arda would figure out a way to get us back without having to wait months for the rainy season to pass. But all the same, I didn't want to dump that burden on her if I could help it.

So, we'd hoofed it, and hoofed it fast. With the breakneck pace, we'd both fallen asleep exhausted each night. And yeah, we'd fooled around a bit too—it was almost impossible not to, with the heat making us wild for each other. But now that we'd finally made the crossing, we could actually slow down and breathe.

Only, as Jalen ushered me into the cave that would be our retreat for the night, my chest constricted, the relief I'd been expecting suspiciously absent.

You've put it off long enough. Ask him.

It was easy to let things slide while we were in a rush. But with every mile we covered, he'd unveiled a bit more of his life to me. With every meal we shared, he made me laugh. At every stop, he went out of his way to make sure I was comfortable. And every time we touched, he made me see stars.

I couldn't deny it any longer. When I looked ahead to the future, there was only one person I envisioned in my life. Only one thing I craved. And it was about time I stopped fucking around and asked for it.

"Jalen."

"Hm?" He turned from the lantern he'd just lit, washing the small cave in a gentle glow. "You hungry? Or do you want first turn washing—"

"We need to talk."

He sank onto a bare pallet, kicking up a few wispy flakes of dust. "About what?"

I sat beside him. "What are your plans after we get back?"

He scratched his chest, drawing my gaze to all those delicious stacked muscles. "That depends."

Focus, Ren! I dragged my attention back to his eyes. "On what?"

"On what your plans are." He leaned back casually, one long leg crossing the other at the ankle.

My heart warmed. "I like Dionus a lot. But I don't want to stay here." Jalen stiffened, and I blurted, "Arda wants to hire someone to run the greenhouse on the *Verne*."

He brightened. "Truly?"

"Would you be interested in the job? It'd mean leaving Dionus. I know it's a lot to ask, but... I think you'd be great at it."

"Ren." Jalen's lips ticked up in a sexy smirk that had me ready to tear off my clothes and kneel at his feet. "Are you asking me to run away with you?"

"Maybe." Heat rushed up my neck. "Will you?" I shifted to face him, hope pooling within me so fiercely he could probably see it burning in my eyes.

He cupped my cheek tenderly. "I'd follow you anywhere. Pretty certain I've mentioned that once or twice."

A smile fought to break free, but I bit it back. "You swear?" It might be selfish of me to demand it, but I had to be certain.

He dragged me closer until our lips were only a whisper apart. "I swear it. You're all I want, Ren." He shook his head, his expression full of disbelief and so much tenderness it made my insides ache. "And now you're inviting me to explore the universe? How did I get so lucky?"

As he pressed a soft kiss to my lips, everything snapped into place. I pulled back before his mouth turned drugging, and whispered, "I'm ready, Jalen."

His hooded eyes stayed locked on my mouth. "Good." He shrugged out of his vest. "I need you naked, writhing beneath me."

My pussy clenched, but I sensed he hadn't caught the gravity of my admission. "Wait—" I pressed a hand on his chest. "I want to do more than fuck, Jalen. W-will you mate with me?"

Inexplicably, nerves burst to life inside me. The man just swore he'd follow me across the universe, and I was bracing for a rejection.

His eyes widened. Then he reached for me, pulling me onto his lap. "You're certain?"

I nodded, excitement quickly replacing the nerves with every tender stroke he brushed across my shoulders and back.

A growl rumbled through his chest. "You'll be mine, and I'll be yours. Forever." He pulled back and stared deep into my eyes. "That's what you want?"

"Yes."

"Thank ellios! Me too." There was that brilliant smile again, just as devastating as the first time he'd leveled it on me. Then those perfect lips descended, stealing my breath with a soul-searing kiss.

We undressed each other leisurely, caressing touches trailing across every inch of skin. By the time I stretched out beside him, my whole body was aflame.

"Jalen, I need you." I dragged his mouth down, and his body came with it, sinking into the cradle of my legs. Gasping, I rocked up to meet him, needing to relieve the ache.

"Soon," he whispered against my lips at the same moment his cocks vibrated against my clit.

I moaned, loving the slick slide of his length. But it wasn't enough. "Now, Jalen." I'd waited so long for this. Yeah, we'd already had plenty of test drives, but each time I was left with a nagging void that only he could slake. "Please."

He chuckled softly. "Patience. I need to make it good for you." He coated his lower cock in my arousal, coaxing more out with each intoxicating roll of his hips. His fingers sank into my hair as he trailed soft kisses to my ear. "I want to make you feel so good, Ren."

"You do." I groaned, my eyes rolling back in my head. The vibrations thrummed through me, making me feel weightless. My spine arched, and my orgasm coiled just out of reach. "Take me, Jalen. Make me yours."

My gaze snapped to his as his weight lifted off my clit. He reached down, adjusting himself. I gasped as I felt the wet tips of his dicks hovering at both of my entrances. Jalen's thumb circled my clit as he slowly eased in one torturous inch at a time.

"Jalen," I cried. "Oh my god!" I lifted my head and stared down, marveling at the sight of our bodies melding. His fingers expertly worked my tender flesh as he sank into me with a slow, measured thrust.

I'd never been so... *full*. It sent a wicked thrill through me, and as the vibrations pulsed, the sensations collided, bringing me close to my peak without him even fully seating himself inside me.

When I tore my eyes off our connection, I found Jalen's gaze again, his eyes shining with lust—and restraint. Even now, in the heat of passion unlike any other, he was taking care of me. More concerned with my reaction than seeking his own pleasure.

That thought made my core clench and Jalen groan. I held his gaze, wrapping my legs around him and dragging his body down until his pelvis pressed flush against mine. "Fuck, Jalen!" I moaned, the intrusion slightly uncomfortable but overwhelmingly *hot*.

"Are you all right?" he asked softly, brushing a sweat-soaked curl off my cheek.

"God, yes. Don't stop." His vibrating cocks quickly chased away the discomfort and had me yearning for more.

Jalen held my gaze as he began to move. With each roll of his hips, sparks flashed, sending me on a spiraling fall. I gripped his arms, holding tight and meeting him thrust for thrust as the most intense pleasure I'd ever felt turned me into a moaning, incoherent mess.

Then the wave of bliss crested, and I screamed, riding the pulsing sensations as the most intense orgasm of my life slammed into me.

"Yes, Jalen. Yes. Yesss!" I'd never felt anything like it, and I knew in that moment nothing else would ever make me feel as good as I did then.

Fuck... No wonder they mate for life.

Jalen's hips stilled a few moments later. "Ren," he breathed, capturing my gaze as he held himself immobile, buried to the hilt within me. The vibrations cut off as his cocks spasmed in my pussy and ass, leaving warmth in their wake.

He collapsed atop me, and I trailed my hands lazily down his back, neither of us speaking while we caught our breath.

Then Jalen lifted, balancing his head on his bent elbow but making no move to withdraw from me. "Wow, that was—"

"Breathtaking," I finished for him.

We both chuckled as we stared into each other's eyes. Tingles spread through my belly. "So, now we're mated." I dragged my nails lightly across his chest, delighting in the way his dicks twitched at the contact. "What happens now?"

Jalen's hand drifted to my breast and lazily plumped the flesh. "First, the heat symptoms will disappear. And we get to do this as much as we want." He bent to nuzzle my neck as his fingers spread across my flat belly. "And one day, when you're ready, you'll grow round with our tike. How does that sound?"

I never imagined I'd ever be lucky enough to start a family with a man who was devoted to me, a man I could inherently trust. "Perfect." My eyes widened as his dicks thickened inside of me. *Does my mate have a breeding kink?* "But I won't be ready for a while," I amended.

He lifted back up, gazing at me with a sexy grin. "I can wait... as long as we get to practice."

"Mmm. You've got yourself a deal, mate."

41

Boinking Like Crazy

Jalen

I held Ren's hand as we climbed aboard the *Verne*. I should've probably been nervous at the prospect of meeting her crewmates after my garden sent one of them on a trip they hadn't planned. Arda's mate honestly sounded a bit scary, and he had a huge reason to not be a big fan of mine. But after finally making Ren mine, I just couldn't stop smiling.

Everything about that night had been sheer perfection. She'd been insatiable ever since, even as the heat symptoms faded. If it weren't for our promise to bring Arda the data we'd collected, I'd have happily spent every waking hour in bed.

Be cool, idiot. We need them to like you.

The advice rang through my mind as we strolled through a long white corridor decorated with silver accents. Ren stopped midway down and opened the hatch to a room filled with muffled chatter.

All conversation cut off as we slipped into a space dominated by a large table and chairs. I recognized the machine in the corner as a food processor. *This must be the mess hall.* But I only gave the room a cursory examination once I realized everyone's eyes were on me. The two females I remembered, along with a hulking golden-haired male who must be the infamous Lux.

Karsen was the first to race across the room. Ren met her halfway, allowing her friend to wrap her in a hug. "I'm so glad you made it back in one piece." Karsen pulled back only to shrewdly scan Ren from head to toe. "Don't lie. Do you have any injuries? We can go to the med—"

"Relax, Kar. I'm fine. It's good to see you, too." Ren grinned crookedly.

Arda leaped to her feet next and stopped beside my mate with her arms outstretched. "Do I get a hug too?"

Ren nodded with tears in her eyes. "I missed you guys." She tugged Arda close and sighed.

I hung back, watching with a smile as Ren soaked up the love of her friends. All except for one.

Lux cleared his throat, his arms crossed over his chest and an unreadable stare on his face. "Good to have you back, Ren," he said, but his gaze stayed glued on me, sizing me up.

Ren split a look between us before a giggle spilled out of her lips. "Jesus, Lux, relax. He's cool."

Lux finally glanced her way but merely grunted before swinging his hard gaze back to me.

I resisted the urge to shudder, and thrust out a hand in the Terran style, uncertain which greeting his species preferred. "I'm Jalen, Ren's mate"—I glanced hopefully at Arda—"and the *Verne*'s new planter?"

"Ship's botanist," Arda said, sidestepping Ren so she could snag the hand I stretched out and shake it. "Welcome aboard, Jalen."

Perhaps it was seeing his female's acceptance, or perhaps the mention of my being Ren's mate, but something about the exchange finally convinced Lux's severe expression to lift. The corner of his lips ticked up in what might pass for a smile on someone who was used to spending their life frowning.

"Mates, huh?" Lux directed the question to Ren.

Ren's cheeks pinked up cutely. "Yep. We, uh, just made it official."

Karsen clapped her hands, face lighting with delight. "You did? Oh, that's fantas—"

A series of hisses and yowls intruded on the happy moment. My brow screwed up as I twisted, hunting for the source of the eerily familiar noise.

"Is Smudge back?" Ren asked. "And still in heat?"

A creature darted into the room that made the hair on my neck stand on end. At first glance, the sickly gray thing looked like it'd been skinned. But then I vaguely remembered Ren telling me about Lux's pet, and my shoulders sagged.

Smudge yowled again, only to press her chest to the floor and lift her swaying crotch high in the air.

"Not in here, you horny devils!" Arda groaned, waving her hands to shoe the purring creature out. But not before I glimpsed a second—more familiar—lifeform. One with black fur, a purple tongue slipping out to lick his lips as he sniffed the air near Smudge's thighs, and three working legs where there ought to be four.

"Trivet? What are you doing here?"

Lux stood, planting himself firmly in my path. "You know this creature?"

I nodded. "He's a lormate. I kind of raised him."

Arda burst into laughter. "Oh, this is rich!"

Lux's scowl deepened.

Ren frowned. "What's going on?"

Karsen hid a giggle behind her fingers before explaining, "Turns out Smudge found a creature compatible with her on Dionus."

Arda added, "Remember that howling I heard outside that I thought was a hallucination? It was him. We found them together—boinking like crazy." She used her boot to gently nudge Smudge into the hall, and Trivet followed readily. "They refused to be separated, so we dragged them both on board. At the rate they're going at it, we'll have kittens before long."

Warmth spread through my chest. "Truly? I always thought he'd end up alone because of his deformity."

"He should have," Lux grumbled, murder in his eyes.

Uh oh.

Ren snaked an arm through my elbow, dragging me into the hall. "I'm gonna show Jalen our room. Here's the data you wanted. See you guys later, 'kay?" She tossed Arda the memory drive that she'd dug out of her pocket, then slammed the hatch shut and burst into a fit of laughter.

"I'm glad you find this funny. He wants to kill me!" I winced as the catlike creatures came into view once again, Trivet looking ready to mount Smudge at any moment. Luckily, Ren wasted no time dragging me away from them down the hall.

"Lux will come around. He's just a little rough around the edges. You'll get him to cool the grump act eventually."

I grinned, puffing out my chest. "True. I have a way about me."

She patted my arm. "You do."

"Perhaps I should show him how to frolick?"

Ren snorted. "I'd love to see that."

And I love you. The words were on the tip of my tongue, but I held off. Probably best not to declare my undying affection with a serenade of horny critters yowling in the distance.

It could wait. We had all the time in the universe.

Ren punched a code into a dial, and then a hatch slid open. Shyly, she turned to me, her gaze dropping to her boots. "It's not much, but it's home. I honestly don't spend a lot of time here, so if you want to decorate or change anything, I'm game for it."

"I bet it's perfect." With a smile, I stepped inside, taking my first look at the sparse interior. Bare walls and shelves stared back at me, more like what I'd expect to find in a guest chamber instead of the resident mechanic's quarters.

At least the bed was nice. It was large enough for both of us to spread out, not that I'd mind being forced to press against her in the night.

But then my gaze caught on something strange. Within a few steps, I plucked the item off my mate's bed. "Ren…" I bit back a chuckle as a memory flashed through me. "Tell me, is this… Nicky-boy?"

Ren's face turned scarlet as she shoved the door closed. "Oh my god, I can explain."

Perhaps another male would make her, but as I watched embarrassment stain her skin, all I cared about was making it go away. She was my mate, and I hadn't been lying when I'd told her I wanted her to feel good. Clearly, this wasn't. But I could fix that.

"Forget it." I tossed the pillow aside and sank down on her—*our*—bed, patting the cool sheets beside me. "I'd rather hear you scream my name."

Jalen

A few hours later, a knock on the door woke my slumbering mate from her nap. She rubbed her eyes, and groggily said, "Verne? Who's at the door?"

"Captain Arda is waiting in the hall," a robotic voice announced from somewhere nearby, making me flinch.

"Tell her we'll be out in a moment."

"What was that?"

"The *Verne*'s computer. If you ever have a question, all you have to do is ask." Ren hopped out of bed and shrugged on her skinsuit while nodding at my clothes. I took the hint and dressed, scanning the walls warily.

Ren chuckled and slapped my back. "Relax. No one's watching you. Promise."

All the same, a rare frown curved my lips. It would take some getting used to living with all this technology.

After stuffing her feet into her boots, Ren opened the hatch. "Capt. What's up?"

My smile returned as Ren's casual greeting filled my ears. I loved how close her crew was. More like a family than mere workmates.

Arda rocked back on her heels. "Thought I'd stop by to see how you were settling in." She peeked around Ren's shoulder at me. "And I wanted to offer Jalen a tour of the greenhouse, if he's up for it."

I met her in the doorway. "That would be great." It'd be nice to surround myself with plants for a change. Perhaps that would negate some of the strangeness from being amid all this metal and machinery.

"Sounds good to me. There're some things I need to check on in the shuttle bay." Ren lifted a brow. "Mind if we split up?"

A pang of discomfort struck me, but I brushed it aside. We'd spent the last couple weeks attached at the hip, but I couldn't hover over her indefinitely. Besides, it'd be nice to get to know my new boss a bit better. "I don't mind."

"Have fun with your babies!" Arda called with a wave as Ren jogged down the hall.

I snickered. "Babies?"

"Just a joke." Arda nodded in the opposite direction. I joined her in the corridor, and our leisurely steps echoed in my ears. "Ren's always treated the hopper and *Verne* like they were her children. I'm glad she finally found something with a pulse to love on."

I sighed, feeling like I was walking on air. "Honestly? Me too."

Arda's nose wrinkled as she examined my gait. A tiny chuckle caught in her throat, and she muttered something under her breath I didn't quite catch.

"What was that?"

She shook her head, smiling. "Oh, nothing important." Then she stopped at a hatch, punched in the code, and flung open the door. "Here it is."

Heat swamped me, along with the sour stench of decay. My smile slid away as I stepped into what I could only describe as a planter's worst nightmare. This wasn't a greenhouse—not in its current state. More like a plant graveyard.

"You can see why we need your help." Arda winced, rubbing the back of her neck. "Think you can fix it?"

With a deep breath, I surveyed the wreckage. Plentiful water trickled in my ears, and rich soil filled chest-high planters, most sporting brown, shrunken plants that had seen better days. It would likely all need to be replanted, but the space had potential. "Yes. I'm up for the challenge." I turned to her with a grin as something I'd forgotten to mention earlier popped into my head. "Oh, before I forget again—" I dug into my vest pocket. "This is for you." I handed Arda the letter Official Minra had requested I deliver after we last spoke.

"What is it?" she asked as she tore open the seal.

"The people of Onatel would like to hire the *Verne*," I explained as her gaze danced across the page. "They want someone to investigate the Thrin smugglers who've been stealing from Dionus."

Arda tapped her chin. "Hm. I need to discuss this with Lux and the rest of the crew, but I will say, I'm intrigued." She continued reading, and as she scanned the bottom of the page, her eyes narrowed. "It says here they sent you with payment?"

"They did."

"Well, don't keep me in suspense."

I chuckled, then dug in a different pocket. I emptied the cloth sack into my open palm and held it out for her to see.

"Seeds?" Her lips pursed. "What kind of cheapskates are we dealing with here?"

A grin split my cheeks. "Actually, if what those smugglers said was true, in about a year, this greenhouse will be the proud home of one of the most valuable plants in the galaxy."

Arda's jaw dropped. "Shut up! Those are the flowers the Thrin are stealing? What did Ren call them... Bellright?"

"Ellbright."

"Wow. Okay." She nodded at my palm. "Take care of those babies, would you? And let me think about this." She shook the letter. "I'll have my answer before we leave Harlxston tomorrow."

"Harlxston." That was where Rhelt was.

"Yep. Ren asked to see her sister before we left. It'll give you a chance to say goodbye to your cousin, too."

My stomach clenched. "It will."

I only hoped that meeting wouldn't be the disaster that ruined everything.

42

Fun Reunion

Ren

The *Verne* touched down in Harlxston late the next morning. Nerves tingled up my spine as I strolled the city streets, down the same route we'd walked on our last visit to Cassidy's house.

The route might be the same, but so much had changed. That terrible sense of dread that had filled me on our last visit was completely gone, replaced with a burgeoning strand of hope. After our talk over the comms, Cassidy and I were closer than ever to seeing things eye to eye. I had a few more things to get off my chest, but if all went well, I could see this visit turning into the first of many.

And this time, I had my mate to lean on. Jalen strolled at my side, his strong presence calming, even though his smile was a little pinched.

I grabbed his hand. "Hey, it'll be all right. He'll understand once we explain everything we've learned."

"I hope so." Jalen squeezed my hand once before dropping it.

"What are you two talking about?" Arda asked. She'd insisted on tagging along, wanting to say a quick goodbye to Cass before we left Dionus. And of course, Karsen didn't want to be left out either, though Lux was forced to stay behind again so he didn't burn to a crisp.

"Rhelt." I sighed. "Jalen's worried he'll be pissed when he discovers we're mates."

"Why would he be mad about that?" Karsen tilted her head, making the twin plaits she'd woven her shiny black hair into bounce on the shoulders of her burgundy skinsuit. We'd all opted for skinsuits today, even Jalen, who'd been delighted to accept his first navy-blue suit as a gift from Arda that morning. "You two are *fated*, right? Isn't that hard to argue against?"

Jalen tugged at his collar. "Yes, it's just that when Rhelt asked me to be your guide, he specifically instructed me to keep my hands to myself."

Arda's brow furrowed. "Weird request."

Arda and Kar had already skimmed the data, including the cryptic warning about twins, but I hadn't filled them in on all the personal details revolving around Cass and me yet. "It's a long story. I'll explain later." We'd arrived at Cassidy's place, and I was itching to see her. "Come on. Let's knock."

I bounded up the steps with my fist raised just as the door swung open. "Ren!" Cassidy wrapped her arms around me, and for once, I didn't feel the urge to shy away. "I'm so glad to see you." She drew back, smiling.

I sent her a tentative smile of my own. "Same. Can we come in?"

She threw the door open wide, revealing Rhelt looking unusually domestic in the kitchen, his hands busy in the sink. "Yes, please come in," she said cheerily.

We piled inside as Cassidy took turns greeting us. Everything went smoothly until Jalen crossed the threshold.

"Jalen." Cassidy lent out her hand just as Rhelt's head shot up.

"No!" His hard voice cut through space. "Don't touch her!"

Cassidy retracted her hand instantly, and Jalen leaned back on his heels, stuffing his hands into his pockets. That didn't seem to appease Rhelt in the slightest. He raced across the room in about two seconds flat, tugging Cassidy behind him. "What are you doing here?" he hissed.

Jalen's face fell. "Nice to see you, too."

Cassidy huffed. "Rhelt, calm down. I can't believe you're being so rude!"

Arda chuckled uneasily. "Fun reunion we're having." She nudged me with an elbow as her eyebrows shot into her hairline.

I shook my head sharply at her, wishing I'd taken the time to explain before Rhelt flew off the handle. Suppose I should've expected it, but now it was time to rip off the Band-Aid.

I stepped next to Jalen, slipping my fingers into his. "Jalen's with me. We're mates."

Rhelt froze for a split second, during which his bronze skin took on a shockingly red hue. Then he roared, "What? One thing. I asked for one simple thing, and this is what happens?"

The animosity in his tone made everyone flinch—but not Jalen. He straightened his shoulders, and replied calmly, "I won't apologize for it. Ren and I are fated."

I jumped in, my words flooding out in a rush. "We discovered some important facts about twins and Dionion mating I'd like to talk about."

Cassidy started nodding, but Rhelt spat out through his clenched jaw, "Fine. We'll hear you out—after Jalen's back where he belongs."

Jalen backed up, shaking his head, clearly stung by his cousin's dismissal. My heart broke as I watched him, recognizing the same feeling from all those years I'd spent waiting for a family I'd hoped would love me to finally come and take me home.

No. Jalen was *mine*. He'd *never* be abandoned again.

I advanced on Rhelt, poking him square in the chest. "Take it back! Jalen's not going anywhere."

Rhelt glared at me. "It's within my rights—"

Tears stung my eyes as the physical contact sent a sickening wash of memories flooding back. "Don't act like you've never made a mistake. You know damned well that's not true." I pulled back my hand and my chin wobbled.

As Jalen tugged me into his arms, Cass turned to Rhelt with wide eyes. "Wait... What are you talking about? What mistake?"

Fuck. This really fucking sucks. I'd planned to sit Cassidy down and explain everything calmly, sharing the warning we'd found first, for context. But Rhelt had forced my hand when he'd threatened to send Jalen away. And from the utter surprise in her expression, it was pretty clear Rhelt had never told her how he'd been unintentionally drawn to me when we'd first met.

Rhelt dragged my sister close, rubbing her shoulders sweetly. "Cassidy... I don't know how to explain. What happened... It's never made any logical sense."

Cassidy blinked repeatedly, her voice breaking. "Just tell me, Rhelt. What the hell happened?"

As the silence dragged out, I shuddered in Jalen's arms. And when I couldn't stand the suspense for a moment longer, I blurted, "The first time we met, he... touched me, mistaking me for you."

Jalen growled out, "And he did more than just shake her damn hand."

Beside us, Karsen gasped. "Of course! That's what that warning meant. The pheromones that cause the mating heat must be too similar between twins."

Her explanation was intriguing, but I couldn't reply. Not after Cassidy sped out of the cabin without a single word to anyone.

"Cassidy!" Rhelt took a step toward her.

I pushed out of Jalen's arms and planted myself in Rhelt's path. "I'm going after her. Stay here and talk to your cousin." With that, I spun on my toes and jogged out the door, Arda and Karsen following closely behind me.

I found her in the front yard, leaning against a haldi tree, her back shuddering. "Cassidy? Can we talk?"

"Why?" Cass spun to face me, blue eyes that looked just like my own red-rimmed and hazy with tears. "Why did you both keep this from me for so long?"

My gaze slid to the ground. "I'm so sorry you had to find out like that. Honestly, Cass? I thought your mate was a handsy creep, but you were so in love with him, and I couldn't bear to break your heart."

"What did he do?" Her palms landed on my shoulders, and I lifted my eyes, finding hers filled with compassion—and pain. "Please, I need to know."

Truthfully, I wanted nothing more than to put the memories behind me. Especially now that I knew Rhelt's unwanted touches were driven by a fluke of nature and not any lewd intentions he harbored for me. But Cass deserved the truth.

"He pulled me into a hug from behind a couple times. And once, when I was bent over, he slapped my ass." I wrinkled my nose. "When I would turn around, he always seemed so shocked. At the time, I thought it was just an act, but looking back now, I really believe he thought I was you."

Karsen cleared her throat. "Sorry to intrude, but I'd like to share some of the data that we recovered. I think it will go a long way in helping you understand why these false mating signals keep cropping up between you two and your mates." She whipped out a tablet and started quickly scrolling across it.

Cassidy's brows dipped, but then it was like watching a light bulb go off. Her expression shifted, brows shooting up and a hand lifting to cover her slack jaw. "Wait... You think this is why Jalen thought I was his mate?"

I nodded. "We do."

Cassidy snagged the tablet. Her gaze traced the screen before she lifted her head, blinking rapidly. "We have to show this to Rhelt. God, Ren. Three years—wasted. If we'd only known this before..."

I patted her arm. "We'll show him. Let's just give them a moment to talk first." Together, we stared at the silent house. "I hope they can forgive each other."

Arda wrung her hands. "They better. I don't want to lose my new botanist."

Karsen asked, "Can he really make Jalen go back to that lonely cabin in the jungle?"

"According to the local laws, yes," Cassidy said. "But I don't think he will. Not after he hears all the facts. Rhelt can be a little obsessive about protecting me, but he trusts science. And he's always had a soft spot for Jalen."

I scoffed. "He's got a funny way of showing it."

Karsen turned to me, cocking her head. "What will you do if Rhelt doesn't listen to reason? Will you stay with Jalen?"

If you'd asked me even a few days ago, my answer would have probably been no. But now, the thought of leaving him alone in that stupid house was enough to give me indigestion. I'd hate leaving my friends, but I'd suffer through it if it was the only way to be with the man I loved.

Fuck. I love him. The realization hit me like a heatwave, warming me all over. "Yeah. I would. But I hope it doesn't come to that."

Cassidy linked our hands. "Me too. And I hope you'll forgive me, Ren."

I gaped at her. "Why? You did nothing wrong."

Her lips quivered. "It doesn't feel that way. If we'd had a normal relationship, you'd have told me everything when it happened. Instead, you had to keep it all inside. I hate that."

"I do too. But now that everything's out in the open, maybe we can have that closeness back."

"I'd like that." Cassidy sniffled.

"Me too."

Damn, it felt good to no longer have those secrets weighing on me. Cassidy and I could move forward with no skeletons in the closet ready to jump out and wreck the tentative bond forming between us.

Arda slung an arm around us both. "That was fucking beautiful." She nodded to the house. "Think we gave them enough time yet?"

I shrugged. "I don't—"

An enormous crash from within made the words die on my lips. We exchanged stunned looks before we hurried across the lawn, back to the house.

43

The Proposition

Jalen

As the door swung closed behind my mate and her friends, Rhelt stared at me, a myriad of emotions swimming in his eyes—anger, sorrow, self-disgust. In some ways, it was like peering back in time. I could recall so clearly feeling the same in the moments after challenging him to a duel over Cassidy.

"You see? We're not so different after all," I said softly, fighting to tamp down my own emotions.

It'd be easy to let the rage at what he'd done to my mate consume me. But Ren was right. We'd both made mistakes. If we wanted to move forward as a family, something had to change. It might as well start with me.

Rhelt dragged a hand through his long blue hair, mussing it horribly. "Cassidy... I should've told her. I-I just never wanted to hurt her."

"She'll understand. I'm certain Ren's out there now, explaining everything."

Sucking in a deep breath, Rhelt spat, "Explaining what? That I'm an idiot who can't tell who my mate is when her back is turned?"

My hands clenched into fists at my sides at the reminder. "No." I forced my tone to lighten. "If you'd have just listened earlier, she'd have told you, too. We found out why this is happening. It's because they're twins. Something about twins and Dionion mating bonds doesn't mix well."

Rhelt scoffed. "Is that your excuse?" He rounded on me, eyes flashing. "Do you even feel anything for Ren, or did you mate with her to get back at me?"

I grabbed hold of his vest, jerking him roughly. "Harlx's bane! Do you think I'm a monster? Ren means *everything* to me!"

He shoved me back, wrenching out of my grip. "You said the same about Cassidy once. You were wrong then. What if you're wrong now?"

"I'm not. Ren felt it too. The mating heat." I sighed heavily. "I can't blame you for thinking that, though. I thought the same at the beginning, but it was so much different from what I experienced when I met Cassidy. So much more intense. Then Healer Asani confirmed it."

Rhelt's brows pinched together. "You went to a healer?"

"After Ren collapsed in the jungle from the heat."

Silence fell over us, and just as I opened my mouth to explain everything that happened on our trip in detail, a curious sound stopped me.

"Are you *laughing*?" I stared at him, my jaw hanging so low I was surprised it didn't ache.

"She's your mate... and I ordered you not to touch her," he choked out between big hearty chuckles. "Ellios' sake! What are the odds?"

I scowled, crossing my arms. "Glad you find my hardships so amusing."

Rhelt pulled himself together, only to narrow his eyes at me as his laughter subsided. "So, you want me to believe that this was some... strange consequence that only happened because Cassidy and Ren are twins?"

"It is. Ren and her crew have research to back it up. I bet they'll be happy to show it to you."

Rhelt shook his head. "Still, that doesn't change what happened. It didn't stop you from trying to take Cassidy from me." His voice was cold—so cold I knew that memory still haunted him.

"I know it doesn't. And it doesn't change the fact that you put your hands on my mate without her permission."

We squared off, facing each other, nostrils flaring, both of us full of rage. It burned inside me hotly—the injustice of everything that had happened to Ren. Fury overwhelmed me as I thought of all those men who'd taken what she hadn't been inclined to give, my cousin included. I'd never be able to go back and tear them apart like they deserved.

But I could take out my frustration on Rhelt.

Perhaps that was exactly what we needed. An outlet for our suppressed rage.

With a grin, I pounced, slamming into Rhelt like an avalanche. We tumbled to the floor, a blur of punching fists, pounding knees, and wild elbows. Pain slammed into me just as hard, but I ignored it, giving as good as I got.

Then the door flew open, and a chorus of gasps joined the grunts and slapping skin reverberating around the room.

Two voices, so similar, called out at the same time.

"Rhelt, get off him!"

"Jalen! Stop!"

Rhelt and I peeled apart, breathing heavily and cradling superficial wounds.

"What the hell is going on?" Cassidy stomped up to Rhelt. "I was ready to talk with you, but if you can't stop behaving like a child, then maybe I shouldn't."

Rhelt stared longingly at his mate before hanging his head. "I'm sorry."

"It's my fault." I shot Cassidy a chagrined look. "I started it."

Then Rhelt—for the first time in three damn years—smiled at me. "No. We're both to blame." He drew a deep breath in through his nose. "I'm sorry, Jalen. For everything."

As pain radiated through my body and I locked eyes with my cousin, a massive weight lifted off me. We might not have settled things the way the girls had, with tears and calm voices, but that scuffle had been exactly what we'd needed to drop our mutual animosity.

I shuffled to my feet, then thrust out a hand to help Rhelt off the floor. "Brothers?"

He lurched to his feet, then clasped my back in a one-armed hug. "Brothers."

Karsen snickered. "Men. I'll never understand how a fist fight can make everything better."

"You might be a genius, Kar, but I think that's one mystery you'll never solve," Arda said.

I pulled away from Rhelt and turned to find Ren. She stood behind me, her eyes glossy. She stepped close to me, smoothing her fingers down my new wrinkled skinsuit. "Well, what's the verdict? Are we heading back to your cabin?"

"You'd go back there with me?"

As she lifted her gaze to mine, I saw the truth shining clearly in her eyes. "Yes. I don't want to, but I would. You'll never be alone again. Now you've got me."

That right there meant more to me than words could ever say. "Together forever," I whispered, dipping down toward her luscious lips. Before they connected, a gruff voice cleared loudly behind us.

"You don't have to go to the cabin. Either of you," Rhelt said gruffly.

I grinned at Ren. "Hear that?"

She nodded. "Yep. You're all mine."

Then I kissed her, and for one moment, everything else in the universe, including the pain from the fight, faded away.

"Not this again. Get a room, you horny devils!" Arda exclaimed.

Ren broke the kiss, only to spear her friend with a murderous glare. "You did not just say that! After everything I've caught you and Lux in the middle of, Kar ought to be back in the med-bay treating me for bleaching my eyes clean."

Arda chuckled. "All right. Fine. Kiss him again." She plunked on the couch and made a show of getting comfortable. "You guys have any popcorn in that kitchen?"

As laughter spilled out of my chest and filtered through my ears, I said a silent thank you to fate. I hadn't just found a mate when I met Ren. I found the answer to reuniting with my cousin and lucked into a whole new family when her friends accepted me. And for a male who started out so lonely he had more friends that photosynthesized than breathed, that was pretty damn amazing.

Jalen

Later that afternoon, my new crewmates and I gathered together once again in the *Verne*'s mess hall for an impromptu meeting at Arda's behest.

"All right." She steepled her hands on the table, her demeanor instantly shifting into that of a natural leader despite her petite size and youthful appearance. "We have some important decisions to make about our next steps, and I'd like your input."

Everyone gave her their full attention, me included. I had a feeling this would be the moment where I learned whether we'd be taking Official Minra up on his job offer.

"Before we get started, we need to consult with an expert." A grin split her lips as she tapped away at the tablet on the table.

"Hello? Zenda speaking."

A quick chorus of hellos erupted from everyone. Well, except for me.

"Thanks for agreeing to chat, Zen." Arda set the tablet down. "Have you had time to look over the blood sample I sent you?"

Blood? I froze, wondering what in the universe this was about. Just as I recalled Zenda was their former medical officer who had left to pursue a job in animal research, her voice rang out over the speaker.

"Yep. It's positive. Smudge is gonna be a momma."

"Truly?" I clasped a hand to my chest. "Trivet's a father?"

Laughter filtered over the line as Lux's hard gaze tore through me like a knife. But I refused to let the grump bring me down. This was incredible news!

"Hey, new guy! You must be Jalen. Nice to meet you. Well, kinda," Zenda said.

"You too, Zenda." It wasn't much of a meeting, but I could already sense that I would like her once we met in person.

Arda cleared her throat, all business. "Thanks, Zen. Can you work up a timeline for us? We need to know exactly what to do and when to ensure we give Smudge the best care during her pregnancy."

Lux finally tore his angry glare off me, gazing at his mate with so much admiration it was obvious he was hopelessly smitten.

"Already sent. If you bring her to the Terran system before she goes into labor, I'd be happy to assist with the birth."

"That's the plan." Arda swiped the tablet, presumably looking over the data Zenda had sent her.

"Where are you off to next?" Zenda asked.

"That's the question we're trying to answer." Arda pursed her lips. "Have you heard of the Thrin?"

"Sure. They're, what... one hundred and fifty light-years from Earth?" Zenda replied.

Lux cut in. "One fifty-seven."

Karsen tapped her chin. "With jumps, that's not too long of a trip. We should be able to make it from Dionus to there and back to Earth with plenty of time to spare."

Arda frowned. "The issue is that I'm not even sure going there would be a smart play. The smugglers you encountered said it was Prince Zan behind everything, yeah?"

Ren nodded. "That's right."

Arda leaned back in her chair. "What we really need is to meet with someone close to him before we make a move. Gather some intel so we aren't flying in blind. Don't suppose any of you have any connections we can lean on?"

Her question was met with silence until a computerized voice echoed through the space. "Captain Arda, an unidentified man is seeking entrance to the *Verne*. How shall I proceed?"

I shuddered, still a bit weirded out with the ship's computer chiming in out of nowhere.

Lux stood. "I suspect that is the port master. I will handle this."

"Thanks." Arda smiled gratefully as he disappeared into the corridor.

Zenda cleared her throat loudly. "Um, that was perfect timing. I actually *do* know someone, but I wasn't sure if I should say anything with Lux listening in."

Arda lifted a brow. "You know I don't keep any secrets from him, Zen."

"Yeah, it's just... I met her in the VIP room back at our favorite old haunt in the outer rim."

Arda's lips formed an O shape before she said, "Ah. I see."

Ren leaned close to me and stage-whispered, "They're talking about a brothel. One where the horny ladies of the Terran system get their lady parts serviced by sex-bots."

"Interesting..." I'd read about those during my studies, back when I'd expected to become an ambassador for my planet, but I wasn't an expert by any means.

Arda rolled her eyes. "It's an *old* haunt—clearly. Which begs the question, do you think your contact will still be there? It's been ages since either of us paid that place a visit."

"Oh, she'll be there. We struck up a friendship of sorts. She told me she had a standing appointment. Last weekend of the month, every month." Zenda's words spilled out excitedly. "And get this, she's basically Thrin royalty. Her niece was promised to marry Prince Zan as soon as some big trade deal was finalized. They might even be hitched already, for all I know."

Arda clapped her hands. "That's fantastic, Zen. Do you think she'll talk to you?"

Zenda chuckled humorlessly. "Um, no. Definitely not."

Karsen scowled. "Jeez, Sis. Why'd you get our hopes up for nothing?"

"Because I might have a plan that could work. See, we'd always shoot the shit, but whenever things got personal, Diarra would clam up. At first, I let it slide. But one day, after I'd spilled a particularly embarrassing story, and she hinted at something similar happening to her but refused to tell me the dirty deets, I asked her what the deal was."

I leaned forward, my gaze glued to the tablet, as she paused for breath.

"I said something like, 'C'mon, if you can't confide in me, who else will you tell?' and do you know what she said?"

Arda asked, "What?"

"She leaned in, real coy, and said, 'I tell the bots.'"

Karsen whistled. "That's actually genius. They're programmed to keep everything that happens between them and their clients strictly confidential."

"So, what do you suggest we do?" Arda's fingers drummed the table. "Hack the bot she hires and find out what they chatted about while they did the deed?"

Ren shook her head. "Not possible. They're equipped with a failsafe. If anyone even attempts to hack into one, they auto-reboot to factory settings. I read an article about it once in *Visionary Tech Magazine*."

Zenda said, "Damn. That was what I was thinking. Sorry, guys."

Karsen's eyes narrowed. "Wait... What if it wasn't a bot?"

"Huh?" Arda blinked repeatedly.

"We could hire someone to take the bot's place, couldn't we? Then we'd have a spy in place who could feed her the questions we need answered."

My lips twisted. "But that would mean the male would have to... you know..."

"Fuck her," Ren finished for me, and the crude phrase spilling off her lips had my loins tightening uncomfortably.

Karsen shrugged. "I'm sure we could find someone willing—for the right price. Unless... is she hideous?"

"Not at all," Zenda replied. "Honestly, she was a knockout. I can't imagine that's changed much since I saw her last."

I cleared my throat. "What about pregnancy? Won't it look odd if our stand-in bot takes precautions against it?"

Ren pursed her lips. "True... I hear the Thrin are into keeping things natural. No birth control implants allowed. They even learn Galactic Standard the old-fashioned way, without a translator implant."

Zenda said, "I've heard the same. Still, there're lots of guys in the Terran system shooting blanks with all the radiation leftover from the old wars. If we find one of them to hire, it might work. But there's one problem. I saw some bots she chose, and she definitely has a type."

"What is it?" Arda asked.

"Fit as fuck. Dark hair. Human. And here's the tough part—she always sets their language controls to Thrinian—not Galactic Standard."

Arda sighed. "Well, fuck. Where are we gonna find someone who fits that bill to a T?"

Footsteps echoed down the hall, and we all turned once it was apparent from the low hum of voices and extra steps that Lux hadn't returned alone. Soon he appeared in the doorway, with someone in tow who made a wide grin cross my mate's face as she spotted him.

"Demetri! You made it!" She hopped up from her chair beside me and pulled her foster brother in for a hug.

Lux grunted where he hovered in the doorway. "He says you offered him a ride aboard the *Verne* out of the Dionion system."

Ren grinned. "I did. This is my brother, Demi."

Demi smiled brightly, making his way around the room and shaking hands with each of Ren's crewmates. "It's so nice to meet you all. I'm really grateful for the ride."

He reached me last, and as he stuck his fist out in the greeting of my people, a tidbit of conversation from our night around the fire flashed in my mind. "Hey, Demetri. You're a linguist, right? Do you speak Thrinian?"

Ren gasped. "No..."

Demetri shot her a perplexed look. "What are you saying, Sis? You know I do. I'm fluent, in fact." He puffed up his chest, grinning proudly.

"You don't say..." Arda slung an arm around his shoulders. "Are you single, Demi?" Lux growled a warning, but Arda waved him off, staring at Demi closely.

"Um... Yep. Hard to find time to date when you're trekking through alien jungles."

Karsen barely let him finish before she asked, "Any chance you're shooting blanks?"

Ren groaned. "No! Absolutely not!"

"Actually, yeah. Though I'm not sure what that has to do with anything." Demi muttered to Ren, "Your friends are *really* weird."

"Let him hear us out, at least." Arda directed the statement to Ren, but patted Demi's shoulder, propelling him out of the mess hall and into the corridor. "Let me show you to your room, and while we're at it, I have a proposition for you..."

Ren rushed into the hall after them, and Karsen sped out on their heels, leaving me and Lux alone in the mess.

"Is it always like this?" I asked, confused, but also slightly exhilarated at the prospect of conducting a spy mission at a brothel as my debut journey into space.

Lux clasped a beefy four-fingered hand on my shoulder. "Welcome to the chaos. Wish I could say you get used to it, but that would be a lie."

I grinned. "Perfect. I can't wait."

44

Surprises

One Month Later

Ren

"I can't believe I let you talk him into this." Nerves pulsed through my skin as I watched Demetri's shuttle depart from the *Verne* on the bridge display with Karsen and Arda.

"He'll be fine." Arda spun in the pilot's chair, tapping the controls with practiced ease. "You know he's our best chance at finding the info we need to take down those smugglers."

"Yeah..." I sighed. "I just wish we didn't have to pimp him out to accomplish it."

Honestly, Demi hadn't been too hard to convince. My brother's dumb eyes had lit up when presented with the opportunity to get freaky with a knockout Thrin, no strings attached. Zenda had contacted the brothel madame—an old friend of hers, apparently—and along with a hefty bribe from the Pherian government thanks to Lux, we'd secured him entry.

I think I was more worried about things going sideways than anyone else was—Demi included. But Arda wasn't wrong... We needed more intel. The plan was kind of unhinged, but it was the best chance we had to stop the theft on my mate's home world and keep a potentially universe-changing advantage out of the hands of some awful people.

"Guys, I have some bad news." Karsen pinched the bridge of her nose, setting down the tablet that she always seemed to have her nose stuck in lately. "I've been weeding through all the data from Dionus now that most of the translations are in. The genetic tampering looks like it's a lot more extensive than we first thought."

"Seriously?" Arda leaned over. "What did you find?"

"Whoever these researchers are, they weren't just on Earth and Vorillion. They were on Dionus as well. And Pheria. They may have had a hand in shaping the genetic codes of all those species, going back centuries."

Shock reverberated through my core. "But... why?"

Karsen shrugged. "No clue. At least, not yet."

Arda pursed her lips. "Did you say Pheria?"

"Yeah. Why do you ask?" Karsen replied.

"I have an important reason to visit—sooner rather than later. I honestly didn't think it would be possible to arrive in time, but if we could get our hands on some of those stolen plants, maybe we could make it happen." Arda twisted her lips. "Now I'm wondering if we should be hunting for one of those facilities on Pheria too."

Karsen tilted her head. "Couldn't hurt to look. I wouldn't be surprised if we found something hidden under all that ice."

My mind spun, worry for my brother compounding with fear of the unknown. We had so much riding on this mission. I really hoped it went smoothly.

"Ugh... The waiting is gonna kill me." I turned from the viewscreen toward the hall.

"Where you headed?" Arda asked.

I lifted my hands in surrender, shuddering. "Anywhere but here. I need to forget I just sent my brother off on a mission to get laid."

Karsen giggled. "I don't know why you're whining. He'll probably come back with a smile on his face and a best-sister-of-the-century award for you."

I whipped around to face her as I hit the hatch and shot her a withering glare. "Eww, Kar. Just... eww."

I tried to block out their chuckles as I made my way down the *Verne*'s corridor. Normally, a moment like this would send me running to the shuttle bay so I could keep my hands busy.

Not this time. I strolled right past the bay to the greenhouse. I paused outside the open door, a grin creeping across my lips as my mate's sexy humming reached my ears.

Fuck... he's so hot. And he's all mine.

"Hey, you busy?" I ducked into the doorway, a pang of regret hitting me as his voice cut off.

Jalen glanced up from the tiny bud of green he'd been tending and graced me with one of his megawatt smiles. "Never too busy for you."

In the month since we'd left Dionus, he'd turned the once-sad little space into something new. Before we'd departed, he'd convinced Arda to stop at his old cabin, and the plants blossoming from his Dionion clippings and seeds were thriving. He'd mixed those in with some Terran favorites of ours—even some oolong, much to Arda's delight. It was still the early days, but I could already see the greenhouse shaping up to become as lush as his garden had been.

"Wow. I like what you've done with the place."

Jalen dusted the soil off his fingers. "Speaking of changes..." He looped an arm around my shoulders. "I have a surprise for you in our quarters."

Our quarters... My belly flipped, hearing that phrase in his sultry baritone. Who would've guessed when I left for Dionus that I'd return shacked up with a man? *I sure as hell wouldn't.*

"Jalen..." I shot him a warning look. "Can we go see it now?"

"Certainly. I know how much you *love* surprises."

Together, we strolled down the hall. "Are you planning to give me a hint about what you changed?"

Jalen smirked. "Let's just say I did some much-needed redecorating."

"Oh." That couldn't be too bad, right? All the same, my heart sped as I punched in the code to the hatch.

I strolled into the room, not knowing what to expect. New pictures hanging from the walls, maybe. Or a fresh coat of paint. But at first glance, everything looked the same.

I faced him, lifting a brow. "Was this a ploy to get me into bed?"

"No. But I'm not opposed to that outcome." Jalen slid the hatch closed, chuckling. "Look again."

My gaze trailed over the bare walls and empty shelves. "What am I looking—" I gasped as I finally spotted it. After crossing the floor to my bed, I lifted his surprise off. "Oh my god. Where did you get this?"

He'd photographed himself standing in the same sultry pose as Nick Cage, his shirt gaping open to show off his impressive chest, complete with a photoshopped beach background. The new pillowcase looked so similar to my old gag gift it was almost uncanny. I lifted it to eye level, biting my lip and fighting the urge to burst into laughter.

"I asked Karsen to help me." Jalen's lips twitched. "So, what's the verdict? Do you like it?"

"I love it." Laughter burst free from my chest, and when Jalen joined in, it brought so much joy to my soul I was vibrating from it.

Any other man as protective as Jalen would've flipped his lid the first time he spotted the silly memento. But not my mate. He'd used it to his advantage, finding a way to chase away all my troubled feelings on a day he knew I'd be down.

"I'm glad you do." Jalen closed the space between us and cradled my jaw. "Now I'll always be beside you even if I wake up early to tend to my plants. I love you, Ren."

"I love you too." As I stared into his eyes, utter contentment washed over me. I hadn't set out to find my soul mate, but now that I had, I was so damn glad I'd volunteered for that hike through the jungle. "Now get in bed." With a grin, Jalen sank down, and I tossed the pillow beside him. "I'm dying to sit on your face."

"Which one?" he teased.

"You'll see... my mate."

The crew of the Verne will return in Brothel Voyage, coming soon!

Also by

Cosmic Lovers
Bloodlust Voyage
Betrothal Voyage
Barbarian Voyage

Upcoming novels in the Cosmic Lovers Series:
Brothel Voyage – coming soon

About the author

Leda Palmer loves dreaming about alien worlds and star-crossed lovers finding each other. When she's not writing, you'll find her with her nose in a book or her eyes on the stars. The Cosmic Lovers series is her debut series.

Find out more about her future projects on her Facebook page Leda Palmer – Author. Or on follow her on Instagram at ledapalmer-author.

www.ingramcontent.com/pod-product-compliance
Lightning Source LLC
Chambersburg PA
CBHW031207310726
48969CB00001B/245